IN HER BLOOD

NIKKI CRUTCHLEY

W☉RLDWIDE

TORONTO • NEW YORK • LONDON
AMSTERDAM • PARIS • SYDNEY • HAMBURG
STOCKHOLM • ATHENS • TOKYO • MILAN
MADRID • WARSAW • BUDAPEST • AUCKLAND

WORLDWIDE™

Recycling programs for this product may not exist in your area.

ISBN-13: 978-1-335-65289-8

In Her Blood

First published in 2022 by HarperCollins*Publishers* Australia Pty Limited. This edition published in 2024 with revised text.

For questions and comments about the quality of this book, please contact us at CustomerService@Harlequin.com.

TM and ® are trademarks of Harlequin Enterprises ULC.

 Harlequin Enterprises ULC
22 Adelaide St. West, 41st Floor
Toronto, Ontario M5H 4E3, Canada
www.ReaderService.com

Printed in U.S.A.

IN HER BLOOD

To the best out-laws a girl could wish for:
Sue, John, Angela, Julia and Rick

PROLOGUE

'THE DARKNESS GIVES you time to think.' Her voice was a whisper, a scratchy hiss. The words, repeated so often in her lifetime, were command and advice all rolled into one. A precursor to this room. Seven words that explained away years of disappointment and anger. This room, like all those that made up the forgotten hallway, was full of secrets, hidden shame. It was a place to lock up your mistakes. The acrid smell of smoke followed them in, finding its way into the corners, a welcome change from the frigid, mildewed air in here.

This place had lived a hundred lives, each one leaving a part of themselves behind, leaching into the walls, easing their way under carpets and into the grooves of floorboards. They had infected the place in their own way, with sadness, madness and misery, turned it rotten from the inside out.

She felt it now, how the chill tickled her spine, just like it used to, moving its way through her body. She had forgotten how cold it was in here, as icy fingers worked their way around her limbs. She groaned and it sounded like it came from the walls.

Her mother always told her darkness was the best place for thinking. That inky blackness where you can't even

see your hand in front of you, where it was so intense
it felt like an actual weight on your shoulders. It left no
room for anything else.

ONE

Charlie

Tuesday morning

THE DREAM WAS so old it felt like a movie she had watched over and over again, one she knew all the words to. Even in sleep her subconscious was telling her it was just a dream—a nightmare—but it never made any difference.

The heat from the flames, blistering her skin. The strong arms of her father carrying her along the hallway and out the front door. The twisting, crashing, moaning of the house folding in on itself. Her sister, Jac, separate from them. Charlie's father putting her down on the ground. His face close to hers, checking if she was okay. His breath hot, wheezing. Smelling the familiar stench of whisky, for once being glad of it. Glad that he was here. That they were safe and out of that inferno. Coughing, trying to expel whatever had seeped into her lungs. The teasing, high-pitched wail of the fire engine telling her that help was on the way. But it was too late, and so were the neighbours who had been roused from their beds by the sirens. No one could do anything.

Jac walking towards them, her movements rigid, like she was made out of wood.

'No!' her dad yelling, stopping Jac from coming closer.

Jac skirting past their father and kneeling down by Charlie, an arm around her shoulder.

'What were you doing?' their father asking, as neighbours closed in on them.

Jac gazing at the scene in front of them. Still not speaking.

'You were just standing there...' her dad says.

The last part of the roof screeching long and loud, the sound wrenching her out of her nightmare in gasping relief.

But straight away she felt disconnected, like part of her was left in the dream. Her hands touched and prodded her face, arms and torso. When her uncertain touch wasn't enough, she raised a hand with some effort, as if someone had hold of her wrist, and she attempted to slap her cheek. She felt the contact, but it didn't sting.

Charlie stared at a darkened ceiling that wasn't hers. The air smelled of damp and mould, and she could feel the weight of it on her bare arms. Her head ached and she felt around her scalp, gently pushing, wincing when she found a lump at the back. Sitting up, her eyes took time to focus. Candles, long and tapered, were dotted around the room. A couple on a desk right next to her, four more on a set of drawers in a corner. They cast a flickering glow that illuminated the wire cage she was in, about the size of her old bedroom and, beyond that, darkness. She swung her leaden legs around, feeling rough carpet beneath her feet. She was close to hyperventilating, and she tried to slow her breathing to calm herself. It didn't work. She could feel the heat from the candles next to her and, without thinking of the consequences, lurched over to the drawers and blew them out, then turned to the desk to do the same. The darkness that engulfed her was heavy and complete. The brief relief she had felt on waking was entirely eclipsed as she realised she had woken up in a whole new kind of nightmare.

TWO

Jac

Thursday afternoon

THE BUS FROM the airport made its way along the winding country road lined with Queen Anne's lace, buttercups and dandelions, lulling everyone but Jac with its idyllic beauty. She jerked her shoulder and the elderly woman who was dozing there stirred, lifted her head, then let it droop to the left. From the time she had parked herself in the seat next to Jac she hadn't shut up. Asking her where she was going, who she was going to see. When she found out Jac was going to Everly too, she bitched about the place for a good ten minutes. 'No decent shops, just a pub, a cafe, petrol station and mini mart. You can't even call it a town. There's less than four hundred people in the settlement. I don't know why my daughter thought it would be a good idea to move there. She doesn't even live *in* Everly. She's on a farm ten kilometres away in the middle of nowhere! She gets up at five every morning to milk cows!' The only way Jac had managed to shut her up was to pretend to fall asleep, and the woman had been using her shoulder as a pillow for almost two hours since.

Now, as the woman snored softly beside her, Jac looked

down at her phone, staring at the texts for the hundredth time that day.

Charlie's missing. No one cares. You need to come home.

And then another last night: Cant find her dont no where she is dont no

The text had cut off and Jac was sure her dad was drunk when he'd written it.

She looked out the window and saw the sign, 'Everly 5 km', and her stomach flipped uncomfortably. But she reminded herself it was different now. She was older. She was not the same scared, bullied seventeen-year-old who had left Everly. The people in that tiny settlement had no idea. She was a woman of the world these days, while they all still had their heads up their arses.

The elderly woman's lolling head made contact once more and Jac jerked her shoulder again, causing the woman to look up and around as if she wasn't sure where she was. Jac looked away, pressing herself into the corner of her seat, taking in ramshackle barns, paddocks full of sheep and cows, and the various wooden billboards, looking aged and weathered now, jammed onto the side of the road between fences and the verge, advertising glow worm tours and black water rafting. The bus slowed as it reached Everly, stopping at the beginning of the small settlement. She averted her eyes, not quite ready to face her surroundings. Not quite ready to believe that she had actually come back.

By the time the elderly woman had got herself organised—applying a fresh coat of lipstick, pulling a brush through her short wavy hair, removing her glasses and polishing the lenses with a screwed-up tissue retrieved from her cardigan sleeve—they were the last ones to get off the bus. Jac clenched her jaw, keeping any cutting remarks to herself. As she got up, she noticed a purse on the floor at her feet. It was fawn-coloured with faded embroidered flowers on it. For a moment, Jac watched the elderly woman shuffling down the aisle, then she picked up the purse and jammed it into her small shoulder bag, before joining the half a dozen other passengers milling around the side of the bus, waiting for their luggage. She'd been one of the last on the bus, and her worn backpack was already on the footpath.

Not everyone was getting off at Everly. This wasn't a tour bus, like those that brought the hordes to the caves, stayed a couple of hours and then left, money spent, photos taken, on to the next stop. For most of Jac's fellow passengers, Everly was just a chance to stretch legs and have a toilet break before continuing south. She removed herself from the throng and looked around. It had been seven years. As if by reflex, she breathed in deeply, knowing exactly what she was going to get before her brain even registered the smells: cut grass and manure with an underlying odour of fuel from the petrol station further up the road and deep-fried food from the cafe. Home, for want of a better word. The old playground, two swings, paint peeling like a bad sunburn, and a slide that set the backs of your legs on fire in summer, had disappeared, and new swings, a slide and a jungle gym, bright primary colours, lit up the dull green of the domain further up on the right past the campground. She had practically lived at the domain and playground when she was a kid. Before and after Charlie was born. Jac held the envy of all the local kids when they had to trudge home or climb on bikes to make their five pm curfew. She never had a curfew. It wasn't until much later that she realised her freedom was actually a big neon sign blinking over her head for all to see that her parents didn't care.

Jac saw the old lady being greeted by a couple in their fifties. Jac turned her back on them and opened the purse. She fished out about ten dollars in coins, and ninety dollars in notes. The old woman had family. She'd be fine. Jac, however, had no place to stay tonight and barely a cent to her name. She stuffed the coins into her pocket and the notes into the zippered compartment of her shoulder bag, then dropped the purse into the bin.

She crossed the road to the police station, a small square building, and pulled the glass door open. There was a desk in one corner and three plastic chairs, with another door leading out the back. Jac knew there was a cell out there, used mostly to dry people out on the weekend or calm someone down after a fight had erupted at the pub. She heard a toilet flush and a moment later a police officer came through the door, pulling up his dark blue uniform trousers. His protruding belly promptly forced them back down to where they had started. He looked to be in his fifties, his thinning hair scraped strategically to cover a balding pate.

He looked shocked to see her, his hand rising to touch a cut on his lower lip before it fell again, and he moved over to his desk.

'Hi there, can I help you?' He smiled at Jac and picked up a pen.

'My name's Jac Morgan.' She saw the spark of recognition and carried on. She didn't know him, but he obviously knew of her. 'My sister's missing. I've been getting texts from my dad, Eddie Morgan. One on Tuesday saying she had disappeared, and again last night.'

'Uh-huh, yes, I was aware of that.'

Jac thought he looked uncomfortable, unable to meet her eye.

'Take a seat, Jac. I'm Constable Robbie Dunlop.'

Jac pulled over a plastic chair, dumped her pack to the side and sat. 'Dad said in his first text that no one cared. I don't know what he meant by that, but I'm hoping he came to you.' She had no idea what her father would have done after having found Charlie missing.

'Yes, yes, he did come to me, on Tuesday afternoon.' Dunlop licked the cut on his lower lip. 'He was very drunk.'

Jac nodded, not surprised, realising where Dunlop's split lip had come from.

'So, what happened?' Jac was becoming impatient.

Dunlop took a deep breath. 'He told me his daughter was missing. That he hadn't seen her since Monday morning.'

'And?' Jac pressed him. 'What's happening?'

He shifted his weight and the chair squeaked. 'You need to understand he was very drunk. I mean, he's often like that…'

Jac knew. Eddie Morgan's benders were legendary in Everly. 'Okay, so what are you saying?'

'He could hardly string a sentence together. I asked him a few questions, her age, if she could be staying with friends, and he got extremely aggressive—as you can see. Once he'd thrown the punch, he walked out before I could do anything else. I figured he needed to cool off.'

'Did you look into where Charlie might be?'

'No, I didn't. I didn't see Eddie again… I just assumed he wasn't thinking straight when he came in.'

Jac remained quiet and Dunlop filled in the silence. 'Look, I'm happy to make a few phone calls, ask around town. How's that?'

He acted like he was doing Jac a favour when he should've made those enquiries two days ago.

'I'm going over to the campground now,' she said. 'I'll come by tomorrow.'

'Here, let me give you my phone number,' Dunlop said, handing her a card.

Jac entered it into her phone and left the card on the desk. He hadn't inspired any confidence and, as Jac walked out, she tried to quell the feeling of panic that was threatening to take over. She had assumed she would come home to find that Charlie had either turned up or that at least some kind of search would have been underway. The fact that nothing had been done finally established the worry firmly in her chest.

THREE

Jac

Thursday afternoon

JAC WALKED A further ten metres up the narrow footpath to the campground, her worn sneakers crunching on the gravel underfoot. There was nowhere else to stay that she knew of. It wasn't like Everly would have all of a sudden got a brand-new motel or even a backpackers. Everly had been on its way out when she'd lived here and, apart from the new playground, it looked like it hadn't done much to pick itself up. So, the campground it was. Sure as shit, she wasn't staying with him.

She slid open the door to the office, which smelled of the raw pine that lined the portacabin's walls. There was a computer in the corner with a sign, 'Internet $2 per half-hour'. Looking out a window, she saw someone marching towards the building from the toilet block.

Charlie had told her that she and Dad had been living at the campground for almost a year, ever since they got kicked out of their place when he couldn't pay rent.

Like father, like daughter. Her gut twisted, thinking of Tania, the flatmate she had abandoned that morning, while owing over two months in rent.

She looked at the board displaying prices above the desk. Studio cabin one hundred dollars a night.

She needed to sort this thing out with Charlie and get out of here. Her eyes wandered to the map of New Zealand on the wall. South Island possibly? Still a whole island away from him, and Everly. Maybe Charlie would want to come with her.

First, I need to find her, Jac reminded herself.

A door behind the desk swung open.

'Hello, there!' The welcome was bellowed out, like the man was trying to get her attention in a roomful of people. 'What can I do for you?'

Dave... She couldn't remember his last name. She stood still, determined not to turn and run, waiting for him to recognise her. Maybe he wouldn't. Her long dark hair had been replaced with a pixie cut days after she had left Everly.

He looked up, eyes narrowing. 'Jac Morgan?' His smile faded, and a thin hand brushed against his beard. 'Your dad know you're home? Been a while, huh…since you were back here.'

She didn't want to get drawn into an argument. 'I'd say you should know exactly how long I've been away, since you and Dad's other mates were the ones that chased me out of town.'

'I…well…' He looked away from her, putting a pen back into a container, sliding his mouse back and forth across the desk, suddenly very interested in whatever was on the computer screen. 'After the fire, your dad was distraught…real tragedy.'

'Yeah, real tragedy,' she said, ignoring the look of shock on his face. 'Look, I'm here to find my sister. She's missing. Can I have a cabin or a caravan?'

'Nah, all booked up.' He reached for a pen and started tapping it against the desk.

'You're kidding me?'

'Plenty of tent sites available.' He didn't meet her eye.

'Do I look like I have a tent?' she growled.

He shrugged.

They weren't booked up. Everly was never booked up. She had been home for ten minutes and the same nonsense had already begun.

'You could stay with your dad.' He raised his brows at her. He was taking the piss and enjoying it.

'Where's his cabin?'

He pointed to the back of the campground. 'He's in a caravan.'

A caravan? Charlie hadn't mentioned that to her, had she?

'There's a line of caravans at the back, past the toilet block, and tent and campervan sites, just before you get to the creek. It's the orange and white one, number four.'

Jac shouldered her backpack and walked out the door. No need to say anything else.

As she walked across the expanse of grass towards the back of the campground, she noticed a group of people through the gaps between the caravans. About twenty in all, with more arriving by the minute. Maybe Dave wasn't lying when he said they were all booked up. She heard footsteps on the path behind her. Dave strode past, ignoring her.

She got closer and heard muted conversation.

'Better go get Robbie.'

'Dead?'

'Long gone, I reckon.'

'Better check.'

She stepped between two of the caravans and tried to peer down the bank into the creek.

'No! Don't touch the body. You're not supposed to touch the body.'

She felt her heart rate pick up.

Charlie.

She pushed through the small crowd until she was at the front, bracing herself, taking deep breaths in preparation.

Dave slid down the muddy bank and splashed into the shallow water. He caught her eye as he grabbed a flannel-clad shoulder, tipped the waterlogged body over and, amid a chorus of gasps, started dragging the dead man out of the water.

'You're not supposed to move him!' someone shouted.

'Who bloody says!' Dave yelled as he dragged the body up the bank, slipping once, his jeans soaked to the knee. 'I'm not leaving him in there for the fucking eels to come and have a go at him! Someone go and get Robbie!' Dave fell down heavily next to the body and hauled the limbs around so the man was lying face up.

Jac stumbled back as everyone else stepped forward to get a better look at the body of her father.

FOUR

Charlie

Thursday afternoon

CHARLIE FELT HERSELF WAKING, but it was as if she was underwater, reaching for the surface, and no matter how hard she swam, she struggled to break through.

She wasn't sure how many days it had been since she had been taken. She had been sleeping a lot, a deep all-encompassing sleep. When she woke, there were those unsure seconds where she didn't know where she was. Then uncertainty gave way to fear that felt like a punch to her stomach. It was always dark here, save for two LED lanterns. They had appeared after she had blown out the candles numerous times. Whoever had been leaving her food and water had noticed and had done something about it. Charlie knew her fear of fire was irrational, that it was the least of her problems right now, but the events of that night, all these years on, were as fresh in her head as if it had been a week ago. She was frightened of any kind of fire where she could feel the heat on her skin. Birthday candles on a cake, the open fireplace in the corner of the local pub. She thought she'd get over it in time, the fear that it was coming for her. The one party she went to last year, they had lit a bonfire, aided by petrol. The sudden whoosh of flames lit up everyone's faces around her. Even standing well back where she thought she would be safe, she could feel the heat on her skin, thought she could feel it blistering, peeling. She saw the sparks leaping out onto the grass and imagined one hitting her clothes, eating away at the material, finding her bare skin, devouring her, just like the fire had devoured her mother. She had completely overreacted and fled the party like someone was chasing her.

There was no way for her to tell the time here, and she often woke up feeling tired even though it seemed as if she had been asleep for days. She wanted to muster the necessary logic it would take to get out of here. Where *was* here? The thought of escaping on her own seemed impossible when she could barely stand for more than a few minutes, when eating, drinking and using the bucket in the corner took every ounce of energy she had, both mental and physical.

Eyes still closed. She was in no rush to open them. Knowing what was waiting for her. Her body ached and was rigid against the taut canvas of the stretcher she lay upon. The fear, when she was awake, made her feel ill. There were no sounds here. It seemed like she was in a bunker, and every now and then she felt as if the air was being sucked from the room, making her breath hitch. That was when she had to calm herself down, tell herself there was enough air, and to breathe deeply and slowly.

Yesterday, or the day before, she had no idea, she got off the stretcher, on wobbly legs, and scoped out her surroundings. She had drunk from the water bottles left on the desk and eaten a stale sandwich. Directly in front of her, six paces away, she was met with the locked cage door. Beyond that was the rest of the room. She could see a metre or two outside the cage, but then any light that was created by the lanterns diminished into a smudgy grey darkness. Inside the cage, sitting on her stretcher, to her left, was the desk; to her right, a chair and the bucket in the corner by the concrete wall, which she had tried her best not to use at the start, only to inevitably succumb, her weak legs barely able to support her as she crouched over it. Directly in front of her, past the desk and to the left of the locked sliding door was a small set of drawers. There was another wire cage, pushed up against her one, on the left, and for a second she had found hope that there was someone else here with her. Someone else to go through this ordeal with. But when she had picked up one of the LED lanterns and shone it through there, all she could see were a few large boxes. As she looked more closely at the structure that contained her, she could tell it was a lock-up storage cage, not, she told herself, a prison, purpose built, just for her. The thought had made her feel better for about five seconds. The dark brown carpet had felt crusty beneath her bare feet. It was a large off-cut that fitted the space almost perfectly, but in the corners and along the edges she could see the dirt floor underneath.

She hadn't got off the stretcher since, or at least she didn't think so. Right now, her bladder was tight and she knew she had to move. It seemed to take an hour for her to prise her eyes open, and then another to get her body off the stretcher.

She positioned herself in front of the bucket, her right hand shooting to the side, steadying herself on the concrete wall as her head spun. Squeezing her eyes tight, she regained her balance, but there, reaching to pull up her school uniform skirt, she stopped, looking down. She wasn't wearing her school uniform anymore. Ignoring her bladder, she walked over to the light of the lantern. She was dressed in jeans, high-waisted, stonewashed—not hers, of course. The belt around her waist was plaited and thick. The cropped, boxy red T-shirt showed off a strip of her stomach. She pulled the jeans away from her waist. Pale blue underwear. Not hers. She peered down the neck of the T-shirt and took in the white crop top, tinged grey. Not hers. She felt the saliva building up in her mouth as panic took over. She was breathing too fast, this god-damn room swallowing up the air. She collapsed onto the stretcher, her addled brain trying to figure out how this had happened. Someone had undressed her—they must have—they'd stripped her naked and re-dressed her in someone else's clothes like she was a doll. She wanted to rip the clothes from her body, but instead she curled her-self into a tight ball, the pain in her head throbbing to the beat of her racing heart.

FIVE

Jac

Thursday afternoon

'JAC! WAIT UP! JAC!' Dave shouted at her. She broke into a halting jog, her backpack slowing her down. As she ran past the campground's office, she almost collided with the solid frame of Constable Robbie Dunlop.

'Sorry…my fault.' He put both hands on her arms as if to move her aside. 'I'm just heading down to…' He didn't finish his sentence, realising who he was talking to and where he was going.

Word was travelling fast. Half a dozen people came out of the cafe further up the road, standing on the footpath, looking over at the campground. Two people stood at the petrol pump, filling their cars, necks craned, trying to figure out what was going on. At the mini mart opposite people were conversing in groups of two or three about what had happened.

Jac didn't say anything to Dunlop and kept walking. She had no idea where she was going, just that she had to get as far away from her father's vacant eyes as possible. With a hiss and a belch of exhaust, the bus she'd arrived in, rest and toilet break now finished, pulled out onto the road. She thought about running after it, putting as many kilometres between Everly and herself as she could, but she needed to find Charlie.

He's dead. He's dead, she kept telling herself as she slowed her pace. A hysterical laugh escaped her lips and became a choking cough. She stopped in the middle of the road and turned around. Dave was now walking back to the creek with Dunlop. She made her way to the other side. She could go to the cafe, sit for a while, gather her thoughts. But she was too far gone. There was nothing about what had just happened that any thinking could calm. She needed to move.

Jac walked away from the cafe, back down the main street and past the mini mart, where the lingering odour of the departed bus's fumes were still in the air. She turned right onto a side street and away from inquisitive stares. She passed Eddie's local on the corner. She continued walking until she came to an intersection. In front of her was her old primary school, now closed. To her left would lead to the site of her old house, and to the right took her up a hill. With no need to revisit those old memories and feeling the need to get her lungs burning, she turned right and started the climb up the hill.

Her eyes stung and she wondered if she was about to cry. There was no way in hell she was going to cry over Eddie Morgan. It was the shock, she told herself— it wasn't anything close to sadness or grief. She passed a few paddocks, dozens of cows grazing on lush grass, which then gave way to thick bush and tall trees on her left and scrubby bush on her right that gave her a view of the main street and campground as she continued walking up the hill. The road narrowed, its white centreline disappearing with room for only one car the further up she got. She slowed and adjusted her pack. The roaring in her ears faded and was replaced with birdsong—tui, she recognised it, even though she hadn't heard one in years. These days she was more accustomed to traffic, roadworks, industrial dryers and vacuum cleaners. She continued up the road, ambling now, getting her bearings, and, rounding a corner, stopped at a weathered sign, half covered as it was in a tangle of ivy and jasmine, the board splitting in places.

'The Gilmore Hotel,' she mumbled.

She remembered this place. Everly's very own haunted house, or so every kid in Everly liked to think. It was over a hundred years old, was once used as a hospital for returning servicemen during and after World War Two, and hadn't been run as a hotel since then. She remembered the ghost stories this building had elicited. A murdered nurse roaming the corridors, forever trapped; the ghosts of soldiers walking the orchard; a guest who hanged himself in one of the rooms.

The road, she knew, was a dead end, and curving off to the left was where the old hotel sat, overlooking Everly and the farmland beyond. Jac wondered if there was anyone living there now. If old Mrs Gilmore was still around.

Afternoon was beginning to give way to early evening. Even though it was warm enough for November, Jac didn't plan on sleeping rough, and there was no way she was going back to the campground. Maybe she could get into the hotel somehow. Smash a window around the back. Even if it was all closed up, hopefully all the beds were still in there. She shrugged off any nerves, the childhood ghosts and dares, and walked towards the low chain hanging across the driveway.

A woman rounded the bend up ahead, a walking stick

in hand. Jac stood where she was, unsure if she should turn back. But the thought of returning to the campground made her stay where she was. It had to be Mrs Gilmore. Jac could hear her humming a tune to herself. The old woman skirted around the chain, carefully manoeuvring onto the grass, and then back onto the driveway. She must have been six-foot tall, having at least a couple of inches on Jac, and despite her walking stick she stood erect and seemed surefooted on the uneven surface. She was only metres from Jac, and still hadn't seen her. Jac wondered if she should make a noise to alert the woman that she was here but didn't want to give the old bird a heart attack.

Mrs Gilmore stopped humming and looked up. 'Oh... hello.' She was looking at Jac as if she should know her, like Jac looked familiar and she was trying to place her name or face. The woman's short hair was white, blow-dried and sitting high on her head like a mushroom cloud. A neat line of stitches sat at her hairline, a purple bruise bloomed from her temple and out towards her left eye.

'Hi,' Jac said.

'Can I help you?' Mrs Gilmore looked around again, and Jac could see she was confused.

'Not really.' Jac was unsure what else to say, aware that she had nowhere else to be or go, hoping the old woman wasn't about to tell her to bugger off, that she was trespassing.

'I'm just going for my afternoon walk. Bit late, but I had an afternoon nap and slept far too long. I'm supposed to stick to the gardens and the paths behind the hotel.' She turned her head and looked at the chain behind her. 'But fuck it.'

Jac raised her eyebrows. Mrs Gilmore looked so proper

and spoke in such rounded, even tones, the f-bomb was surprising.

'Don't look at me like that.' Her soft face turned hard for a second. Jac noted the sagging skin around her neck and cheeks, swollen pouches under her eyes, powdered make-up sitting in the wrinkles, as Mrs Gilmore looked out past the short ponga ferns, flax bushes and brushy scrub that lined the right side of the driveway and stretched all the way down the side of the hill. 'Have you come from down there?' she asked. 'What's happening?'

From their spot on the hill down to the campground it would've been over five hundred metres. Jac wondered if the old woman could actually see anything at that distance. 'They found a body,' she replied. 'In the creek behind the campground.' There was a larger crowd there now, gathered between the line of caravans and the creek—small dots, motionless, and she could just make out Dunlop, shooing everyone back like they were a swarm of flies.

'Huh,' Mrs Gilmore said, placing her walking stick on the ground. 'Who was it?'

'Eddie Morgan.' Jac fought the urge to laugh again.

Mrs Gilmore nodded and turned to Jac. 'Who are you? Do you live around here? I don't get out much these days.'

'My name's Jac. Jac Morgan,' she said, curious to see if she'd catch the last name.

Mrs Gilmore nodded again. A manicured finger, the nail polish an understated beige, scratched at the edge of the row of stitches, which pulled slightly, puckering the skin at her temple. 'I'd better get back. My jailer will be wondering where I've got to.' One side of her mouth twitched in an attempt at a smile. 'Morgan, you said?'

'Yeah.'

'Eddie Morgan's daughter? That's him, down there.'

She waved her stick in the direction of the campground, putting two and two together. 'Dead.'

'Yeah. I just got home. I haven't been in Everly for a while.' It felt weird, somehow good to say the words out loud. Ever since she had arrived she'd felt like she was in a dream, or maybe a nightmare.

'Jac Morgan...' She could see the old woman searching her memory. 'Oh!' Her face brightened. 'You're the lass who killed her mother...the fire.'

Jac stepped back, shocked, even though she shouldn't have been. Even up here on the hill Mrs Gilmore still got all the gossip.

'And now your father's dead. He was a bit of a no-hoper. That's right, isn't it? Liked the drink. I'm sure I have the right man. He may have done some work up at the hotel for me at some stage. Years ago, now.' She looked at Jac again, and her eyes darted to the pack on her back. 'Where are you staying while you're here?'

'I'm not sure. I was going to get a cabin at the campground but...'

'You can stay here,' Mrs Gilmore said. 'It's perfect timing. I need someone to clean the hotel. You can do that, can't you? My usual cleaner's pregnant and she had to quit yesterday. Strict bed rest, apparently. We've got a busy few days ahead of us. How long are you staying? I guess with him down there dead, you'll be here for a bit to sort all that out. That will take some time. But no reason you can't chip in here. I'll give you accommodation and meals, and will pay you in cash.'

Jac stood there dumbfounded, feeling like the decision had already been made. She had no idea what the next few days would bring. But since she had nowhere else to stay, and very little money, she nodded in answer.

'Good. That's sorted. Come on.' Mrs Gilmore looped her arm into Jac's. Her perfume was so strong, Jac could taste the bitter notes on her tongue. 'The slope up here's a bit much for me sometimes. My name's Iris Gilmore, by the way,' she said as they walked up the drive. 'Owner of this fine establishment.' She waved her walking stick in front of her as they turned the corner and the Gilmore Hotel came into view.

The two-storey hotel was made of weatherboard, painted white. The second storey had wraparound verandas and the wooden balustrades that stretched the length of the building were decorated with intricate fretwork. On the right-hand-side corner a turret, three rectangular windows placed to give views over Everly, sat slightly higher than the red corrugated iron roof, where multiple brick chimneys rose.

To the left of the covered, pillared entryway, Jac took in the floor-to-ceiling windows on the ground floor and French doors opening onto the tiled patio. It was so quiet up here. She couldn't hear any traffic from the main street down the hill and wondered if there was anyone living with Iris. Surely, she didn't live on her own. Jac glanced at the wound on Iris's head, the bruising the same colour as the bank of hydrangeas in the lush garden over to her left, and wondered who looked out for her. She had the thought that she could be sucked into caring for Iris. That was the last thing Jac needed. It almost made her turn around right then. Almost.

Remember why you're here, she reminded herself.

She continued walking with Iris, around a circular garden in the middle of the driveway, built up from the concrete with a low limestone wall, which was bordered by roses, a flagpole in the centre, sans flag.

'The lawns are going to have to be mown. Remind me to tell Nathan to do that,' Iris muttered to her. 'He should know to, but just in case.'

Jac didn't ask who Nathan was, didn't care, but nodded in reply.

They stood under the portico, amid its thick off-white concrete pillars. Iris had a sheen of sweat on her brow and was leaning heavily into Jac.

'Where have you been!' A woman rushed out of the entrance. Her dark blonde hair was pulled into a low ponytail; a pair of track pants and an oversized T-shirt drowned her small frame. The woman's face changed from worried to surprised when she saw Jac.

Iris straightened her back, no longer leaning on Jac, and muttered something she couldn't make out.

'Who's this?' the woman asked, her smile frozen in uncertainty, making her look pained.

'This is Jac Morgan. She's just found out her father's died. She's going to be staying with us.'

With each statement, the woman's smile gradually fell away.

Iris waved a hand in the woman's direction. 'This is Lisa. She's my...carer.'

Lisa stiffened slightly as she nodded at Jac. 'Nice to meet you. I'm actually Iris's daughter.'

SIX

Lisa

Twenty-two years ago

PAIGE AND LISA GILMORE stood at the open door of the music room, halfway down the long main hallway of the hotel, listening as Peter Finch was shown out. They had all just had dinner together. Lisa liked Penguin Pete, as Paige had nicknamed him, because of his hooked nose and his heavy bottom half, causing him to waddle side to side when he walked. Tonight, he was dressed in a black suit and a white shirt, which made the comparison all the more obvious, and had started Paige and Lisa off in a fit of giggles at the table, which Lisa had been reprimanded for. Penguin Pete had grandchildren in their teens and was always interested in what Lisa and Paige were up to. That evening, Lisa had spoken up as he questioned her, telling him about her hopes for the coming year. School was due to start in a few weeks, Paige's last, with Lisa having two more to go. She spoke of her flute lessons and her favourite subjects and teachers, one eye on her mother, Iris, hoping she was listening.

The sisters had been sent to the music room to practise while Iris and Peter talked. They were coming to the end of their conversation and were standing at the front door, their voices echoing along the hallway to where the two girls eavesdropped.

'Ten years is enough,' Iris was saying. 'I refuse to support Andrew anymore.'

She was talking about their father, who had left over a decade ago.

'Of course, Iris, you've been more than generous and, to be honest, he hasn't really got a leg to stand on. He's not going to fight for custody after all these years. How long since Andrew's seen the girls?'

'Never. He never came back to see them. He had checked out of this family long before he left. I mean, he never even fought me when I told him I wanted the girls to have my surname and not his.'

'Well, I don't think you'll have anything to worry about.'

Lisa couldn't remember her dad that well. Even when he had been around, she'd rarely seen him, never felt like she knew him, and over the years Iris had muddied the way she thought of him. Was he selfish? Was he only with Iris for her money? Paige said she remembered him, said he was those things, that he never loved them, but whenever Paige talked about their dad, it sounded like Iris's words coming from her mouth.

Iris closed the heavy front door and the girls heard the dead bolt shifting into place.

'Paige. Lisa,' Iris called.

To show they hadn't been listening in, the girls waited a few seconds before they came into the hallway from the music room.

'Some music before bed, I think, Paige?' Iris smiled at her eldest daughter. 'Piano, tonight. Maybe some Beethoven?'

Paige nodded. 'I've just been practising *Moonlight Sonata*. I can play that?'

'Sounds wonderful, dear.'

As the conversation proceeded, Lisa felt her insides turn to liquid, and when her mother's gaze landed on her, she took half a step back.

'Come,' Iris said.

Lisa sighed, not loud enough for Iris to hear and to accuse her of being dramatic or precious, but enough to expel the air and take in another deep breath of preparation. She looked over at Paige, knowing what was about to happen, knowing neither of them could do anything about it. Paige had tried over the years, but this was the only time Iris wasn't interested in what Paige had to say. Lisa had hoped that tonight, with Pete visiting, Iris would just send them up to bed without any further need of them.

'Don't look at her!' Iris snapped as she took Lisa by her arm and led her up the stairs.

She knew it was important to Iris to have alone time with Paige. She knew she tested Iris at times, made her angry, that she wasn't as smart as Paige or as beautiful. Iris made it clear that Lisa was difficult to love. And Lisa had tried. She had started learning the flute a few years ago. She had nothing on Paige, who was an accomplished musician, knowing how to play violin, flute and the piano. But Lisa thought that, if Iris could see her trying, it would help. So far, it hadn't.

Now, on the second floor, Iris and Lisa passed the bedrooms and stopped at the end of the east wing's hallway. From a distance, it looked like the hallway ended here, the expanse of wall at the end covered in navy wallpaper with bursts of orange and white florals. You had to know the keyhole was there to see it, hidden in a patch of navy.

You also had to be right in front of the door to notice its outline. Iris withdrew the small key from her pocket and unlocked the door. She pushed and as it sprang open, they stepped from warm, wide-open spaces into the damp hallway beyond, the air heavy, oppressive, causing Lisa's breath to catch in her throat.

There was no electricity in this part of the hotel. When Iris got the building rewired a couple of years ago, she didn't bother with this hallway, where there were another five abandoned rooms, and instead had this door installed, making the whole wing disappear. Iris left the main door open to the hallway to light their way and swung open the door to the nearest room: 12A. There was no number 13 in the hotel. Bad luck, Iris always said. Instead, there was 12A and 12B. To Lisa, they had always been bad luck. Just because something was renamed didn't change what it was.

'Get in,' Iris said, pushing her into the small bedroom. 'The darkness will give you time to think.'

'Can I have a light on, please!' Lisa begged, an edge to her voice, verging on hysteria. She would never get used to this. She knew there was no way to light the room but still she asked, always hoping Iris would realise that of course she could have a torch or lamp to help fight the darkness.

'No, the darkness gives you time to think,' Iris repeated, pulling the door closed, plunging Lisa into darkness.

Lisa sat on the floor, the smell of mould and damp overpowering here. The rooms never got any sun, as the windows were boarded up. When she was put in here in the daytime, she could often just make out her hand in front of her face, but at this time of night the darkness was complete.

She had never understood what Iris meant: *The darkness gives you time to think.* Think about what? she had always wondered. Was she supposed to learn something as she sat here in the terrifyingly black stillness?

Lisa had screamed and cried the first few times in the soldiers' hallway, the name Iris used for this part of the house. She had never been so scared in her life. Her dad had left, and the next day Iris put her in here. Lisa's six-year-old imagination had thrown up images of creeping, crawling, burrowing things in the dark, monsters reaching out clawed hands, scratching and tearing at her.

She let out a choked laugh now. Those made-up things in the dark from years ago had nothing on her mother.

SEVEN

Charlie

Thursday evening

CHARLIE OPENED HER eyes wide with a start. Had she heard something? What had woken her? She tried to sit up but couldn't and was frustrated that her body refused to co-operate. She had no memory of having fallen asleep again and wondered how long she had been out for, if minutes or hours had gone by. She put a palm to the back of her head, her fingers gently pressing a tender area. She couldn't remember hitting her head. Couldn't remember much of anything at all. She looked over at the desk. There was a tray with a plastic bottle of water and something under a silver cloche. Her stomach grumbled. Her eyes shifted to the set of drawers by the locked sliding door of the cage. Piles of clothes were neatly distributed across the top. The LED lanterns were still glowing, lighting up the cage and not much else. She picked up the heavy cloche, unsure what to expect. On a white plate bordered by pink roses was a sandwich—white bread, crusts removed. She picked it up. Sniffed it. Peanut butter and jam. She took a nibble. Not bad. Her stomach clenched—desperate for more— as she swallowed the first small mouthful. Another four big bites and the sandwich was gone. She picked up the bottle of water, unscrewed the lid and gulped down half the contents.

She inspected the clothes. The underwear looked old, faded, some of the elastic puckered, like the pair she had on now. She moved on quickly, trying not to think about who might have worn them before her. There were denim overalls, more cropped T-shirts, slip dresses, one red, cotton, the other silky black and cut on the bias. There was a pair of navy satin pyjamas, which she threw onto the stretcher. She picked up the crop tops and underwear and placed them in the first drawer. Everything else went into the second drawer. She stopped, a manic sob escaping.

What the hell am I doing?

She was acting like she was at home, putting her laundry away. Backing away, she looked around her. Tears blurred everything in front of her, and she felt her stomach cramp, the sandwich rising up her throat. She ran to the bucket and threw it up in one chunky evacuation. She sobbed again, wiping her mouth. Looking over at the drawers, a gold piece of metal caught her eye. She hadn't seen it at first. A watch. Gold and stainless steel band. Digital. Picking it up, she looked more closely at it: 5.30 pm. And in small capitals in the corner of the screen: THURS.

It's 5.30 in the evening and it's Thursday!

She felt her body relax a fraction. It wasn't much but it was a start. Maybe she could get her bearings if she knew what time it was. She put the watch on. It felt heavy, and she winced when the bracelet part pulled the hairs on her wrist, but she wasn't going to take it off. This was her lifeline, giving her a modicum of control.

Sitting on the stretcher, the dull ache all over her body

that had subsided for a few minutes was back, and her vision blurred. She closed her eyes, trying to stay focused, trying to think back, her last memory. She remembered school on Monday morning. It was the last day for year thirteens before study leave started. Getting up. Dad snoring. The caravan reeking of cigarettes and body odour, and whatever was coming out of her dad's pores, poisoning the air around them. She had dressed and got out of there as soon as she could. Waiting for the bus. School as usual. A flute lesson with Ms Wallace at lunchtime, which was the only thing she'd got out of bed for that day. And that was it. She thought she remembered the bus trip home. The seat beside her vacant as always. There was the usual chatter that fell about around her. Invitations to parties, sleepovers, trips to the movies. None directed at her. There were the girls behind her, kicking her seat with such force she had to shift forward, leaning her head against the seat in front. Had that happened, or was this memory just a mix of days and weeks gone by? One day being ignored, the next being put under the spotlight. Nothing interesting ever happened in Everly, so something like the events of the fire that happened all those years ago still stuck, and Charlie got the trifecta: alcoholic dad, mother dying in a fire, sister responsible. It had ensured many years of people only wanting to be her friend to find out the details, or a constant stream of bullying and teasing for who she was, for what her sister had done. After the fire, Jac Morgan became a warning that parents gave their teens. And when Jac had gone, Charlie was left with no one and a surname that was synonymous with tragedy and gossip. For the last year, though, it had got marginally better, but maybe that was because she had stopped reacting: no more tears, fear or anger, just the end goal to get out.

She lay down, looking at the watch again, with some relief that at least she had this. It was 5.38 pm. Surely her dad would have reported her disappearance to the police? It spoke volumes about the man he was that she wasn't sure what he would do. And Jac—would her dad have told her? Would she come? She had more faith in the sister she hadn't seen since she was eleven, than her father. Maybe he thought she had packed up and left. Maybe he would be relieved that she was no longer there—she threatened to do it at least once a week. Just like her mum used to do. Mum would get angry drunk and yell at Eddie, telling him he had ruined her life, that he had promised her adventures. Those were the nights when Charlie used to take herself off to the bedroom she shared with Jac and make herself as small as possible. But her mum had done happy drunk as well, where she would dance around the room to songs Charlie didn't know. Charlie would sit to the side, back against her dad's old armchair littered with cigarette burns, watching her mum's hips moving and the glass in her hand spilling amber liquid onto the already stained carpet. Her mum had a beautiful voice and she would sing like she was on a stage performing to an audience of thousands. Charlie loved it, but Jac would roll her eyes and leave.

Jac always said she'd come back for Charlie. And Charlie believed her. Jac had always whinged that Charlie was an annoying brat, but she was all talk. Jac had been more of a parent to her than either her mum or dad. Jac would probably ring or text her at some stage, and then, not getting a response, how long would it take for Jac to become concerned, for her to worry enough to reach out to the father she hadn't spoken to in years? Or maybe she would become so worried she would get on a plane and finally come back home. That's what she would do.

Charlie thought of Jac, all her sharp edges, her forced smile, her cackling laugh. She thought of the way she used to drape an arm over Charlie's shoulder for no reason at all—a hug that wasn't really a hug.

Jac would know something was wrong. She was sure of it. Jac would come.

EIGHT

Jac

Thursday evening

THE FRONT DOOR of the hotel groaned shut behind them, instantly darkening the already dim hallway, shutting out the birdsong and the distant whine of a chainsaw, as if a mute button had been pressed. The silence in here was warm, heavy, so that Jac felt like opening the door again and taking a deep breath before coming back inside. She stood there in the foyer, as Lisa and Iris moved further down the long hallway towards the staircase.

Jac had stood right in this place years ago. In her teens, her friends and she would often get drunk out on the domain on a Saturday night with a hip flask of cheap rum between them, lying on their backs, talking and drinking. Once they'd had enough Dutch courage, they would sneak up to the hotel via the path opposite the domain. The dare had always been the same: try to get inside the hotel. Whoever felt the bravest, and drunkest, would give it a go. Jac got to this very spot one night but didn't go any further. She wasn't sure if it had been the alcohol or the stories they had told to scare each other, but she'd turned and run back into the bush, feeling like something was chasing her, collapsing into relieved laughter when she got back to her friends.

Lisa looked back at Jac then to Iris, her mouth a thin line, her back rigid, hands clasped in front of her. She was obviously thrown off by Jac's presence. But from the little Jac had seen, Iris ruled this place. Directly inside the front door and to her left was an ornate wooden coat rack, with each of the five hooks ending in a carved stag head. To the right, was the old check-in desk. Jac moved over to it, removing her heavy pack from her back and resting it on the grey and white chequerboard tiled floor of the foyer. Glancing behind the desk Jac saw a pile of boxes and a wall of cubby holes with numbers under each one. Empty hooks were fitted inside each cube, where the room keys would have hung. She turned back to the two women, trying to listen in to their whispered conversation ten metres away.

'Mum, what are you doing?' Lisa asked, her right thumb rubbing the knuckles on her left hand back and forth.

Jac looked along the hallway, past the two women, noticing that, even with the lights on and high ceilings, it was dim, the dark panelled walls and polished floors not helping. She met Lisa's eye and looked away.

'Where is she going to stay?'

'In the staff quarters out back.'

'Nathan's in one room and the other room is a mess—there's not even a bed in there anymore.'

'Well, this is a hotel. We'll put her in the west wing.'

'It's a mess in there too.'

'It's fine. With Tui gone, we need someone to clean. We can't hold the open day without the whole place getting a onceover.'

'I told you this morning that I could do it. I don't know

if this is a good idea.' Lisa lowered her voice, but Jac still heard her. 'We don't even know her.'

'Well, lucky for you I own this place and decisions like this have nothing to do with you.' Iris's voice was loud and clear.

There was a brief silence and the women separated. Lisa continued along the hallway, disappearing through a set of double swing doors past the stairs, towards the back of the hotel, and Iris came towards Jac.

'All organised,' Iris said, as if the disagreement hadn't happened.

HALF AN HOUR later Jac came down from her room and waited at the bottom of the staircase unsure of where she should be going. Iris had told her dinner would be served at six. Iris appeared on the landing, the end of her walking stick in her right hand a few centimetres off the ground as if to prove she didn't really need it, but gripping the handrail with the other as she descended the stairs, each step deliberate, wearing fashionable wide-legged trousers and a short-sleeved silk top; a slash of maroon lipstick and a streak of bronzer on each cheek livened up her face but failed to cover the bruise at her temple. Lisa, who had stood at the entrance half an hour ago in track pants and a T-shirt, appeared a minute later and was now wearing a sleek, black wrap dress. Her hair was pulled into a neat bun, but her face, devoid of make-up, looked pale and tired under her freckles. Jac smoothed down her baggy T-shirt and yanked up her jeans. *Too late now*, she thought. Plus, there wasn't a single item of clothing in her bag that would even come close to what the Gilmores were wearing. Lisa glanced at her, giving her a quick up-and-down, clearly not approving.

The dining room was on their right, a few metres from the staircase, and it was huge. Beyond huge. There was a cavernous open fireplace on the right and, on the left, a sweeping bar, a length of shiny dark wood, the mirrored wall behind it reflecting the dim lights, the glass shelves empty of alcohol. Brocade curtains hung at the floor-to-ceiling windows on the far side of the room. Paintings of various sizes with ornate frames hung against the ivory walls on either side of the fireplace. Most were landscapes, dull greens, greys and blues that brought no life to the room.

Six chandeliers hung from the ceiling; the lone dining table placed directly under one in the centre of the room. Jac imagined all the other tables that could fit in here— used to fit in here, when it was the hotel restaurant.

Only three of the chandeliers were illuminated, leaving the far corners of the sparse room in darkening shadow, the curtains having been drawn, even though it was still light outside. Despite the enormous size of the room, Jac felt claustrophobic, hemmed in, which was silly, she told herself, after where she'd come from: a bus, a plane, and a tiny flat, in which her room was more a closet than a bedroom.

She took her place opposite Lisa at the long table, which, she counted, could fit twenty. A linen tablecloth covered less than a quarter of the expanse.

'I always had the dream that we would open up the hotel again,' Iris said, her voice echoing, bouncing off the bar and back over to the table, 'but it never eventuated. Can you imagine this place, full of people, eating and drinking…' She sighed and straightened her cutlery, picked up a fork and polished it with her cloth napkin. She held her wine glass up to the light then placed it back down, adjusting her water glass, moving it left and then right.

Lisa mirrored her mother's actions, and Jac was unsure if she even realised she was copying her. Or maybe Jac made her nervous.

'Wine?' Lisa asked.

Jac picked up her glass and reached over for Lisa to fill it. As she poured, Jac noticed the red mark across the knuckles on her left hand. Up close, the skin looked raw and Jac wondered if it was from her rubbing her knuckles before. Lisa saw Jac looking then, and lowered her hand under the table.

Iris picked up a small silver bell and rang it. Less than a minute later, a door in the far right-hand corner of the room by the windows opened and a man wheeled in a trolley. He looked to be in his late twenties, his dark hair was cut close to his head and he wore a chef's whites. He smiled at Jac as if he knew her. Jac didn't return the smile.

'Tama here has been cooking for me for the last…' Iris looked at Tama for the answer.

'Almost five years now, Ms Gilmore.' He gave Iris the same open smile he had just given Jac.

'That long?' Iris shook her head. 'Tama does all the cooking. Breakfast, lunch and dinner, five days a week, and his wife, Tui, up until yesterday, did all the cleaning.' Iris turned to Tama. 'How is Tui today?'

'Good, thanks. But not happy about the bed rest and upset that she let you down right before the open day this weekend.' Tama moved around the table placing plates in front of them.

'Well, Jac's timing has been quite fortuitous. She'll be with us for a few days and will be helping out.'

Tama nodded, his smile faltering. Jac could tell he knew who she was.

He left the room, and Iris placed her cloth napkin on her lap. Lisa followed suit. When Iris picked up her knife and fork, Lisa did the same, always a fraction of a second behind. Jac dug into her roast pork, relishing the taste of the rich gravy and the tender meat, the salty roast potatoes, hardly swallowing before she pushed the next forkful into her mouth. She couldn't remember the last time she had eaten like this. With a stab of guilt, she thought of Charlie. What was she eating tonight? Where was she? Was she warm and fed? Jac rested the knife and fork on her plate, her appetite diminished.

'Your name, is it short for Jacqueline?' Iris asked. 'Such a regal name.'

Jac smothered a laugh. She had been likened to many things before but regal wasn't one of them. 'The name on my birth certificate is actually Jack with a k. But I spell it j-a-c. Don't get as many questions when it's spelled like that.'

Iris looked at her, head tilted, obviously waiting for an explanation.

'And my sister's name is Charles. But she goes by Charlie.'

'Why on earth would your parents do that to you? That's ridiculous.'

'I agree. It's ridiculous. I wasn't planned. Mum didn't really want to be pregnant at all—she was young when she had me—but when she came around to the fact, she became desperate for a boy. No idea why. She always said she was a hundred per cent sure I was going to be a boy, so I was named before I was born. The name Jack stayed. Exactly the same thing happened with Charlie. She made

sure we both knew she was disappointed we weren't boys.'
Jac shrugged and Iris nodded, as if she understood.

'I'm sorry to hear about your father,' Lisa said, no doubt
trying to fill in the awkward silence after Jac's oversharing.

Jac turned to her. 'You really don't have to be.' She
picked up a piece of crackling and began snapping it into
smaller pieces.

Lisa looked shocked. Iris half hid a grin behind her
napkin, and Jac wondered why this amused her.

'We didn't get on. I hadn't seen him in years,' Jac said,
eager for the women to understand that she didn't need or
want their sympathy.

'Eddie Morgan,' Iris said, looking at Lisa. 'That was
her father.'

'I'm not sure I know him,' Lisa replied.

'Did a bit of work for me a while ago. You weren't here.'
It sounded like an accusation. 'Anyway, if you don't know
who Eddie Morgan is, you would've heard of Jac. She's
the one who killed her mother—in the house fire.'

'Mum!' Lisa exclaimed looking first to Jac in horror
and then back at Iris.

'It's true. Isn't it?' Iris looked to Jac for confirmation.
'If I remember rightly, the blame was put on your poor
mother, or was it your father? I can't remember now. But I
heard the whispers.' Iris winked at Jac as if they shared a
secret. 'It was actually you. You came home drunk, passed
out in front of the TV with a cigarette in your hand.'

So many different stories floating around. But the
general consensus was that Jac had killed her mother, a
nice tidy conclusion, details be damned. Jac stared at Iris,
shocked at her bluntness. Her face was slack, her lips a
thin line, but her eyes danced, like the whole conversation

amused her. Jac put a piece of pork into her mouth. She started chewing but it refused to go down. 'My mother died in a house fire. I was seventeen at the time. My sister Charlie was eleven.' She hoped that was enough to end the topic.

'How tragic,' Lisa said.

'So tragic.' Iris's tone suggested it was anything but.

'And how old's your sister now?' Lisa asked.

Jac cleared her throat, ready to tell the story, eager to move on. 'She's the whole reason I'm back in Everly. Charlie's just turned eighteen. She lives at the campground with Dad—or did, I guess. I got a text from him on Tuesday saying she was missing. I saw Constable Dunlop this afternoon and I suppose there was a bit of confusion… So far nothing's been done.'

'Oh!' Lisa held a hand to her chest. 'That's terrible!'

'Well…yes.' Jac was not expecting such an emotional reaction. She thought she could see tears in Lisa's eyes, but Lisa dropped her gaze to examine her plate.

Lisa sniffed once and then said, 'It's a horrible, horrible thing when a loved one goes missing. So is Constable Dunlop doing anything about it now that you've talked to him?'

'He said he'd look into it.'

'That Robbie Dunlop, he's useless,' Iris said, taking a sip of wine. 'Wouldn't put too much faith in him.'

'Mum…' Lisa admonished.

'Don't "Mum" me. He's hopeless. What would you know anyway?'

Lisa nodded, as if agreeing with her mother.

'I'll go and see him again tomorrow. See what's happening,' Jac said.

'Is it possible she ran away?' Lisa asked her.

'Maybe… But I'm sure she would've said something to

me if she was planning on leaving Everly.' Again, the little bit of doubt nudged its way in. *Would she have told me?*

'Of course.' Lisa nodded.

'It's a small place,' Jac said, and then asked: 'Do you know Charlie?'

'I don't think so,' Lisa replied. 'Even though I come back to Everly every school holidays to spend time with Mum. I must admit we do keep to ourselves here a bit.'

Jac pulled her phone out of her pocket and scrolled through the various texts from Charlie. 'She sent this to me a couple of months ago.' She reached across the table so Lisa and Iris could see the photo. It was a closeup of Charlie, blonde hair framing her face, blue eyes squinting in a smile, neat smattering of freckles across her nose. Iris reached over and took the phone, her fingers brushing the screen, a small smile on her face.

Jac looked at Lisa, questioning.

'Mum,' Lisa said. When she got no reaction, she said again, louder, 'Mum.'

Iris looked up.

'Jac's phone,' Lisa said.

Iris handed back the phone, gazing straight ahead.

'Do you know her?' Jac asked.

'No… No, I don't think I know her.' Iris sounded confused.

'Do you think you may have seen her somewhere?' Jac pushed.

Iris was silent and Lisa said, 'You don't look much alike.'

Jac turned away from Iris, who was obviously having a moment. 'Lucky for her, huh.' Jac ran a hand through her short dark hair. Wanting to get back to Charlie's disappearance, Jac said, 'If Constable Dunlop's as useless as you say, I might ask around Everly myself, see who saw her last. Maybe contact her school. Friends.' She didn't even know who Charlie's friends were, but she needed to do something.

'Good idea,' Lisa agreed. 'I wish I could help, but as I said we don't really venture out much, and I've only been back a few months.'

'What did you do before you came back here?' Jac asked.

'I'm a teacher—music.'

'Not anymore,' said Iris. 'You can't say you're a music teacher when you don't even have a job,' she muttered into her wine glass.

Jac glanced at Lisa, trying not to show surprise, but Lisa was looking at Iris with a tight-lipped smile.

'I've given up work for now to care for Mum.'

Iris grunted.

'I moved back a few months ago to help Mum out. This is a big place to be rattling around in all by herself, even if she does have help with the grounds and housework. I felt better being here with her. Which was lucky as she had a nasty fall last week. She got quite a bad concussion, along with the cut on her head…and she—'

'Don't talk about me like I'm not here!' Iris's voice echoed through the dining room so forcefully that Jac startled, her knife slipping and clattering onto her plate. She hadn't known the old woman had it in her.

Lisa looked down, both hands in her lap. Jac noticed a slight movement in her right upper arm and now guessed the reason for her reddened knuckles. 'Sorry, Mum. That was rude of me.'

'You go on about how you're doing me a favour. I didn't ask you to come back, did I?' Iris dabbed at the corners of her mouth with her napkin, frowning, the stitches at her hairline puckering.

'No, you didn't. But I'm happy to be here with you,' Lisa said, glancing at Jac, trying to keep the peace and restore order.

The rest of the dinner was eaten in silence, with Lisa excusing herself before Tama came in to clear up the dishes.

Iris and Jac stood, Iris taking Jac's arm, just as she had done on the way back up the driveway that afternoon, and led her out of the dining room towards the staircase. Halfway up, they stopped on the landing.

'My mother, Helen,' Iris said, staring at the painting there. It took up the whole wall. The stern woman looked down at them. Jac could see the resemblance to Iris—the skin colour, the hard-set mouth. The woman looked to be in her forties, dark brown hair styled in a severe bun that sat on top of her head. Her eyes were blue, like Iris's, but paler. She wore a white shirt, with a stiff collar, making her look almost masculine.

'A strong woman,' Iris said, nodding. 'My mother lost her parents in the space of a few months. They left her and my father the hotel and they both ran it for four years, then when my father went to war my mother ran it on her own for two years, until it got too much.'

They turned right and continued up the stairs, Iris with her walking stick in one hand and the other remaining linked through Jac's arm. At the top of the stairs, in front of them, was the east wing's long, carpeted hallway, four doors on either side. Brass sconces were placed on the walls between each door and gave the hallway a muted glow. Iris bade Jac goodnight as she stopped at the first door on the right and let herself in. Jac rounded the ban-

ister on the left, her hand trailing along the smooth wood.
A few metres ahead were the heavy smoke doors that separated the east and west wings. She pushed open one of
the doors, the small rectangle of glass at eye level showed
the hallway she was about to enter was pitch black. She
reached into the darkness, slapping the wall on her right
trying to find a light switch, but when she found it and
flicked it down, nothing happened. Iris had explained to
her earlier that this part of the hotel was never used and
they often had trouble with the electricity. She knew her
room was the first on the right and with arms outstretched
she found the door handle and let herself in, the large window on the opposite side of the room letting in the last of
the evening light.

   The air felt stale and the carpet in both the hallway
and in her room was different from that in the east wing's
hallway. Here, it was peeling up in the corners, and it
was tacky underfoot, the soles of her shoes grabbing on
for an instant before releasing. She walked across the
room, ignoring her bed with the large brown stain on the
mattress to her right, and wrenched open the stubborn
window with some difficulty, flakes of white paint fluttering down to the carpet. Poking her head out, she could
see a narrow gangway where two metres along a fire escape ladder was attached to the wall. Jac thought if she
pushed it hard enough the whole thing would break away.
Below her, at the back of the hotel, was a large rectangle
of pitted concrete that stretched the length of the hotel
and out ten metres which then gave way to neatly mown
grass. To the left was a small building, white stucco with
a red roof, in keeping with the hotel and behind that in
the golden light Jac could see long grass and neat rows
of fruit trees. In front of her, beyond the concrete and

manicured lawn, there was a wide dirt path, which vanished into thick bush. She left the window open and went into the ensuite, switching on the light. It fizzed, flickering on and off, before deciding to stay on. There was a cracked basin and a shower; the yellow shower curtain and scum-coated shower tray looked like they hadn't been touched in years. A toolbox sat on the floor under the pedestal vanity. Jac hoped the plumbing in here was okay—she was dying to take a shower, even looking like it did. She leaned in and turned the tap; the pipes groaned and clunked into life and she felt the hot water flow over her hand before turning it off. Stepping out into the bedroom, she went over to the dressing table, the mirror above tarnished with black splotches, where Lisa or Iris had left a set of sheets, which thankfully smelled freshly laundered, and a pale blue synthetic bedspread that smelled of mothballs. A large patch of the wall to the right of the mirror and dresser had the faintest brown stain on it, like a mug of tea had been poured down the wallpaper.

Jac made her bed, ignoring the foreign smells and the damp feel of the room. She would only be here for a few days while she tracked Charlie down. If she had to be in Everly, the Gilmore Hotel was the place to be, up on the hill, removed, a world of its own, away from the whispers of the locals.

She plugged her phone in to charge at the power point by her bed, thankful that it actually worked, and put it on the bedside table. Laying down on the bed, she sighed in relief. It had been a long day. A long forty-eight hours since she'd got her dad's first text. There were no curtains on the window and she turned onto her right side and watched the light change as the sun set, the shadows lengthening in the room, the house stretching and cracking as the temperature cooled. She thought of her father lying in the creek. She had spent the whole trip home trying to figure out how she would speak to him after all this time. She had been angry for seven years, probably longer than that, and this feeling was hard to let go of when she had held it close for so long. Her anger had given her some kind of purpose back then. It had propelled her first to Auckland and when that didn't seem far enough on to Australia. But it had also provided excuses. It was the reason she held off returning to Everly. To Charlie. It was the reason she kept to herself. She called it being private. Others called it antisocial. Some thought she was afraid to let people in, to trust. They were probably right, but she didn't want to pick at that particular scab, fearing what it would reveal.

He was dead. He was finally gone. There was no sadness at this fact. But the anger still burned, and now there was regret at not having stood up to him sooner. Now, she could never tell him what she thought of him. What a hopeless, worthless piece of shit he was. And yet, what would've been the point to saying any of that? Eddie Morgan never cared about anyone, especially not Jac. She could see herself standing in front of him, reciting some pathetic speech filled with half-truths about how he'd ruined her life but that she was okay now, she was doing just fine, and he would've got himself another drink, already moving on. He had never been a father to her. Throughout her life he had only ever caused her stress, heartache and fear.

Jac pushed thoughts of her dad away. He didn't deserve another second of her time. She was here to find Charlie, not to rake over the past. She closed her eyes, hoping sleep would come quickly.

WHEN JAC WOKE, it was dark, and the open window brought in a cool wind that chilled her bare arms. She was curled into a tight ball on the bed, still fully clothed, trying to find the energy to either get up and close the window or at least climb under the covers. It was a full minute before she realised there was someone in the room, the figure only a smudge in the muted grey darkness of the moonlight. She stiffened as they moved towards her.

This fucking hotel is haunted.

Jac urged herself to roll off the other side of the bed, to scream, to kick out. Instead, she closed her eyes tight, hoping to erase what she was seeing. Telling herself it wasn't real. But when she heard shuffling footsteps, her eyes flickered open again. She squinted into the darkness. It was Iris. Jac didn't know if she felt relieved or even more scared. What was the old woman doing in here?

Iris sat down on the bed, the weight of her body making Jac tip towards her. Was she sleepwalking? Jac wanted to reach out and shake her awake, but then vaguely remembered you weren't supposed to wake a sleepwalker, although she had no idea why. Something to do with giving them a heart attack? The last thing she needed was Iris Gilmore's death on her conscience. Before Jac could do anything, she felt Iris's hand touch her head. Jac winced as if she had been slapped. The hand caressed her forehead, then moved down to the nape of her neck. Jac wanted to squirm away, but before her brain had time to cobble together an action, Iris leaned down, kissed her forehead and said, 'It's okay. I'm here. I'm here.'

What the fuck?

And then Iris got up and walked out of the room.

Jac jumped out of bed, her brain and body finally cooperating, and reached her door in time to see Iris walking through the smoke doors. Jac poked her head out through the doors. She edged along the hallway and watched Iris as, instead of going to her room across the hallway, she descended the stairs. Jac didn't care where she was going and returned to her room, closed the door, this time locking it. She crossed the room to the open window, glancing out, looking for what she wasn't sure. More ghosts? Intruders? And with some effort she yanked the window down and it screeched closed.

She checked her phone: 11.30 pm. No messages from Charlie, but other voicemails waited for her. Two from her flatmate, Tania, and five from her boss—ex-boss. They could wait.

She went into the bathroom and splashed her face with water. When she looked in the mirror, she could see the remnants of the fright Iris had given her: eyes wide, forehead creased, mouth straining down. She relaxed her face and tried to smile, wiping her shaking hands on a towel. She changed into a pair of boxer shorts and a singlet that she dragged from her pack, and then double-checked the door was locked. She climbed under the covers. Every time she thought of Iris's touch, she shivered and pulled the covers over her head. Throughout the night, she got up several times to check and recheck the door was locked. It wasn't until the room started to lighten with the dawn that she finally closed her eyes again and slept.

NINE

Lisa

Twenty-one years ago

LISA LAY IN BED, SHEETS, blankets and duvet pulled up to her chin. It was August and so cold in her room that, when she poked her head out of the bedclothes and breathed out, she could see a wisp of condensed air above her. Iris refused to let her have a heater in her room, told her it was a waste of money and for her to put more blankets on her bed. Iris had a heater in her room—Lisa could hear it whirring away in the mornings when she passed on her way downstairs. Paige had one too. Iris said Paige needed it, as she sometimes practised her flute or violin in there. 'How do you expect your sister to practise efficiently when her fingers are frozen?' Lisa had no answer to that. But Paige would often bring the small fan heater into Lisa's room at night, warming it for her before taking it back to her own room.

It was ten o'clock, Saturday morning. Lisa had no place to be, and she knew Iris wouldn't bother her. Out of sight, out of mind, was Iris's motto with her youngest. She yawned and stretched. She had stayed up far too late the night before, but that had been mostly Paige's fault. Paige had tapped on her door just before ten pm, dressed in a denim mini skirt, black tights and boots, her midriff showing as her khaki anorak fell open. Paige always looked effortlessly pretty. Her tan was always even, and somehow she held on to it during the winter months. It wasn't the rich glow of summer but enough to allow her to go without make-up or, like last night, to show off her midriff in the middle of August.

'You're going out now?' Lisa had asked.

Paige had flashed her a smile. 'You should come, Lise. There's a party at Felicity's.'

Paige asked her if she wanted to go with her every time she snuck out Lisa's window but they both knew what the answer would be.

Lisa's room didn't have a balcony like Iris's and Paige's but it did have a fire escape—and the ladder was still solid, unlike the one in the west wing at the opposite end of the hotel, where the ladder had become unbolted on one side and listed slightly. Paige had been using Lisa's fire escape for the last year to sneak out to see friends and go to parties.

At last night's invitation, Lisa had snuggled down deeper into her blankets, an open book balanced on her chest. 'No thanks.'

'Come on, Lise, it'll be fun.' Paige had grabbed the blankets and yanked them off her.

'Paige!' she'd yelled as the icy air travelled over her ankles and feet.

Paige had laughed, then told her to be quiet, making her way across the room and opening the sash window, peering out. 'Shit, it's cold tonight.'

'You're telling me.' Lisa had pulled the covers back over herself.

'See you later.' Paige had smiled back at her and then hoisted herself onto the small, rusted platform to begin her descent.

Lisa had jumped out of bed, stuck her head out the window and peered down. 'Be careful,' she'd hissed, and then pulled the window down, leaving it open a few centimetres, so Paige would be able to hook her fingers under to open it fully when she came back. It also chilled her room even more, leaving enough of a gap for icy fingers of winter breeze to creep in. Duty done, Lisa had dived straight back into bed.

She had gone to a party with Paige this time last year. Paige had known she was nervous, and Lisa made her swear not to leave her, but as soon as she got to the party, Paige had spotted her friends, telling Lisa she'd be back soon—only to disappear for the rest of the night. Lisa didn't blame Paige. Her sister was pretty and popular and she shouldn't have expected Paige to stick by her when there were so many people vying for Paige's attention. Parties weren't for Lisa. Too noisy. People she thought she knew got drunk and seemed to undergo a personality change, becoming extra bitchy or extra friendly—both of which threw her off. She struggled to talk with people and didn't even consider dancing. With no alcohol in her system, she couldn't imagine moving next to the people who writhed and wrapped themselves around anyone who came near. Afterwards, Paige had apologised profusely for abandoning her, saying it would never happen again, but Lisa hadn't felt the need to go out again. Paige, however, needed to escape sometimes. Iris smothered her, and Lisa understood that she needed to get away from their mother. Nevertheless, the times she was left here, even if it was in the middle of the night, Lisa felt abandoned. She tried to imagine Paige in her own bed, along the hallway from her, but it never really worked. Her loneliness was almost as bad as what she felt in the soldiers' hallway.

Paige had fallen in through her window just before two am. She had stumbled to Lisa's bed and whispered in her ear, 'I'm home,' her hot breath laced with alcohol, forcing Lisa from sleep. Paige had leaned down, kissed her forehead, and then run a hand over her cheek. Her fingers had been so cold, Lisa felt the ghost of her touch even after she was gone. With arms outstretched in the darkness, Paige had made her way across the floor, tripping once over a pile of clothes, and then running into the door. Her giggling could be heard as she yanked it open and made her way along the hallway to her room.

Paige would be hungover today, but she was good at hiding it from Iris, who never suspected that Paige would be sneaking out to parties on a Friday night, let alone drinking alcohol. Lisa rolled out of bed and pulled on her fluffy blue robe. Even though she didn't like going to parties, she loved to hear all the gossip Paige always came home with. Who had gone. Who had hooked up with whom. Who had got so drunk they passed out or vomited.

She walked along the hallway, her bare feet still getting used to the plush new carpet that had been laid. She thought her mother could have gone with something more understated, but Iris had insisted on colour-matching the carpet to the same it had been for decades, a deep red: 'In honour of the past.' Lisa inhaled. The scent of paint still hung in the air even after all these weeks.

Lisa stopped at Paige's room. The old plastic numbers on the doors had been replaced with shining brass. Her mother's room was the next one down, number sixteen; Paige was number fifteen. Lisa was on the other side of the hallway, number eight, as far away from Paige and her mother as possible—her mother's choice, not hers.

She looked back along the dim hallway towards her room and, just beyond it, the almost invisible door that led to the soldiers' hallway. In her room, in bed at night, she swore she could feel the dank loneliness emanating through her wall from that disused hallway. She had asked her mother numerous times if she could move further up the hallway by her and Paige. Iris always said no.

Lisa rubbed at her arms enclosed in her dressing gown and turned once more to Paige's door. She tapped with a finger, softly at first, but Paige had already started her scales. She admired her sister's dedication. Saturday morning, with a hangover. She listened at the door as her sister went through a series of finger combinations, the notes ascending and descending. She knocked louder. If she got her early enough into practice, she may just bunk off for the morning. No answer. Lisa looked to her right, waiting for her mother to appear at the stairs, and, when she didn't, knocked again.

'Paige.' Her stage whisper, she hoped, was loud enough for Paige to hear but not loud enough for her mother to catch, wherever she was. 'Paige, let me in.' The music stopped.

And then her mother was there, by her side, as if she'd materialised out of thin air. Lisa jumped as Iris grabbed her wrist.

'What do you think you're doing?' she hissed. 'You know you're not to interrupt Paige when she practises. What's wrong with you?'

Lisa froze. She didn't want to end up in the soldiers' hallway. She should've kept a better listen out for her.

'Go,' her mother said. 'Out—away! I don't want to see

your face until dinner time.' She released Lisa's wrist, smoothed back her short, bobbed hair that was always blow-dried into a hard helmet, and knocked on the door. 'Paige, darling. Can I come in?' She turned the handle and walked in.

Lisa hurried back to her bedroom, feeling like she had dodged a bullet. If Iris didn't want to see her till dinner, Lisa would gladly obey.

TEN

Jac

Friday morning

BEFORE JAC HAD even opened her eyes, her brain kicked into action. Charlie. Where was she? Where had she slept last night? Her father. She shut that down straight away. Iris in her room last night. Weird. Creepy. Would she say anything?

Her phone vibrated on the bedside table. Turning on her side, she disconnected it from the charger and looked at the name on the screen. She blinked twice, squeezing her eyelids together in an effort to focus. She felt groggy after a mostly sleepless night. Her boss, Jim—again. She swiped the screen, declining the call. A few seconds later, she got a text saying she had voicemail. She replayed the message, knowing what was coming. Jim's voice, always one octave higher than you would expect, came down the line, the anger, just below the surface, cutting each word off abruptly as he spoke. 'As you have not responded to any of my messages, I have no choice but to take this further. If I haven't heard from you by midday today, the police will be called, and we will be pressing charges— assault and robbery.'

'Fuck,' Jac muttered, throwing the phone onto the bed. She knew she had gone too far but had been desperate. Jim was a piece of shit with an inflated ego, for someone who managed the cleaning staff of a hotel and whose office was in a basement with no windows. After Jac had found out about Charlie on Tuesday, she had gone to him the following morning to ask him for an advance on her pay, so she could get back home. He asked her why. So, she told him, and he still said no. So, she completely lost it. Knocked over a chair and grabbed a stapler, meaning to hurl it at the wall, but it rebounded off the filing cabinet and hit him in the face. He had a tiny cut above his eyebrow and now he was saying she had assaulted him. She should've just left it there, but after he'd fired her, telling her to clear out her locker and leave her key card with reception, she had gone to room 403. The couple staying in there had been guests at the hotel for a few days. Each time she had cleaned the room, she had looked in the wardrobe and bedside tables. She always did it out of curiosity, wanting to see how the other half lived, the clothes, jewellery and perfume they wore. She had never taken anything, although had often been tempted. There was cash, poking out from beneath the Bible, at least a couple of hundred. She'd let herself in, taken the money, then waiting for Jim to go on his break, she went back to his office and cleared out the petty cash. She had her ticket home, plus about a hundred spare. That's all she cared about. Getting home to Charlie.

Jac's heart rate returned to normal as she reminded herself that her phone was the only way Jim could contact her. She wished she could throw it away. A fresh start. There wasn't anyone in Australia she needed to keep in contact with, even after living in Sydney for almost two years. But Charlie had this number. It was the only way she could contact Jac.

Everything would be fine, Jac told herself. She always managed to land on her feet. She had a fleeting thought that her dad would be proud of her—and jumped off the bed to chase the thought away. Jim and the cops had no idea where she was. It wasn't like she was a murderer or anything. They'd try looking for her and would soon give up. There was no chance she'd be going back to Australia now, though.

It was just after 6.30 am and Jac wondered if Lisa and Iris were up. She crossed the floor and opened the door. It was so quiet she could hear every stretch and groan of the hotel—it sounded like an old woman with creaking bones and aching joints. There was no sign of anyone as she walked through the smoke doors and down the sweeping staircase. As she passed the portrait of Helen Gilmore on the stairs, she nodded good morning to the stern face—one that seemed to be wondering who this mess of a scrappy blow-in was and what she was doing in her fine establishment.

She walked along the long hallway, past the dining room on her right. There were closed doors on either side but at the end, near the lobby and old check-in desk the double doors to the lounge were open. It had multiple sitting areas, set up like the place still housed guests, when there was only Iris and Lisa. After seeing the way Iris behaved towards Lisa last night, Jac could imagine the two sitting in here, opposite ends of the room, each in their own space. The paintings in this room were enormous, like all the others, having such big spaces to fill on the sprawling walls. On one wall was a landscape, with men on horseback surrounded by hounds, and the other showed a scene of three women in pastel, corseted dresses, hair bundled high on their heads, drinking tea, with looks on their faces as if they had smelled something objectionable. Jac thought everything here looked like it belonged in a country house in England a hundred years ago—maybe that was the look Iris was going for. There was yet another fireplace, too, the limestone hearth cool beneath her bare feet. The mantel was lined with half a dozen photos in wooden frames. One was of a young Iris, Jac thought, standing at the entrance to the hotel. She looked to be in her mid-teens, hair brushed into a beehive. The one next to it was Iris again—slightly older this time, possibly seventeen or eighteen—and she was standing in the turret, gazing down at the photographer, who would've been standing in the driveway to get the shot. Jac shivered. The blurriness of the photo, colours faded, Iris's fair hair and white top—she looked like an apparition.

Jac crossed the room to the side table by the door where there were at least another twenty photo frames. She leaned down to inspect them. Iris, with a baby, presumably Lisa, cradled in her arms in this very room, the soft light from the windows bathing them in a golden glow. One of Iris and Lisa as a toddler, the two figures off-centre in the frame. Looking closer, Jac could see the photo had been folded, cutting off someone else in the picture. She could just make out the edge of a shoulder, the curve of a shoe. In the photo, Lisa was looking past Iris and appeared to be laughing at the invisible person. In others, Jac watched the little blonde toddler grow up. Posing around the hotel, inside and outside, mostly with Iris, some on her own. By the age of ten or so, Jac realised this wasn't Lisa, but someone else. Her face shape was different, her skin olive and free of freckles. A sister? There was one image of this girl, around sixteen, in profile, staring out a window, a flute on her lap. Jac felt a jolt of recognition—then yelped with fright when, close behind her, someone said, 'Good morning.'

Jac spun around. She hadn't even heard Lisa come in.

'Sorry,' Lisa said. 'I didn't mean to scare you.' Her eyes were on the photos, not Jac.

'That's okay.' Jac shuffled her feet, embarrassed she had been caught snooping. She took in Lisa's full face of make-up, her creaseless white shirt and three-quarter black jeans, ballet flats on her feet. Her hair was done up in a neat, high ponytail. And here Jac was standing in her pyjamas. 'I woke up early,' she said, as if this was an excuse for why she was down here inspecting Lisa's family photos.

'Don't worry about it.' Lisa waved a hand. She gestured towards the table full of photos. 'Looking for me, were you? Or didn't you notice?' Her friendly tone had changed; some sort of bitterness or sadness seemed to make her face contort.

Jac didn't reply. She decided now wasn't the best time to mention Iris's night-time wanderings, either.

'I guess you could call me the family photographer.' Lisa turned and left the room, saying, 'Breakfast is in half an hour. Mum will expect you to be dressed.'

ELEVEN

Charlie

Friday morning

CHARLIE CLAWED HER way into consciousness. Her earlobes stung, a white-hot pain that made them feel like they were on fire, demanding that she leave the comfort of sleep. She opened her eyes and stared at the ceiling. The dream came back to her. But it wasn't a dream. Her arm felt heavy, as if there were weights attached to it, and she had to make a concerted effort to raise her hand to her ear. Wincing, she could feel small studs in her ears.

They pierced my ears while I was sleeping?

The fear and uncertainty about what was going to happen next brought tears to her eyes. She closed them tight, trying to choose a memory that would calm her down. Her mother had had her ears pierced, three in each ear. She'd worn gold studs, and flashy diamonds and rubies, although Charlie knew now it was all costume jewellery. She remembered her dad being away for a couple of weeks in a shearing gang and one afternoon her mum took Charlie and Jac to the next town over to get their ears pierced. Charlie was seven and Jac was thirteen. Charlie remembered her excitement, that it had little to do with the ear-piercing and more to do with her mum taking them out somewhere. 'Just the girls,' she had said. Jac got hers done first. Seeing usually stoic Jac wince in pain and her eyes tear up, Charlie chickened out and they had returned home. Charlie was deflated, feeling like she had let her mum down, that her mum had done something nice, and Charlie had refused it. The memory, fully relived, felt just as painful as her ears. As she turned to look at the desk now, she gasped as one ear was squashed against the stretcher. She sat up, slowly, deliberately, each movement considered, the motion automatically triggering the headache that was always with her when she was awake.

More things, she saw, had been left on the desk for her by whoever came in while she slept. She grabbed the half-empty water bottle, taking a long gulp in an attempt to ease her headache. She picked up a flannel, wondering what the point of it was. How could she bathe herself with half a bottle of water and a flannel? She picked up a small compact mirror, uncertain if she wanted to see her reflection, what her eyes, her facial expression looked like, no doubt telling the story of her fear and hopelessness. She flipped it open, glancing over her face. Turning the mirror to look at her ears she saw dried blood on her lobes. She then picked up the flannel, now realising the point of it, and poured the remaining water onto it, dabbing at the dried blood until her ears were clean. When she was finished, she walked over to the set of drawers, her stomach dropping, uncomprehending at what was set up here: a red lipstick, a hairbrush and a thick, black velvet headband; a plastic container of bobby pins; a half-empty bottle of perfume. She picked up the small, frosted perfume bottle: it had the words '*Charlie Red*' printed across it in red. She didn't wear perfume and hadn't heard of this one. Was it a coincidence the perfume bore her name? A black plastic make-up palette next to the perfume held an array of pink-toned blush, and eyeshadows from taupes and beiges to pale blue and shocking pink.

On the edge of the drawers, next to all of this was a photo. The girl in it was around her age, thick blonde hair, like her; blue eyes, like her; full lips, like her. Gold studs glowed bright in her ears. Like her.

Charlie touched her ears and winced. She turned the photo over. In faded, looping handwriting, it said: *Paige, aged 18.*

Eighteen, like her.

She picked up the piece of paper next to the photo, and read the tidy print:

> *Look at the photo and use the make-up and hair accessories to look like her. No more food or water until it's done.*

That's why she was here. They wanted to turn her into someone else. Paige.

And once I'm her? What then? Charlie thought. There was more. She knew it. There was going to be more.

TWELVE

Lisa

Twenty-one years ago

PAIGE'S BRIGHT RED lips pouted as she sucked on her straw. She always wore lipstick these days. It was a new thing. She told Lisa it made her look older. The lipstick was bright red, which made her blue eyes pop and tanned face glow. Iris told Lisa she wasn't old enough to wear make-up—although the difference in age between the sisters was only ten months. It was Lisa's birthday in two weeks and they would both be seventeen, and then Paige would edge away again, turning eighteen in November. Lisa was playing a game of catch-up without an end in sight.

They followed the dirt path from the back of the hotel into the bush and towards the creek, the cicadas and bird-song making it feel more like summer than the start of spring. At the water's edge, Paige placed her empty Fanta bottle on the grass, the last remnants trickling out. Lisa stood it upright next to her own finished bottle, trying to keep the ants away.

Paige stood in the shallow creek. 'Let's go for a swim,' she said, brows raised, lips turning up into a smile.

Lisa looked left and right. 'I…'

'Come on. We haven't done it since last summer.' She grabbed Lisa's hand, causing her to stumble into the water next to her. The water was freezing.

'There's no one around,' Paige said, their hands still clasped. She started swinging their arms back and forth, her grin wide and eyes wheedling, imploring. 'Come on, Lise.'

She pulled at Lisa's shorts, and the elastic snapped against her hip.

'Paige!' Lisa laughed, pulling her shorts back into place.

'It's hot. There's no one around, and the alternative is to go back to Poison Iris,' Paige said, using the nickname they had for their mother.

Lisa looked around again. It was private here. The creek flowed through the property and, deepest in the centre, only came up to their waists. To their right there were large pines and oaks, and to their left paddocks and further along towards the hotel, the small orchard. There was the copse of native bush they'd just come through, the path there leading back to the hotel—they could just see the top of the dark red roof from here. In front of them, over the creek the property gave way to thick bush where Lisa rarely ventured.

'Okay.' She grinned as Paige squealed.

Paige leaped back up onto the bank, slithering out of shorts and T-shirt like a snake shedding its skin. Lisa tried not to stare at her sister's perfect body, her olive skin and blonde hair luminous in the sun. She smothered a sigh and, taking another furtive look around, shrugged off her T-shirt and edged her shorts down over her hips.

'It's freezing.' Paige gasped as the water stole her breath. But she waded out further.

Lisa took a step towards Paige, who was now standing

in the middle of the creek, her arms outstretched, fingers tapping the water with one hand and beckoning Lisa with the other. She looked like a siren.

'Those boobs are coming along nicely, Lise!' Paige joked as Lisa crouched down in the water and crab-crawled out to Paige.

Lisa couldn't help but smile. She had been flat-chested for what seemed like forever and finally in the last six months she had something resembling breasts, much to her relief.

Paige splashed her and she got a mouthful of creek water. Coughing and spluttering, she did the same back to Paige, and soon they were yelling and screaming, hair soaked and plastered to their scalps.

'Don't look now,' Paige said, her voice low, eyes directed into the brushy mess of native trees they'd come through. Lisa froze, watching Paige's eyes flit from her face to something over her left shoulder, a glimmer of a smile. Lisa lowered herself further into the water until just her head was showing.

'Who is it?' she hissed. *Please don't be Iris.* Although, she didn't fancy the idea of any other alternative, either.

'Nathan,' Paige said, her eyebrows dancing. 'Don't turn around. Act natural. He doesn't know I've seen him.'

Nathan Thomson was the gardener and general handyman at the Gilmore Hotel. He was in his early twenties and had been working for them for the last two months. He was quiet, a bit odd, Lisa thought. Paige called it brooding. Lisa wasn't so sure.

Paige giggled and turned away from Nathan. 'Did you know he's been in prison? Got out late last year.' Moving closer to Lisa, she looked excited by the revelation.

'What?' The news alarmed Lisa.

'Nothing too major.' Paige brushed it off.

'Nothing too major?' Lisa echoed. 'If he's been to prison, it's major.' She was getting cold, and she rubbed her wet hands up and down her arms.

'Well, he didn't, like, murder anyone.'

'Oh, right, that's okay then.' Lisa frowned at Paige, shaking her head.

'He was involved in a robbery at a dairy. His friend had a gun. He didn't use it… Anyway, don't tell Iris. She doesn't know.'

'How do you know all of this?' Lisa asked.

'We've chatted.'

'When?'

'Just when I see him around.' Paige wound her long hair into a rope, wringing out the excess water. 'It's good to know who we've got working for us.'

'I want to get out,' Lisa said, her voice low. 'How long's he going to perv at you?' There wasn't a chance Lisa was going to get out with him leering at her from the bushes, even though she knew it was Paige he was here to see.

'Hang on,' Paige said, walking to the bank of the creek and towards their clothes, where they lay on the grass.

'Paige!' Lisa hissed, her eyes searching for Nathan. She could just make out the top of his dark head in the bushes, twenty metres away. Paige was in no hurry to cover herself up, making a performance of wringing out her hair again. Lisa sat shivering, crouched in the creek. The confidence her sister displayed always surprised her, made her feel less-than.

Paige wiped her body down with her T-shirt, then struggled into her clothes, which stuck and twisted as she pulled them on. When Paige was fully clothed, Lisa watched the dark head retreat.

Paige turned back to her. 'Come on. Coast is clear. He got what he came for.'

Lisa waited a few more seconds, scanning the bushes, and then leaped from the creek, pulling T-shirt and shorts straight over her wet bra and underwear.

'That was creepy,' Lisa said. 'He's creepy.'

'Nathan's fine. Just a bit shy,' Paige said.

'You seem to know him well.' Lisa turned to her sister, getting the feeling that Paige had more to say.

'I don't.' Paige shrugged and started walking back to the hotel.

Lisa shivered and followed after her, forever in awe at her sister's confidence.

THIRTEEN

Jac

Friday morning

JAC SAT WITH Lisa and Iris at the dining room table, in the same places they had at dinner the night before. Light was streaming through the windows at the back of the room and the whine of a lawnmower could be heard out the front. Tama had brought out toast, a silver-lidded dish filled with steaming scrambled eggs and a tray of butter and spreads. He had served them coffee and tea, then said, 'Enjoy, and let me know if you need anything else, Ms Gilmore,' before leaving the room as quietly as he had entered.

'Did you sleep well?' Iris asked. The bruise on her temple had dulled slightly, the purple giving way to a muted yellow.

Jac stared at her for a second, wondering if she remembered what happened last night. But she obviously didn't, and Jac certainly wasn't going to bring it up now. 'Yeah, I did. Thanks.'

'What do you do for work? I take it your employer was understanding at you having to come home?' Iris asked.

'I had a bit of annual leave owing from the hotel I work at in Sydney. When I told them about Charlie, they were happy to give me the time off.'

'You work in a hotel? Marvellous,' Iris said, heaping a spoonful of sugar into her teacup. 'What do you do there?'

'I'm on the front desk,' Jac said, the lie coming easily, even though it wasn't necessary. She shouldn't have cared how Iris and Lisa Gilmore viewed her. But these people and their surroundings made Jac want to appear a couple of notches above what she actually was. Particularly ironic, considering Jac was staying here in exchange for cleaning.

'Well, the open day's coming up on Sunday and, with Tui gone, we need all the help we can get to make sure the hotel is looking its best. Given your experience I'm sure you understand that.' Iris looked at Jac expectantly.

'Mum,' Lisa said softly. 'I'm not sure if this is going to work out. Jac's father has died and her sister is missing. She's got more important things to be worried about than cleaning this place for the open day.'

'I wasn't speaking to you,' Iris said. 'Jac and I were having a perfectly pleasant conversation.' Iris ate a mouthful of her scrambled eggs.

Jac appreciated Lisa speaking up for her but said, 'Of course I'm happy to help.' She said she would, and the only reason Iris had invited her to stay was because she said she would help out. She needed a base in Everly for at least another night or two, while she talked to a few people who might be able to provide information on Charlie's whereabouts.

Jac busied herself putting milk into her coffee so she didn't have to see Lisa's face after Iris's reprimand.

Iris finished her mouthful and continued talking. 'The open day is wonderful. The hotel comes alive! Nathan makes sure the grounds look perfect. We open up a few of the bedrooms, we set up the ballroom and the music room.

We even light a fire in the library—lovely ambience— even though it's probably too hot for that now. We bring out old photos and display them. It's important to remember those who have come before us. Nice to reminisce.'

Jac wondered what all the excitement was about. Did people in Everly really turn up to this open day? She couldn't remember it when she was younger, although it wasn't something her parents would've cared about. Jac thought maybe Iris was the only one looking forward to it. She noticed Lisa winding her napkin into a thick rope between her hands.

'And,' Iris leaned forward across the wide table towards Jac, 'it's the day my Paige comes home.' Her gaze shifted past Jac's shoulder. Iris smiled as if she had seen someone she knew. Jac spun around, expecting to see this person, but there was no one there. She turned to Lisa, unsure what to say. Lisa shook her head, still inspecting her lap.

'Frankie Hastings always helps out,' Iris said, as if she hadn't just spaced out for a few seconds.

'Miss Hastings?' Jac asked.

'You know her?'

'I think she taught me at school. History?'

'Yes,' Iris said. 'That would be right. She's been around for a while. It would be nice for you to catch up with her. She's still teaching at the area school. I'm not sure if Frankie's one of your sister's teachers. But she might know of her.'

Jac's heartbeat increased—a possible link to Charlie. 'I'm going down to the police station this morning to talk to Constable Dunlop. Hopefully, he's found something out.'

'Robbie Dunlop.' Iris sniffed, her mouth turned down. 'Like most men I know—useless.'

Iris had said exactly the same the night before and Jac wondered if she remembered the conversation.

'Mum,' Lisa said. Jac assumed that was supposed to be a reprimand, but Iris carried on.

'He is. Don't go standing up for him. You haven't lived here in years. You don't even know the man and wouldn't have any idea what goes on around here anyway.'

'You're right, I don't,' Lisa replied. 'But I think that's the last thing Jac needs to hear when she's trying to find her sister.'

Iris continued without acknowledging what Lisa had just said. 'Now, what are you going to do about your father?' she asked Jac. 'You don't seem too sad about the fact he died yesterday.' She raised her brows, sipping tea from the delicate bone china laced with a pattern of pink roses.

Lisa looked like she wanted to admonish Iris but kept quiet this time.

Good choice, Jac thought. She wasn't sure if she could witness the awkwardness of Lisa, a grown woman, getting another dressing down from her mother.

'I wasn't close to my father,' Jac said, hoping that would put an end to any questions.

'Another useless man, huh?' Iris replied.

'Something like that.' This time Jac enjoyed Iris's abruptness.

'I've been surrounded by them my whole life. My ex-husband, particularly, was a waste of space. Couldn't handle a strong woman.'

Jac concentrated on spreading Marmite on her toast with a heavy butter knife but looked up at Lisa when the silence wasn't filled.

Lisa was staring at Iris, a mixture of anger and sadness flitting across her face. Her left hand closed into a fist but just as quickly relaxed. When Iris looked over at her, ready to challenge, Lisa's eyes softened, her lips turned up in a half-smile, and she broke away from Iris's stare.

It was just past eight am when Jac, ahead of walking down the hill to the police station, went upstairs to get her phone from her room. In the east wing hallway, she overheard Lisa and Iris in Iris's bedroom, the door slightly ajar, and it sounded like Lisa was trying to help her mother with something. Jac stood there for a moment, listening, and heard Iris say, 'Ouch!'

'Sorry,' Lisa murmured. 'Just keep still. I'll be done in a minute.'

'The doctor should be doing this,' Iris said.

'The doctor showed me how to do it, Mum.' There was a pause. 'There, all done.'

Jac thought Lisa sounded pleased with herself. 'Your hair looks different,' Iris said. It sounded like an accusation.

'Does it?'

'It doesn't suit you that long. Never did.'

'I quite like it.' Jac could hear the edge in Lisa's voice.

Iris sighed and Jac heard the groan of bedsprings as she got up, followed by the shuffle of footsteps.

Jac made her way past the top of the staircase, through the smoke doors and into her room, where she grabbed her phone off the bed and then briskly descended the stairs once more. Lisa and Iris's relationship was obviously complicated. But it was nothing to do with her. She was only here for one reason. *And, hell*, Jac thought, *who am I to judge?*

FOURTEEN

Charlie

Friday morning

SOON AFTER READING the note that told her to turn herself into Paige, Charlie decided that she wasn't going to do it. Everything had been taken away from her here, but this she could control. She wouldn't do it. She tried not to think of the consequences, tried not to think how long she could go without food or water. She could do this. Couldn't she? She was strong. She had got through her mother's death, and Jac leaving. She had been living with her father for the past seven years. Putting up with all his shit. The drinking. The ranting and raving. The weird promises, often when he was drunk, that he would sort himself out and make a better life for them. He did that a lot and, when she was younger, it had made her feel better. But, one afternoon, he had called her Isabel and she realised he was making promises to his dead wife, promises he couldn't keep.

Her mother had never been happy with what she had, where she lived. Charlie was only aware of this, as her mother, drunk or not, would complain about how small her life was, how pointless. How there was so much more to the world than Everly. Charlie often wished she had done more to make her mum happier while she was still here. She remembered a handful of times when her mother used to flick through her old *Lonely Planet* guide with her. It was used as a storybook in place of Winnie the Pooh or Harry Potter. Her mum's favourite cities were Paris and Rome. She knew everything about them, even though she had never left New Zealand, and her finger would run down the columns of the guidebook as she talked about the Eiffel Tower, the Louvre, the Vatican and the Trevi Fountain, like she had actually been to see them. Charlie's favourites were places with beautiful or interesting names that she found hard to wrap her tongue around—Bucharest, Zagreb and Gdańsk—and all the ways you could get around that massive continent—bus, plane, car, train. That travel guide was the only book in the house and well-thumbed by Charlie by the time it was turned to ashes the night of the fire, along with her other meagre possessions.

Jac was gone less than a month later, with promises to Charlie that she'd be back for her soon. 'I won't leave you with him, Charlie. It won't be forever. I promise.'

So much for promises.

'Take me with you,' Charlie had said, even though she wasn't sure she wanted to go with Jac. Where would they go? How would they survive? Would Jac's 'somewhere' be better than Everly? She wasn't so sure.

'You're too young for me to take you with me.'

When Charlie had said goodbye to her, Jac took her into her arms and gave her a quick hug. 'Don't believe stuff he says,' she whispered. 'Don't believe what they say around town…about the fire.'

Charlie had nodded. But she still remembered the anger at being left. First her mum and then Jac. The kids at school whispered behind her back. There wasn't a lot of sympathy, just wide-eyed wonder at the girl whose sister killed their mother. When her dad got drunk, proper drunk, when he couldn't walk in a straight line and his words came out in a slippery mess, he would cry, telling her how much he missed her mother, and that he could never forgive Jac.

'Your sister was reckless,' he said.

But Charlie wished so many times, maybe even more than wanting her mum back, that Jac had stayed, helped her stand up to the bullies and rumours, the stories about what happened changing every week, that Jac had purposely set the house on fire with her whole family in it, or that it was an accident but Jac, drunk, had escaped the fire and hadn't alerted her parents or sister; the only similarity being that whatever the version, Jac Morgan was to blame. Charlie was sure they could've got through it together.

After her mum and Jac, she got into the habit of dreaming up 'what ifs'. What if her mother didn't die in the fire? What if Jac didn't run away? What if her dad found a job he loved—one that he loved so much it made him stop drinking.

But that was pointless. Instead, she started to look ahead. Some of her teachers had spoken to her about university, telling her how easily she would gain entrance. But it didn't appeal to her. Didn't they know her? Her last name was Morgan. They should've known she wasn't from a household that valued education. Going to uni would be considered a waste of money by her dad. Even though she found her subjects interesting, she never felt a need to carry on with study after high school. Her dean had tried to talk her out of travelling next year, telling her that her talents would be wasted, but Charlie ignored her.

Everly had got smaller and smaller the older she got.

She felt she had long outgrown it and it was time to move on. She'd saved up just over two grand from working at the cafe. Her plan had been to head up to Auckland, possibly even to Sydney to see Jac.

Some nights she lay in bed in the caravan, often by herself because her dad was at the pub or passed out on someone's couch, and she'd think about packing a bag and leaving. But she knew she had to finish her final year. And as much as she wanted to leave, she was anxious about taking the first step.

Charlie took the photo of Paige from the top of the drawers. She knew by now she was likely wearing Paige's clothes. She touched the perfume, brushed a hand across the velvet headband, wondering who Paige really was, what might have happened to her. She picked up a bobby pin, fiddling with it, bending it out of shape. She looked up at the cage, at the small lock. Then back at the bobby pin. Could she? How many movies had she seen where it had been done? Surely it wasn't as simple as they made it look? She pulled off the little knobs of plastic covering the ends of the bobby pin and bent it open to make a ninety-degree angle. She felt her heartbeat increasing, her head throbbing as her sluggish brain started working. A spark of excitement flared at the thought she could get out. She put one of the lanterns on the very edge of the drawers so she could see what she was doing and inserted the bobby pin into the lock. She was gentle, directing it forward, turning it left then right, then moving it back out slightly, doing the same again and again. She continued jiggling it, getting more and more frustrated. After a few minutes, she pulled the pin out and threw it on the floor.

'Stupid,' she said, her voice coming out in a croak. She

grabbed hold of the wire cage and rattled it as hard as she could. It did nothing but made her feel slightly better.

She grabbed the water bottle, and drank the last few drops, her eyes surveying Paige's things beside her on the drawers. She could go without food. She knew that from experience. But what about water? And how long would they let her protest? This would be her small attempt at defiance, and one she was sure they weren't going to let her get away with.

FIFTEEN

Jac

Friday morning

JAC, WITH THE Gilmore Hotel out of view, stopped at the bottom of the hill on her way to the main street. To her right was her old primary school. There were two buildings on the land, one junior room, one senior. All the panes of glass were smashed, with rock-shaped holes and jagged edges, or missing altogether. The slab of concrete where she used to play handball with her friends was barely visible among the weeds that had taken advantage of every crack. The sports field was overgrown, and five sheep meandered around a single rugby goal post, which was listing to the left, and the wooden benches where she used to have her lunch.

She continued on to the main street which, apart from a sporadic car driving through, was quiet, as usual. Jac crossed the road to the police station, which was locked. She banged on the door, wondering where Dunlop was. If he wasn't here, he had better be doing something that involved finding Charlie. Jac walked along the footpath looking over at the corner of the campground but saw nothing that might have shown that a person had been found dead there yesterday. *Probably bad for business*, she thought. No tourism provider wanted police or emergency tape anywhere near their premises. She wondered briefly where her dad had been taken, if there would be any kind of investigation, but then admonished herself. Her time was better spent thinking about Charlie.

She walked further up the main street and crossed the road to the cafe, perched as it was on a small rise overlooking the campground and the domain, which was used for everything from rugby and soccer in winter, to the county fair in summer and the annual wood-chopping competition every spring. Jac took in a small area of fresh, ripped-up dirt on the domain, its rich brown guts spilled open like it had been clawed by a giant. Kids joyriding on quad bikes, she guessed. Some things never changed. As she was taking out her phone to ring Dunlop she looked up at the cafe, empty apart from one person sitting in the window. As she got closer, she saw who it was—Constable Dunlop.

Dunlop looked up as she came through the door.

'Ah, Jac, good morning,' he said, half rising as she walked over to his table He was halfway through devouring a full English breakfast. 'Take a seat.' He pushed his egg-smeared plate aside as if the cafe table was his office and pulled his notebook closer to him.

Jac sat opposite, declining food or drink from the man who came over and asked if she wanted to order.

'This kind of stuff doesn't normally happen in Everly,' Dunlop said. 'Been run off my feet since yesterday afternoon.'

Did he want her sympathy? Jac frowned at him, and he carried on.

'Your dad, first.' Jac wanted to stop him there, but he

continued. 'Your father's body was removed late yesterday afternoon, taken to the morgue at Waikato Hospital where an autopsy will be done in the next couple of days. We—I—have no reason to think it was suspicious. Your father...well...he was known...' Dunlop rubbed a hand over his jowls.

'He was an alcoholic who more than likely had had a skinful, fell into the creek, knocked himself out, and drowned,' Jac said, enjoying the shocked look that passed over Dunlop's face.

'Yes, well... I've talked to Dave at the campground and the various people who are staying there at the moment. A couple of people noticed your father returning from the pub after closing, around eleven pm, and it did appear he was very intoxicated. But no one heard any kind of altercation. Dave said Eddie had lost his job on Wednesday. I think he was working as a labourer on a new build out of town. Dave said he'd gone on a bit of a bender.'

'Plus, he was probably a bit concerned about his missing daughter,' Jac said, reminding him.

'Yes, of course,' Dunlop replied.

'Look, I'm not here about my father. I hadn't seen him in seven years. I didn't care about him. He didn't care about me. I'm here about Charlie. Can you please tell me what's happening?'

'Yes, sorry, of course. I talked to Dave at the campground. He can't remember the last time he saw Charlie. He said possibly Sunday afternoon. Brian, the owner of the cafe,' Dunlop nodded towards the counter where Brian was passing a takeaway coffee to a customer, 'he knows Charlie. She works here on weekends.'

That was news to Jac.

'He last saw her on Sunday, when she finished her shift here.'

Dunlop went on. 'I rang the school. As she's year thirteen and the students had their last day on Monday and are now all off on study leave for end-of-year exams, they couldn't really tell me much. Her dean mentioned that, while Charlie's a good student, she did have quite a few absent days over this last year. I got the impression she struggled a bit socially at school. I asked around at the pub last night, too. As you know, Eddie was a regular.' Dunlop picked up the mug in front of him and drained his coffee. 'One of the bartenders said she saw Charlie heading out of town on Monday afternoon. She thought that would have been just before four, as that's when her shift started at the pub. She said Charlie had a small bag on her back and was heading to the main highway.'

Jac was silent.

'So, at this stage,' Dunlop concluded, 'it looks like she was leaving town.'

'She would've contacted me. She would've told me her plans,' Jac said, more to herself than Dunlop.

'When was the last time you spoke with her?' Dunlop asked.

'A couple of weeks ago, I guess.' Then Jac realised it was probably over a month ago.

She and Charlie weren't proper close, like some sisters were, but they tried to talk at least once a month. Checking in on each other. Charlie usually bitched about school, apart from her flute lessons, which she loved, and Everly in general. Jac usually told her all about the rich people who came to stay at the hotel, all the jewellery and expensive clothes she saw while cleaning the rooms. There was a six-year age gap and an ocean between them, but more than that, there were words unsaid, certain events brushed under the carpet.

'You've told me she just turned eighteen. She's an adult. I think this is more a case of lost contact than a missing person. It sounds very possible she's just up and left.'

'So what? That's it?' Jac asked. 'Can't you… I don't know, check her phone records or something?'

'To do that I'd have to prove a crime has occurred and there's nothing telling me that one has. If I write an affidavit, without something solid to show the court a crime is likely to have occurred, then it won't even get signed.' Dunlop splayed his hands on the table. 'If you have any more information regarding Charlie, I'd be happy to look into it, something that points to something other than her leaving Everly at her own will…'

Jac had nothing. She didn't know who Charlie's friends were. She didn't know if she had any enemies. Which seemed like a ridiculous thought anyway. Did Charlie have money to support herself? If she had been working at the cafe, maybe she had a plan. Was she saving up to leave?

'People do just up and leave sometimes,' Dunlop said.

Jac hated the way he said it. Like he wasn't taking it seriously, like he was just going through the motions. There was no sense of urgency. She felt in her gut something was wrong but hated the fact that she didn't know things that others would about their little sisters. She hated that she couldn't demand action from Dunlop because, really, there *was* a good chance Charlie had left Everly. And what would their father have known anyway? He would've been drunk the two times he texted Jac. Had he been overreacting? Had Charlie actually told him she was leaving, and he forgot? Whatever it came down to,

Jac knew—Charlie would've texted her if she was planning on leaving.

'Who was the bartender you talked to?' Jac asked.

'Michelle…' Dunlop flipped through his notebook. 'Michelle Lafferty.'

If Dunlop wasn't going to do anything, Jac would.

She watched Dunlop pocket his notebook and pay for his breakfast, then she sat for a minute, wondering what to do next. What could she do? If she wasn't sure who Charlie was these days or where she would go, maybe she could find out. She introduced herself to Brian, taking his offered hand and shaking it, feeling a sense of relief when he told her he'd bought the cafe only a year ago—he didn't appear to know anything about her past.

'Great girl,' he told Jac when she asked about Charlie. 'She started working here a little over six months ago. She said she was saving up to travel. She was great with the customers.'

'Are you surprised she left without telling you?' Jac asked.

'Yeah, I am a bit. She wasn't like some of the other younger ones around here. She always seemed a bit more mature for her age. I guess you have to be with a father like—' He stopped himself, too late, when he realised who he was talking to. 'Sorry about that,' he apologised, his pale skin turning a ruddy red. He picked up a cloth and started wiping the counter back and forth like he was trying to erase what he had just said.

'Don't worry about it,' Jac told him.

'Constable Dunlop said she was seen leaving Everly on Monday afternoon,' Brian offered. 'Looked to be heading for the main road.'

'Yeah, so I heard,' Jac said. 'I mean… I thought Charlie

would've told me if she was planning on leaving, but… I guess I didn't know her that well, after all.'

Jac thanked him and left the cafe. Maybe no one, including Jac, really knew Charlie—which made all of this so much harder.

SIXTEEN

Lisa

Twenty-one years ago

LISA HAD SPENT the morning dodging Iris, as usual. It wasn't like Iris would give her a job or bother to enquire what she was up to this Sunday morning, but Lisa preferred to keep out of her way, if she could. It didn't take much to piss Iris off, especially if you were Lisa.

She was at a loose end, with Paige practising. Paige's private tutor had just left, and she still had another hour to go. The round, rich notes of the piece she was playing on the piano floated through the open door of the music room on the ground floor and wound their way throughout the hotel. Lisa had spent most of the morning in the library, opposite the music room, avoiding the comfy, overstuffed leather sofas and armchairs in favour of sitting behind one of the sofas on a feather cushion. If Iris poked her head in, Lisa wouldn't be seen. She was halfway through Ken Follett's *The Pillars of the Earth*. She thought it may have belonged to her dad, and that most of the novels in here had. Iris wasn't a big reader. The library, to her, was an effect, something that had to be in the hotel to go with the image she wanted. It wasn't a place to go and lose yourself, to remove yourself from this world and find another one that suited you better, like it was for Lisa.

The library door rattled open, and Lisa slid further down behind the sofa.

'As you can see, everything's done,' Iris said, her voice smooth, in control, talking about what she knew and loved best. 'Nothing needs doing in here. The ballroom can be set up easily enough and, as you know, over half the rooms have been renovated.' Lisa heard admiring oohs and ahhs at that, from the women of the PTA—the Parent Teacher Association at the school she and Paige attended.

The annual Gilmore Hotel Open Day had been going on for decades, with all proceeds given to the area school. Helen, Lisa's grandmother, had started the first one and it had been held once a year ever since. Iris had stuck faithfully to the tradition.

Lisa listened to the women lavishing praise on Iris, telling her how beautiful the hotel looked, what a wonderful job she had done with the renovations.

'So tasteful, Iris,' one woman said. 'You clearly have an eye for interior design.'

'I'm looking at reopening the hotel. Possibly in the new year.'

This surprised Lisa. Of course, she knew that Iris had done a few renovations with the hope of reopening, but she didn't know Iris had been announcing it to people.

More oohs and ahhs and comments on how it would do wonders for Everly.

'It would be such an undertaking,' another woman said.

'I have Paige,' Iris replied. 'She's always so helpful. And she will be a big part of why people come to the Gilmore Hotel. The music room has also been done and we'll hold concerts there every weekend. I'll get performers from all over the country—only the best—to come to the hotel. But Paige will be the main attraction. You all know how accomplished she is.'

Lisa found it hard to stay put on the floor at this revelation. Was this really going to happen? Did Paige know about this? If she did, surely she would've told Lisa.

'I assumed Paige would've been going to university next year,' yet another woman said.

There was silence, and then Lisa heard the doors close, Iris changing the subject back to the open day.

There hadn't been a lot of talk about what Paige would do next year. Lisa liked the idea of Paige staying on at the hotel. Would she agree to it? Throughout the years, she and Paige had always talked about taking over and restoring the Gilmore to a working hotel. Of course, Iris would need to be a part of these plans. And from what Iris had just said, maybe it was really going to happen. Lisa felt a pleasant flip in her stomach as she started imagining what life would be like in this place if it started up as a hotel again. She thought of all the rooms full. Concerts every weekend and new people to talk to. Smiling, relaxed people gathering in the lounge in the evening for cocktails before dinner. Maybe Iris would give her a job at the hotel. She could work on the front desk, welcoming visitors, handing out keys, making bookings. Life, she thought, would be almost perfect.

SEVENTEEN

Jac

Friday morning

'Jac!'

Standing on the front steps of the cafe, she watched Dave walking up from the campground on the other side of the road.

She crossed over and joined him, unwilling to talk about her father or get roped in to organising a funeral. But she needn't have worried.

'You need to clear out your dad's caravan. I need to get it cleaned today. With them both…gone, I can't just leave it standing there empty. I'm losing money every day,' Dave said. 'Sorry.' The apology tacked on the end was meaningless. 'I've unlocked it for you. Anything you don't take I'll donate to the Sallies.'

More like keep for yourself, Jac thought.

'Yeah, okay,' she said, and carried on to the campground, heading in the direction of the caravan. Her stomach felt queasy after having talked to Dunlop, the scrambled eggs she'd had at breakfast threatening to reappear. Jac stood at the door, a hand on the handle. She wrenched the flimsy door open, and it banged against the side of the caravan.

She hoped it left a mark. The combined odour of stale, deep-fried food, alcohol and cigarette smoke escaped out the door, leaving a lingering scent of pine air freshener. She latched the door so it stayed open and, breathing shallowly, entered the small space. To her left was a small bench cluttered with takeaway boxes. The sink was filled with empty beer bottles. Further down, at the back of the caravan, was what she assumed was her father's bedroom. An unmade double bed, yellowing sheets, an almost empty bottle of Jim Beam lying on its side among the sheets. But it was the overflowing ashtray sitting on top of the duvet that did it, an orange plastic lighter abandoned in the mess. She picked up the heavy ashtray and threw it against the window that took up the whole back wall of the caravan. The impact splintered the glass, leaving thin lines radiating from the small hole in one corner, which the ashtray had made. Dave was going to be pissed. She didn't care. She pulled the concertina door closed across this section and turned back to the front of the caravan.

It took her a while to figure out where Charlie slept, until she realised she was sitting on it. The dining room table and the bench seats either side of it converted into a bed. Jac placed her hand on a tidy stack of sheets and blankets next to her. She leaned in and breathed the fresh scent of what she assumed was Charlie: apple shampoo and a sweet, floral spray-on deodorant.

Jac picked up a reusable supermarket bag. What should she keep? She opened a cupboard above her head and stuffed what few clothes Charlie had there into the bag, avoiding the school uniform. If she had run away, what had she taken? Jac didn't know what clothes Charlie owned, what was or wasn't missing. In another cupboard, she came across a small pile of sheet music for the flute. That was one thing Jac knew about Charlie. She had enjoyed learning the flute for the last two years. Jac shoved the stack of papers into the bag.

As she looked around the small space, a voice at the back of her head wondered if Dunlop was right. Had Charlie got sick of it all? Living in this caravan with their lazy, fucked-up father; going to a school with mean and bitchy kids she hated; a sister thousands of kilometres away who seldom contacted her.

There wasn't a lot else in the caravan. They had lost everything in the fire: photo albums, toys, furniture. A lot of that stuff hadn't been replaced, couldn't be replaced, the idea of any kind of insurance being the last thing their parents would spend their money on.

Jac opened a drawer that held underwear and bras, and emptied its contents into the bag. As she swung it over her shoulder, she looked at the cork board on one of the walls. Most of it was covered with the postcards she had sent Charlie over the years. Silly touristy stuff like the Sydney Harbour Bridge, the Opera House, Bondi Beach. She read the back of a few of them, unable to identify the chirpy, positive person who had written them. Jac guessed Charlie and she were busy trying to persuade each other that the lives they were living were fine, happy, normal.

On her way out the door, Jac grabbed the set of keys on the small kitchen bench. Her dad's old ute was parked at the side of the caravan, dark red paint peeling, a large dent in the passenger door. He'd had it for as long as she could remember. She unattached the caravan key from the cheap plastic keyring and left it on the bench for Dave. Her final thought, as she slammed the door closed, was that she should've come earlier. Charlie needed her and was either too embarrassed to say or, worse, she was too scared to ask, knowing what Jac's answer would have been.

EIGHTEEN

Jac

Friday morning

JAC DOUBTED THE ute would start. She threw the bag full of Charlie's clothes onto the passenger side seat and wound down the window to try to get rid of the cigarette smell. Her hand brushed over the worn bench seat, its stuffing spewing from the tears in the vinyl, and hardened circles from cigarette burns scraped her palm.

She started the engine and on the third attempt it finally kicked into life. She drove along the pitted gravel driveway and turned left, heading out of Everly and to the main road. She checked her watch. It was just after ten am. She made the decision then to go to Charlie's school. She wasn't sure what she was going to accomplish there but at least it would feel like she was doing something.

HALF AN HOUR LATER, Jac pulled into a parking space in front of the area school, just off the main state highway heading north. A place she had suffered in for too many years. She had hated school, but liked the social side of it, until the fire, when even her best friends questioned the events of that night. She walked up three concrete steps to the admin building and, after explaining who she was, asked the woman on the front desk if she could talk to someone about Charlie.

Hinemoa Wells was Charlie's dean and in her late forties. She wore a pair of black-rimmed glasses that covered half her face. She was quietly spoken and expressed her sympathies over Charlie's disappearance but seemed unable to register any kind of emotion, her face frozen. Maybe that's the way you got when you dealt with teenagers all day, Jac thought.

'I just wanted to see if you could give me any more information on Charlie. I live in Australia and haven't seen her in some years.'

Ms Wells nodded, and Jac wondered if she knew her story. Probably.

'Charlie is a very bright and capable student. She's just not that interested in school.'

Sounds a bit like me, Jac thought—at least the not interested in school part.

'Do you know if Charlie would have any reason to leave, run away?'

'She's had quite a few absences this year,' Ms Wells said, reading from a laptop. Jac wondered if this woman really knew Charlie at all or was getting all her answers from the computer. 'But in spite of that, she's kept up with her schoolwork and she's expected to do well in her final exams. She did keep to herself a lot. Comments on her mid-year report show that she worked best by herself and didn't often contribute during class discussions.'

'And what about friends?' Jac hoped Ms Wells would be able to give her some names. As far as she could remember, Charlie had never mentioned any friends by name.

'As I said, she does keep to herself a lot. I'm afraid I

couldn't name one of her friends. She does seem to struggle a bit in that area. I know that during her time here she's had some trouble with bullying…'

Jac didn't need to ask what that was about. Of course Charlie got bullied. Jac had left and poor Charlie picked up the slack. Alcoholic father, the fire, Jac leaving et cetera. But Charlie had never mentioned any of that. Yes, she had always kept herself to herself as a kid, wanting to keep everyone happy, always avoiding confrontation, but Jac should've known Charlie wasn't telling the whole story. Guilt cut into her again.

When she realised Ms Wells couldn't offer her any more, Jac thanked her and left the school. Eyes on the road, with paddock after paddock flashing by her, Jac felt a headache coming on as thoughts of Charlie and her whereabouts tumbled around inside her head. Back in Everly, passing the pub—its carpark empty, obviously not yet open—she saw someone parking a car by the front door and pulled in beside them, winding down her window.

'Do you work here?' she asked a young guy who looked to be in his twenties.

'Yeah, but we don't open for another half-hour, sorry.'

'Do you know if Michelle's working today?'

'Nah, she's on tomorrow. She'll be opening up. Did you want me to give her a message or something?'

'No, that's okay,' Jac said, thanking him and making her way back to the hotel. She felt like she wasn't getting anywhere. She had pretty much retraced Dunlop's steps and got the same answers. Everything pointed to Charlie being unhappy in Everly and to her having decided on Monday to leave for good.

NINETEEN

Lisa

Twenty-one years ago

THE TINNY CLINK of cutlery cut through the silence at the dinner table. Lisa kept her head down, finishing her dinner as fast as possible. She didn't have to field questions about her day—if she had homework, what her friends were up to, what her plans were for the weekend. Even though it was a constant, something that had happened her whole life, she still felt the urge to tell Iris all about her day. To be the one who made her face light up when she told her she'd got an A in a test or that her music teacher had told her that, with a bit more practice, she would be just as good as her sister at the flute. She half listened as Iris quizzed Paige about her upcoming exams. Paige made all the right noises, but Lisa knew she hadn't been studying, that she was more interested in hanging out in the music room or sneaking out her window to parties on the weekend.

Iris placed her knife and fork down, dabbed her lips with her napkin and took a small sip of red wine.

'Mum?' Paige said.

Lisa looked to her sister. Just that one word, the tone, she knew something was coming. Paige's lips were turned up in a smile, but the look in her eyes made Lisa worry. What was she going to say?

'Mmm?' Iris folded the napkin and placed it to the side of her plate.

'The application forms for university are due back next week. I have a chance of winning a scholarship for a Bachelor of Music.'

'Why would you need a scholarship? We have money,' Iris said.

'So, you're okay with me going to university?' Paige asked, eyes wide in disbelief.

'I didn't say that, dear. I was just wondering why you'd bother with a scholarship when there are so many others out there who need the money for their tertiary education.'

Paige took a deep breath. 'Would I be able to go to university next year?'

Lisa frowned at Paige, but her sister wasn't looking at her. University? Why was she talking about university? They had never spoken about that—not really. Paige used to talk about studying music, but that was one day, in the distant future. Not next year.

What did you think she was going to do? Stay here with you? Lisa felt herself growing hot.

'University? I don't think so, Paige,' Iris said. 'There's a lot happening at the moment, and I need you here.'

Lisa could tell Paige was trying not to cry. Her face coloured and her lips disappeared. 'What for?' Paige's voice came out in a broken whisper.

Iris directed her gaze straight down the long table. 'I've almost completed the renovation on the hotel, and I think it's time to reopen,' she said. 'I hope to start booking guests soon, in time for the summer crowds.'

Lisa had to hide her smile from Paige, who looked confused. Since Lisa had overheard Iris speaking to the PTA women a couple of weeks ago, she'd thought she might have imagined what Iris's plans were. She hadn't mentioned anything to Paige because she didn't know if it was going to happen, but she had been building a whole new life in her head, and the last two weeks had been manageable because of it.

'The Gilmore Hotel will once again become a destination in itself. There are the caves, yes, and the glow worm tours here,' Iris rolled her eyes. 'But along with the region's best food and wine, we will be offering weekend and evening concerts featuring classically trained musicians from around the country and possibly the world. Paige, you will be a big part of this. You'll be our inhouse musician. It's going to be a lot of work and you girls will be expected to pull your weight. This was always a family business. And someday it will all be yours.' This last part was directed at Paige.

Lisa didn't even care that Iris was mostly talking to Paige. Iris had just said 'you girls'. Iris had included her as part of this family.

'But, Mum, I have talent. You've said so yourself, and Mrs Pratchett says I'd have an excellent chance at winning a scholarship.'

'Yes, you have talent, my darling, in absolute spades, and that is why people will be coming far and wide to see you perform. And I think,' Iris hesitated slightly, 'yes, I think at the open day this year I'll announce it all—the reopening of the hotel and your special part in it. Oh, it's going to be fabulous!'

Lisa stared at Iris. She hadn't seen her mother like this—ever. Openly happy and excited. She was always so buttoned-up and steely, especially around Lisa.

Paige pushed her chair back with such force it toppled to the ground. Lisa got up, eager to speak with her, and as Paige ran from the room, Lisa followed behind.

At the top of the staircase, Paige ran along the east wing hallway, past their rooms, and just before the invisible door to the soldiers' hallway, she took a right down another short corridor. She wrenched open the narrow door and went up another short flight, to the turret room, their footsteps echoing on the bare wood stairs as they ran up. Lisa reached the top as Paige flung herself into one of the threadbare armchairs in there. Lisa sat in the other one. The turret room was her favourite room in the hotel. It was empty apart from a few old pieces of furniture that Iris had wanted to hold on to but didn't deem fashionable enough for the hotel's facelift. There were three rectangular windows, separated by blank walls, that took up half of the turret, looking out over the vegetation surrounding the hotel and to the valley and hills beyond.

'University?' Lisa exclaimed, surprised. 'You never really talked about that.' She didn't want Paige to get more upset than she already was, and so tried to tread lightly. 'But don't you think Iris's plan sounds exciting?' She leaned over and placed a hand on Paige's knee.

Paige sniffed, frowning now, more angry than upset. 'I'm going,' she said.

She got up from the chair and walked over to the edge of the first window, where she pulled the bulky velvet curtain out of the way. Iris had installed curtains up here years ago, and Lisa couldn't see the point of them. She and Paige were the only ones who ever came up to this room and, even pulled back as they were now, the curtains hindered the view. A recessed shelf was completely hidden by this particular curtain, though, and Paige brought out from behind it a plastic hip flask filled with a lethal concoction of vodka and gin siphoned from the bottles Iris kept on the drinks cart in the lounge.

'Going where?' Lisa asked.

'To uni. I'm going whether she likes it or not.' Paige unscrewed the cap and took a sip, passing it to Lisa, who shook her head. She hated the stuff.

Lisa chose not to say anything. Paige could get away with most things, but there wasn't a chance Iris would let her leave.

'I did the audition for the scholarship a couple of weeks ago,' Paige said, taking one more sip and then stowing the flask back on the shelf, adjusting the curtains once she was done.

'How?' Lisa asked.

'I told Mrs Pratchett I couldn't make it up to Auckland, so the assessor said I could video my audition. I had to interpret a piece of unknown music, and perform a prepared piece. Mrs Pratchett gave me a reference and sent it all off. I did it in the music room at school. Used their piano.' Paige sat up straighter, looking pleased with herself.

'And?' Lisa prompted. This was too much information all at once. What would Iris say about this deception?

Paige shrugged. 'I'll find out next month.'

'So, you'll go? Even after she said you're not allowed? Even after everything she has planned?'

'Of course. If I get the scholarship, I won't need her money. It will pay for all the fees and accommodation, and I'll get an allowance.'

'You have it all worked out,' Lisa said.

Paige came over and squeezed herself in next to Lisa.

'Lise, it's okay.' She put a hand on her knee. 'I know we kind of used to talk about running the hotel, but it was just talk, right? You don't really want to stay here with Iris forever. I know you'll be on your own with her next year. But it won't be for long. One more year of school next year and you'll be free. You won't ever have to come back.'

It was never just talk for Lisa, though. She had honestly believed that they were going to run the hotel. She felt stupid. Had Paige just gone along with the idea to keep her happy, but all the while had been planning her escape?

'What am I going to do without you?' Lisa felt her throat constricting. Her head was spinning. This was too much to take in. Sitting at the dinner table ten minutes ago, she thought life was finally starting to improve.

'You'll be fine. I promise. And I'll visit heaps.' Paige laid her head on Lisa's shoulder. 'I've got to do this.'

Lisa absently started smoothing Paige's long blonde hair. Iris constantly pointed out the differences between the girls, how Paige's hair was blonder—'kissed by the angels', she would say—and how flawless her skin was, opposed to Lisa's, whose face was covered in freckles from forehead to chin, as if someone had whipped a paintbrush full of brown paint at her face. Paige was always going to be taller, thinner, more eloquent, more talented, better in every way. One evening, when Iris had had too much to drink at dinner, she'd turned nasty, and had referred to Lisa as 'the poor man's Paige'. Lisa was only thirteen at the time, but she'd understood what Iris had meant.

Iris kept Lisa's hair in a bob. It was blunt, and slightly crooked at the back where Iris had hacked at it. Paige always helped her to even it up afterwards. Iris did it once every few months when it had grown too much and started softening. The first time she had done it was when Lisa was six. She and Paige had always wanted to dress alike, but Iris always refused to buy them the same clothes. One day, they both donned pale blue jeans, and Paige had given Lisa one of her white T-shirts to wear. They did their hair up in high ponytails. Paige had lent Lisa one of her Alice bands. They had giggled at themselves in the mirror, taking in how similar they looked. They went downstairs to show Iris, who had stared and said, 'No.'

The girls had looked at each other, then back to Iris, confused, but knowing by her tone they had done something wrong.

'No,' Iris had repeated. 'You,' she had pointed at Lisa, 'will never be her, so stop trying. There is only one Paige.' She had turned to Paige, smiling, making sure Paige knew she wasn't angry with her. 'My Paige.'

She had taken Lisa by the hand and marched her into the kitchen, grabbed a pair of heavy scissors and hacked at her hair. Lisa had tried to pull away when she felt the first locks fall onto her bare feet, but Iris had pulled her back, the sharp tip of the scissors nicking her neck.

Paige stood up now, her blonde hair falling through Lisa's fingers, interrupting her thoughts. 'It'll all work out,' Paige said. 'I promise.'

Lisa nodded. But it wasn't going to work out. She could feel the dream slipping away and Paige along with it. Paige was going to ruin everything, and the realisation left her feeling sad and angry and used.

TWENTY

Jac

Friday afternoon

Ferns and tree branches scraped the passenger side as Jac drove the old ute up the hill to the hotel. Shifting down gears, the engine struggled until the road flattened out and gave way to the hotel's driveway. She wondered where she could park the ute, considering what an eyesore it was. She could drive further up, follow the driveway along the left side of the hotel and park around the back, but that seemed a bit forward, so she pulled over to the left as far away from the front of the hotel as possible, leaving the ute half covered in overhanging ponga ferns.

Jac took in the strip of lawn and gardens, further along, on the left; they were filled with bush roses, camellias and lavender, all in full bloom. Above that was a bank of hydrangeas, sheltered by a row of pine trees. To her right, across the driveway, with Everly below them, were pines, totaras and golden conifers. The front of the hotel, while run down, was still a sight and already looked better compared to yesterday, when she had arrived. The weeds had been removed from the guttering and the circular patch of lawn at the front of the hotel had been mown; the red and white roses had been pruned too. There was a man on the porch, outside the lounge windows, water-blasting the terracotta-tiled patio. The whole front facade had already been done and it glistened bright white in the afternoon sun.

Iris and the gardener were standing close together at the front door, Iris's hand on the gardener's meaty forearm. She was speaking and he was nodding. They both looked up at the same time and saw Jac. But then Iris turned slightly away from her, and the gardener did the same. Jac felt like she was intruding, and slowed her pace, wondering if she should go around the back way so they could carry on their conversation uninterrupted.

'Ah, Jac, there you are.' Iris turned back to her now, as if she hadn't just seen her.

The gardener nodded at Jac, giving her a tight smile as he walked away.

'I was hoping you'd make an appearance. It's about time you started to earn your keep.' It was said jokingly but Jac felt the sting in Iris's words.

She had her walking stick in one hand and a few sheets of paper in the other. 'Follow me,' she said and Jac dutifully obeyed. They stepped into the hallway and one of the pieces of paper drifted to the floor without Iris realising. Jac scooped it up. Before she could hand it over, Lisa met them by the lounge door.

'Mum, I can show Jac around. You've probably got other things to get on with.'

'Yes, I suppose,' Iris replied. 'But make sure you show her everything. And we're opening rooms six, seven and fourteen, so they'll need to be cleaned.' She turned to Jac. 'Lisa will show you where the cleaning products are. And it'll be dusty in the rooms. I can't remember the last time they were opened up. Make sure all the windows and balcony doors are opened. But also make sure they get shut up tonight.' Jac could see Iris getting more and more stressed as she rattled off instructions. 'The ensuites will need to be done too.'

'Mum.' Lisa put a hand on her arm. 'Jac and I will have it taken care of.'

Iris mumbled a reluctant assent and made her way along the hallway.

'She really should be resting,' Lisa said, looking at Iris. 'She loves the open day, insists on it, but it's a lot of work and stress for her. And I know you have a lot on your plate. I feel like Iris has bulldozed you into this, taken advantage.'

'It's fine,' Jac said, even though it was the last thing she wanted to be doing.

'Did you speak to Constable Dunlop this morning?'

'Yeah. Apparently, Charlie was seen leaving Everly, heading towards the main road, on Monday afternoon.'

'Oh, well, is that good news?' Lisa asked.

'I'm not sure, really,' Jac said. 'I guess, but I still think she would've told me if she was planning on leaving.' Again, that niggle of doubt.

They walked into the lounge. Most of the wall to their left was made up of three sets of French doors leading out onto the vast patio at the front of the hotel. On the far wall was a row of floor to ceiling windows that looked out onto the side of the hotel and the gardens. Thick velvet curtains were tied back with gold, tasselled ties. Everything about this place was aged but extravagant—just like Iris.

'Are you sure you want to be doing this?' Lisa asked. Her expression was pained. 'I feel terrible.'

'At this stage, there's not a lot else I can be doing,' Jac replied, appreciating Lisa's sympathy.

'Okay, so all these rooms down here—lounge, library, dining room, events room and music room—will all need to be vacuumed and dusted,' Lisa explained. 'I keep finding little things that need doing. With Mum getting older, lots of things are on their last legs, literally. The leg on this is buggered,' she said, walking up to a green velvet armchair. 'I need to get Nathan to fix it before Sunday. Someone will want to take a load off and the whole thing will collapse. Or maybe I can just put it away in one of the old rooms. And I only noticed the cracked window over there yesterday.' She pointed to one of the bottom panes of glass in the French doors. 'I'm not going to be able to have that repaired by Sunday.'

'It's hardly noticeable,' Jac said. 'It must take a lot of time and money for the upkeep of this place.'

'I'm not sure if there's much upkeep these days. I mean, look at that.' Lisa stared up at the chandelier above them.

'It's amazing,' Jac said, taking in the multitude of crystal pieces hanging in an intricate, circular pattern.

'Look closer. There're bits missing. No idea how they come off. Or where they go.'

Jac could see now. Gaps in the pattern. 'Hardly noticeable,' she said again.

'Everything about this place is nice, on the surface. If you paid a bit more attention, looked a little closer to see what it's really like, you'd realise it isn't that impressive. That's the way it's always been, people included.' She murmured, the last two words and made her way across the room.

Jac glanced at the piece of paper she had picked up earlier and, while Lisa continued talking, she read the neat, looping handwriting on it.

Timetable, Open Day, Sunday 26th
9 am Doors open
10 am Talk in library about history of the Gilmore Hotel (Iris and Frankie)
11 am Talk in orchard about hotel's orchard and vegetable gardens (Tama)
Midday Picnic in orchard
1.30 pm–3 pm High tea (only for those with tickets)
6.30 pm Paige arrives home
7 pm Special welcome home dinner for Paige
8 pm Paige plays flute (choose a few favourite songs if she's not sure what to play)
9 pm Bed
NOTES: Make sure Paige's sheets are changed, air out Paige's bedroom, check with Tama we have Fanta for Paige, flowers in Paige's room—yellow roses, not pink or red.

'Jac?' Lisa asked. 'Are you coming?' She was standing by the side table full of family photos.

'Sorry,' Jac said, walking over to Lisa, the piece of paper held out. 'Iris dropped this before.'

Lisa took it from her and scanned it. She sighed as she folded up the piece of paper.

'Who's Paige?' Jac asked, curious.

'She's my sister. Was my sister.' Lisa moved closer to the table. 'She's the one who stars in most of these photos.'

She didn't sound bitter, more sad, Jac thought.

'Did something happen to her?' Jac asked, unsure where this was going.

'Paige went missing the day of the open day. Twenty-one years ago, this coming Sunday.' Lisa spoke quickly, matter-of-factly, but Jac could see she was upset. Lisa pressed her lips together as she gazed at a photo of Paige.

'Oh, I'm sorry,' Jac said, immediately aware of her and Lisa's similar circumstances, each with a missing sister, and her stomach clenched, realising there wasn't a happy outcome for this family. 'What happened?'

'Nobody knows.' Lisa paused. It was obviously still a sore subject. Lisa gazed at the photos and started rubbing at her knuckles. Jac didn't think she even realised she was doing it. Up this close, Jac could see small calluses on each knuckle. 'Paige was here during the open day and then…she wasn't. The cops were called, the whole hotel was searched and all the grounds. Everyone has a theory. Some think she ran away. Some think she was abducted. Maybe even murdered…' Lisa stopped rubbing and looked at Jac.

'And what do you think?' Jac asked, looking at the photos on the side table, those of young Paige and Iris.

'I don't know. I prefer not to think about it.' Lisa covered her eyes with her hand. 'Whatever happened to her, the conclusion is always the same—she's not here. For years, I questioned. Did she suffer? Did someone do something horrific to her? Did she run away? And if she did, why didn't she say anything to me? It was horrible to live with. After uni I ended up going overseas. I spent two years in London, and then another two years in Australia trying to forget. I tried to move on. But running away to different countries didn't change anything. Paige was everywhere I looked. And staying away was selfish. Mum needed me.'

Jac wondered about the truth of Lisa's last statement,

but she understood what Paige's disappearance must have done to Lisa. 'You were close.'

'Really close.' Lisa smiled, and Jac could see the resemblance to the girl in all the photos. 'We were best friends. Only ten months apart.' She sniffed. 'Mum never got over it. You could say Paige was her favourite.'

No kidding, Jac thought, looking at the photos. She couldn't see Lisa in any of them.

'Mum's always believed Paige would come home. I guess, while there's hope, she's been able to carry on. The older and more absent-minded she gets, she's developed an expectation that Paige will come back on the anniversary of the weekend she disappeared. The disappointment last year when Paige didn't materialise took her weeks to get over.'

Jac picked up one of the photos of Paige. She looked to be in her mid-teens. 'She looks a bit like Charlie,' Jac said.

'I noticed that when you showed me the photo on your phone last night at dinner. So did Mum.' Lisa paused. 'I'm sorry about Charlie. I know better than anyone how you feel. The uncertainty.' She stopped and then hurried on to say, 'Not that it will be like this for your sister. I'm sure there's a perfectly good explanation for Charlie's disappearance.'

Jac nodded, hopeful that Lisa was right. What had she just said about Iris? While there's hope, she'd been able to carry on. And that's what Jac would do.

TWENTY-ONE

Lisa

Twenty-one years ago

ON THE WAY home from school on the bus, Paige had been quiet, staring out the window, not interested in Lisa's questions or stories about her day. Lisa had continued making small talk on the walk from the bus stop up to the hotel. Paige had smiled and nodded in all the right places, but Lisa could tell her mind was elsewhere.

'You okay?' Lisa asked as they approached the front of the hotel.

'Fine,' Paige said, turning her head left and right.

'Who are you looking for?' Lisa asked, pulling open the solid oak front door and feeling the weight of the hotel press down on her shoulders.

'No one,' Paige said, and sprinted along the hallway and up the stairs.

Lisa peered into rooms as she went, looking for Iris, waiting for her to materialise. Through the double swing doors, she stepped into the back hallway and turned left into the kitchen. She said hello to Nancy, who was busy at the centre island rolling out pastry, a smudge of flour on her cheek. She sat on a high stool opposite Nancy and peered into the mixing bowl.

'I'm making your favourite tonight,' Nancy said. 'Lemon meringue pie.' Her Scottish brogue could just be discerned beneath the dull Kiwi accent she'd succumbed to from thirty years of living in New Zealand.

Lisa smiled her appreciation. Nancy came in every afternoon for a few hours to cook their dinner and bake. They also had a cleaner who came in three times a week. Apart from Paige, Nancy was probably her favourite person in the world. Nancy had never said anything to Lisa about it, but it was clear she knew Iris didn't treat Lisa as well as she did Paige. Nancy always found ways to cheer Lisa up, cooking her favourites—when Iris wouldn't have had a clue what her favourite anything was—and often slipping a chocolate bar into her desk drawer in her bedroom. When Nancy first began working for them last year, Iris had once caught her giving Lisa a magazine. After putting the magazine in the bin, Iris had told Lisa to leave the kitchen, but, standing outside the door, she heard the clipped lecture that followed.

'How do you think that would make Paige feel? You giving Lisa something and not her. It's unfair. If you value your job, I'd rather you not play favourites with my daughters. Stick to doing your job—feeding this family.'

Nancy hadn't stopped sneaking Lisa things, but since then had been extra careful.

'Where's Paige?' Iris appeared by the kitchen door now.

Lisa knew her mother wouldn't come in. Iris Gilmore believed the kitchen and laundry were not her domain.

'I haven't seen her, sorry, Ms Gilmore,' Nancy said, the usual singsong voice she used with Lisa and Paige had disappeared and was replaced with a softer, more serious tone. She put her head down and continued rolling out the pastry.

Lisa turned on her stool to face Iris and shrugged. She didn't expect a welcome from Iris, didn't expect her to ask how her day was.

'The violin tutor's going to be here in half an hour,' Iris said, looking at her watch. 'I'm up to my neck in work.'

Lisa had discovered Iris liked to appear busy, but, apart from a few charities she helped and brainstorming ideas around the interior design of the hotel, Iris didn't do a lot with her days.

Out of the corner of her eye, Lisa could see Iris still standing there, glaring.

'Find her!' Iris shouted. Her reedy voice, even higher than usual, made Lisa wince. 'For god's sake, do I have to do everything around here?' She marched off, slamming the door.

Nancy didn't look up as Lisa slid off the stool and went to search for Paige.

She sprinted up the stairs, taking them two at a time, and dashed into Paige's room. It was empty, and her school uniform was lying in a heap on the floor, her violin case next to it. Lisa then ran back downstairs, went through the double doors, passed the kitchen and the tradesmen's hallway to her left which led to the laundry and on her right the door to the disused indoor swimming pool, and raced out the back. There, she stood on the concrete. Nancy's car was parked by the door. Twenty metres away to the left were the staff quarters. Nathan was the only one who lived there at the moment. She crossed the concrete and walked on to manicured grass that separated the orchard, paddocks and bush from the hotel. Glancing over at the orchard and seeing no sign of Paige, she carried on to the dirt path that led into scrubby bush. Halfway down the path, a small clearing opened up. To the left was a small plaque commemorating Iris's parents, and the native trees they had planted there over eighty years ago. To the right was the wishing well. When it had been a working hotel all those years ago, before it had been leased to the government for the care of wounded soldiers, guests would walk down to visit the well. Iris had told her and Paige that children used to drop coins in, closing their eyes and making wishes. But now, the wishing well was not much more than a collection of tiles and wooden beams lying under many seasons of leaves and twigs. All that was standing now was the circular base made with heavy grey rocks, the spaces in between them filled with crumbling mortar. There was also the story that Iris had told Lisa and Paige of the family who had come to stay at the hotel for a week one summer. The seven-year-old boy and five-year-old girl had come down to the well on their own but only the boy had returned, saying the little girl had refused to come back. The girl was found an hour later. They said she had tried to cross the creek further along where it was wider and shallower, but she had slipped and hit her head on a rock and drowned. For every happy memory the hotel held, Lisa felt there were five tragedies.

She carried on along the path and came out into the back of the property, the creek in front of her. And then stepped back into the bushes when she noticed Paige and Nathan standing under one of the oak trees ten metres away. Nathan was in his usual work clothes, long trousers and a ragged-looking T-shirt. Paige, to Lisa's surprise, had on the black dress she usually only wore for her performances at school. It was long, slinky, cut on the bias, accentuating everything womanly about her body.

She watched as Nathan shoved her hard up against the tree, his hand running up her leg. Lisa stepped out, alarmed, protective of her older sister, for a second assuming she needed saving, but almost immediately realised that wasn't the case.

She watched, both fascinated and repulsed, as Nathan's mouth devoured Paige's, and as Paige reciprocated. Stumbling back, Lisa tripped on a rotten stump; twigs snapped as she landed awkwardly, and the couple broke from their embrace at the sound.

Lisa shifted further back into the bushes and saw Paige glance at her watch.

'I have to go,' she said. 'I'm going to be late.'

Nathan grabbed Paige by the hand, kissing her again, as Lisa got up and began sprinting back to the hotel, scared they would catch her out.

At the rear door of the hotel, Lisa decided she didn't want to go back inside. She wasn't going to get a blasting from Iris just because Paige was late. She headed for the concrete steps that led down the hill to the main street of Everly.

'Lise!' She heard Paige's breathless voice behind her and turned. 'What're you doing?'

'Not much. Just going for a walk. She's looking for you. I was supposed to come find you. You're going to be late for your lesson.'

'Sorry,' Paige said, genuine worry on her face, knowing Lisa would cop it. 'I'm going right now.' She re-tied her ponytail, smoothing her hair back into place.

Lisa reached up. 'You have some bark or something stuck behind your ear.'

'Oh.' Paige giggled.

'Why are you dressed like that?' Lisa asked. 'Bit nice for a walk in the bush.' She tried to sound casual, but her tone came off as accusatory.

Paige narrowed her eyes and then shrugged. 'Better go

before Poison Iris tracks me down. You'd better make your-self scarce as well. See you at dinner, Lise.' She opened the door and disappeared inside.

In no hurry, Lisa walked around the side of the hotel and down the concrete steps, saddened that Paige didn't share what was happening between her and Nathan. Since Iris had spoken to them a couple of weeks ago about re-opening the hotel next year, about how Paige was going to be a part of it, Lisa felt Paige had distanced herself. She was practising more, in her bedroom or the music room. On weekends, she often said she was studying and would lock herself away in her room. Lisa felt like she had hardly seen her. When they did talk, Paige always brought their discussion around to the scholarship, the nervous excite-ment around waiting for the assessor's decision. She was fully committed to leaving the hotel. Lisa tried her best to gently persuade her to stay and, when that didn't work, challenged her, telling her there was no way Iris was going to allow it. Over the last couple of weeks their conversa-tions had ended with Paige switching off and leaving or changing the subject, not willing to listen, as if she had already mentally started the process of cutting herself off from the hotel, from Lisa. As much as this saddened her, she refused to believe that Paige would actually go through with it. And at the back of her head, Lisa always found comfort in the fact that, no matter how much Paige wanted it, Iris would never allow her to leave.

TWENTY-TWO

Jac

Friday afternoon

JAC HAD SPENT the whole afternoon cleaning, thinking about Charlie and, as she moved through the three rooms, about Paige Gilmore's disappearance as well. Two young women, bearing a resemblance, both missing, both from Everly.

The guest rooms were filthy. She vacuumed, dusted and polished, made up beds and attacked ensuites that looked like they hadn't been cleaned in a decade. Iris popped her head in when Jac was halfway through the first room, all smiles and ready for a chat.

'My mother always called this the hanged man's room,' she said, smiling, as if reminiscing about a happier time. 'Yes, when my parents operated the hotel, a man hanged himself in this room.'

'That's terrible,' Jac said, vaguely aware of the story, looking around, finding herself wondering how he did it.

'Hung himself from the light fixture, apparently,' Iris said, as if reading her mind.

Jac looked up at the ceiling rose she had just spent the last fifteen minutes scrubbing stubborn mould off and polishing the brass light-fitting in the middle of it.

'Word got out, of course. Mother thought it would be bad for business, that no one would want to come. But people did. I remember Mother saying they got some strange people visiting, wanting to be put in this room for the very reason that someone had hanged themselves in here. And as the years went on, people often used to say they heard strange noises when they slept in here.' Iris wiped a finger across the window. 'Look at the state of it,' she said. 'Would you mind also doing the windows, and those in the other rooms as well? Try to avoid any streaks.' And then she was gone, leaving Jac staring at the ceiling, imagining the worst.

Apart from Iris's ill-timed ghost story, it was mindless work and Jac's thoughts wandered, back to the fire, the aftermath. Charlie had begged Jac not to go after their mother's death. Had said she needed her. But back then it wasn't enough for Jac to stay. Whenever she and Charlie talked, there was always that hesitation, that barrier that stopped them getting closer. She knew Charlie had been brought up on gossip after she had left and the incessant talk of their father, blaming Jac for everything, like a preacher trying to convert a non-believer. Jac thought Charlie had had questions, of course she had, but they'd both been too scared about what would happen if the subject of the fire was brought up, and so it simmered, just below the surface. The guilt had always been there—her decision to leave Charlie behind to try and forge out a life for herself away from her father, away from the person he had made her out to be. And she never regretted leaving Charlie more so than over the last few days. She knew how much Charlie used to rely on her when she was little. A responsibility that never sat well with Jac but one that she didn't have a lot of choice in. Charlie had often needed comfort and Jac was the one to provide it. When they were younger, Charlie would slide into Jac's bed. They shared a room in their small two-bedroom rental. In winter in the middle of the night she was often woken with a start by Charlie, ice cold feet resting on her shins. She was always half asleep, and instead of sucking her thumb for comfort or hugging a teddy she would take a piece of Jac's then long hair and, grasping it in her fist, holding it close to her face, she would fall asleep.

JAC CALLED IT a day two hours later and headed to her room, desperate to clean off the grime of the hotel that had settled on her skin. She got out of the shower just before six pm, realising she would be late for dinner. She was starving but didn't feel like sitting down with Lisa and Iris tonight. And the fact she was no closer to finding out anything more about Charlie was frustrating her.

There was a knock at her door. She stepped across the room to open it, pulling her towel tight around her.

'Jac, hi,' Lisa said. She looked uncomfortable, unable to meet her eye. What was going on? 'Thank you for the work on those rooms. They look amazing. I didn't realise they'd come up so well.'

'No problem. I'll be ready for dinner in two minutes,' Jac said.

'Oh, well, that's why I'm here. Mum has a guest to-night…an old friend who helps with the open days. They're going to be chatting about it over dinner, a bit of a bore, really, and Mum thought…she suggested, after the day you've had…you might be quite tired…'

'It's fine,' Jac said, saving Lisa from having to say that Iris didn't want Jac at dinner tonight.

'No, it's not, really. I'm sorry. She thinks she can treat people this way.'

Jac felt sorry for Lisa. She knew what it was like to have to apologise for a parent's behaviour.

'Don't worry about it. I'm pretty tired anyway,' she said, honestly relieved.

'If you'd like to go down to the kitchen when you're ready, Tama will have something for you.'

'Thanks.' Jac closed the door and got changed, towel drying her hair and raking it forward with her fingers, pushing the spiky bits down as best she could.

Five minutes later, she walked down the stairs and could hear voices coming from the dining room, but she had no interest in whatever they were discussing. She turned a sharp right and went on through the double doors to the rear of the hotel. Lisa had brought her back here this morning, pointing out the old tradesmen's hallway where the laundry was and the indoor swimming pool opposite. She now opened the first door on her left.

Tama and Nathan were standing at the stainless-steel island in the middle of the kitchen, beers in hand. They stopped talking when she approached them.

'Dinner will be ready in five. Is that okay?' Tama asked, placing his beer down and walking over to the huge ten-burner stove on the back wall, clicking the gas burner on.

'Yeah, sure, no rush,' Jac said, not used to being waited on.

'Beer?' Tama asked, making his way over to the walk-in fridge that took up half the right side of the kitchen.

'Thanks,' Jac said, taking the bottle from him and twisting the top.

'I'm Nathan.' He held his hand out across the island bench.

Jac shook it, her hand disappearing into his. Calluses scraped the soft skin of her palm. 'Jac,' she said.

Silence. She felt awkward, out of practice, unable to chat about the everyday. She had got used to keeping to herself. Nathan slipped a hand into his pocket then pulled it out again. He clawed one hand through his brown hair, which was streaked with grey.

'You work here,' Jac asked. 'You're the gardener?'

'Not sure if you can call me that. Jack of all trades, I guess,' Nathan said.

'Have you worked here for long?'

'Half my life, I reckon.' He scuffed his work boot on the lino. 'You know Iris, or Lisa?' he asked.

'No, not really.' Jac leaned against the island, tried to look casual, easygoing. 'I used to live here, in Everly.'

He nodded. His face didn't give much away and, as usual, Jac wondered what he knew about her. If he was silently judging her.

'My sister's missing. That's why I've come home. And my dad…died yesterday.'

'Right. You're Eddie Morgan's daughter.'

It wasn't a question, but she nodded anyway. She wondered if Nathan knew her dad. They probably would've been around the same age.

'Yeah, heard about that,' he said. 'Sorry about your dad…and sister.'

She put her beer down on the bench and pulled out her phone, finding the photo of Charlie. 'You don't know her, do you? Her name's Charlie. She's just turned eighteen.' Tama stopped what he was doing and came back over to look. 'She lives at the campground.' Jac turned the phone to Tama and then to Nathan.

'Might have seen her around. Maybe at the cafe,' Tama said.

'Yeah, she worked there on weekends,' Jac said. 'Do you remember the last time you saw her?'

'Probably a couple of weeks ago now,' he said then picked up a block of parmesan and started grating.

Nathan's gaze was still on the photo. Jac didn't understand the look on his face. Recognition?

'You know her?' she asked.

'No, I don't, sorry.' He didn't meet her eye as he spoke, and Jac noticed him glancing over at Tama for just a second. Tama paused and then went back to the stove, his back to both of them.

'Are you sure?' she pushed. 'Maybe you've seen her at the cafe as well?'

'Nah, just looks like someone I used to know.'

'Paige Gilmore?' Jac asked.

He looked surprised.

'Lisa told me about her this afternoon. Sad story. Did you know her well?'

'Not really.'

'Were you working here when she disappeared?'

'Yeah.'

'Lisa told me no answers were found after her disappearance. It's a horrible thing for her family to have to go through. I'm just really hoping the same doesn't happen with Charlie.' She left her words hanging in the air, but Nathan was silent, draining the rest of his beer.

'I'd better be off,' he said, turning to Tama.

'Sure you don't want any food? Heaps here, mate,'

Tama said, returning from the stove with a pot of pasta in one hand and a pot of meat sauce in the other.

'All good. See ya later.'

He walked past Jac without saying anything.

Tama used tongs to dish up spaghetti into a bowl and ladled the meat sauce on top. He sprinkled fresh parmesan with a flourish. 'Here ya go,' Tama presented her with the bowl. 'Feel free to eat in here or you can take it up to your room.'

'Thanks,' she said, and then asked, 'Do you know much about Nathan?'

'How do you mean?' Tama started wiping down the island bench and stacking pots in the sink.

Jac wasn't sure where she was going with this. 'I mean, I don't know him at all, but it's just that he seemed to get a bit funny when I asked him about Charlie.'

Tama hesitated and then said, 'Look, Nathan's a good guy. He does know Charlie, or at least knows of her.'

'How?' Jac asked, sensing there was more to this.

'Same as me, I think. From the cafe. From what I've heard, Nathan may have…made her feel a bit uncomfortable when she started working there.'

'What does that mean? Uncomfortable how?'

Tama looked like he was regretting saying anything now. He rubbed the back of his neck and sighed. 'I don't know. I haven't actually spoken to him about it. I just heard things from my wife, ya know. I don't think it was actually a big deal.'

'Says you,' Jac said.

Tama shrugged and turned away from Jac. 'Sorry, but I need to get moving and get this dessert ready for Ms Gilmore and her guest.'

Jac didn't say anything more and left Tama to it.

SHE LAY ON her bed later that night, her belly full from Tama's pasta and so tired she could barely move, but sleep still wouldn't come. She stared at the intricate ceiling rose. She had cleaned three exactly the same that afternoon, wiping mould and grime, and while they hadn't come up quite sparkling white, they were better than the dull grey one she was staring at now, trying her best not to think of the hanged man's room further along the hallway in the east wing.

She wasn't used to the sounds of the hotel. There was an occasional creak, old floorboards and walls groaning with age, and an occasional morepork calling through the night outside, and then long periods of silence. But then again, she'd become used to Sydney's soundtrack: sirens; cars peeling out from the stop sign on the corner, metres from her bedroom window; drunk people yelling obscenities at each other. She wasn't sure which one she preferred. The silence, here, was so wide open; it made her want to fill it up with something—talk or music or laughter or screaming.

It was just past eleven pm when she gave up on sleep and decided to go downstairs. Maybe she could make herself a cup of tea. She couldn't stop thinking about Nathan and what Tama had said, and she'd made a plan to add Brian at the cafe to her list of people she wanted to talk to tomorrow. As she made her way down the stairs, which were each lit up with small, embedded lights to guide her way, she heard music coming from somewhere. Walking along the main ground-floor hallway, her imagination conjured up the ghosts of the Gilmore Hotel. Halfway along on her left, a strip of light glowed underneath a closed door, where the music seemed to be coming from. She opened the door and found what must have been the music room. The walls of the long, rectangular space were a buttery yellow under the one central chandelier that was on. On the left was a small stage, a metre off the floor, and on the back wall, under the window was what looked like a grand piano covered in a dull white dust sheet. A spray of mould fanned from the far back corner, giving the room its musty smell. Lisa was in the middle of the room, seated, playing the flute, surrounded by stacks of chairs.

Lisa, as if sensing someone behind her, stopped playing and let out a gasp when she saw Jac.

'Sorry,' Jac said, stepping back towards the door. 'I'm so sorry. I didn't mean to intrude. I heard the music and wasn't sure where it was coming from.' She didn't mention her theory that it could've been a ghost.

'It's okay, no problem,' Lisa said, taking the flute apart and putting it back in its case.

'Don't let me stop you. I'll go back up to bed,' Jac said. She could see she had embarrassed Lisa—she could see her blushing cheeks from where she stood.

'I was never really used to an audience. That was more Paige's thing,' Lisa said, snapping the case closed, then standing, the sheet music on the stand fluttering to the floor.

Both women were silent. Lisa got up, case under her arm, and walked past Jac.

'Goodnight,' she said, her smile tight. Jac thought she could see tears in her eyes.

'I'm really sorry…' Jac said again, watching her walk along the hallway to the stairs.

Jac walked over to the music stand and picked up the sheet music. It was titled *Syrinx* by Claude Debussy. Jac had no idea about classical music, playing it or reading it, and wished more than anything that Charlie was here to play for her. She placed the sheet music back on the stand and looked around the room, shuddering involuntarily. At the door she flicked off the light and made her way back to her room.

TWENTY-THREE

Lisa

Twenty-one years ago

PAIGE, LISA AND Iris sat in the stifling lounge. Lisa wiped at the gathering sweat on her hairline. Iris had insisted on a fire tonight. It was mid-November and Lisa could already feel that gradual shifting from spring to summer, moving into clear, sunny days; the temperature increasing. It was not fire weather, but Iris said she loved the feel of it. 'So intimate and cosy, don't you think?' she asked Paige, who nodded and smiled in return.

Paige and Iris sat side by side on a couch directly in front of the fire and Lisa sat in a velvet wingback chair to the side.

'Paige, play something for me,' Iris said. 'The violin tonight, I think.'

Paige hesitated and then said, 'How about Lisa play something. She's getting really good on the flute.'

Lisa had been taking lessons at school for the last three years. She had joined the orchestra and had to be happy with one of the borrowed flutes from school that were lent out each year. Iris didn't think Lisa was serious enough about it to buy her one of her own. Paige's flute, meanwhile, was solid silver with a gold embouchure—one of the best money could buy.

Lisa shook her head, frowning at Paige, who nodded back in encouragement.

'No,' Iris said. 'I want you to play, Paige.'

'You're so much better than me, Paige. I'd hate to inflict my terrible playing on our mother.' Lisa failed to keep the sweet sarcasm out of her voice and regretted it even before she saw Iris's lips disappear in disapproval. What was she doing? She didn't even want to play, knowing it would only end in criticism and comparison.

'Come.' Just one word, but the tone, the look in her mother's eyes, told her where she was going.

Lisa got up from her chair, but instead of walking towards Iris, she skirted the couch and moved away, knowing not to turn her back on her enemy.

'No,' Lisa said.

'What did you say to me?' Iris had a small smile on her face, but her eyes narrowed as she approached.

Lisa stopped, realising she had backed herself into the corner by the window. She glanced at Paige, who looked at her, horrified, shaking her head.

'Don't you look at her!' Iris ordered. 'Come!'

'No,' Lisa said again, but this time it came out as a gulping sound laced with fear. As she shrank away, her mother seemed to grow before her eyes.

'Come. With. Me.'

It was the first time Lisa had come close to disobeying Iris. It felt completely wrong and terrifying, but she couldn't stop herself. She stood as tall as she could, still only just coming up to Iris's shoulder, and she walked straight past her. If Iris wanted time alone with Paige, fine. Lisa would go to her room.

Iris grabbed her by her upper arm, but Lisa shrugged out of her grasp. Heart hammering, she headed for the door. She heard Iris's footsteps coming after her, and she resisted the urge to run—but she should have. Seconds later, Iris grabbed her hair, twisting it at the roots, and then slammed her head into the corner of the door.

She heard Paige yell out, but Lisa didn't make a sound.

'How dare you,' Iris hissed in her ear, and the words were surrounded by a buzzing static.

Lisa turned to look at Iris. At first, her face was a blur, but after she blinked twice, Iris came into focus. Lisa tried to read her face. Iris had never been physically violent in this way before, apart from a firm grasp around Lisa's wrist as she led her upstairs. She had never needed to be. Lisa had always complied. Iris's abuse was always more concealed, words like barbs, withholding of affection. Did she look regretful now? Sorry that she'd taken things too far? Lisa didn't think so.

She let Iris lead her up the stairs, unable to do anything else, struggling to put one foot in front of the other, her forehead aching. At the end of the hallway, past their bedrooms, they stood in front of the soldiers' hallway. Iris took a key out of her pocket—she had obviously planned her alone time with Paige tonight—and unlocked the door.

Without Iris saying anything, Lisa stepped into the disused wing of the hotel, the cold air immediately seeping into her bones, making her wish she was still sitting by the fire in the lounge. She waited while Iris opened the door to 12A.

'The darkness gives you time to think,' Iris said. 'And you've got a bit of that to do. I never want to see a display of disobedience like that again.' She slammed the door.

Lisa held a hand to her forehead and winced. There

was no blood, but she could feel a lump under her fingers. She sat down in the middle of the dark room. The rooms here were the smallest in the hotel with no ensuites. She knew there was a stretcher in the far-right hand corner, a boarded-up window in the middle of the far wall, and that was it. She closed her eyes and tried to fight the fear, thinking of good things: swimming in the creek with Paige; the possibility of the hotel opening, welcoming new and interesting people; walking in the orchard; playing the flute. Anything but what went on in these rooms.

The history of the soldiers' hallway had been told to Paige and Lisa like a bedtime story. During and after World War Two, the hotel was turned into a place where returned soldiers could recuperate. This hallway became a prison of sorts. Iris had told the girls that some of the soldiers were mentally unstable, violent, and that those patients were put into the five rooms in this hallway, with the windows in each boarded up 'for their own good', and the wooden doors reinforced to stop them from trying to escape. 'Not many of them had a lot wrong with their bodies,' Iris told the girls. 'But,' she tapped the side of her head, 'it was all up here. The war drove a lot of those men out of their minds.'

Everyone knew these stories; the kids around Everly had been brought up on them. Everyone had their favourite one to retell, the gorier the better. But Lisa had never enjoyed the stories. It was a lot different when you lived in the same place as the ghosts.

The one that always stayed with Lisa was about a solider who had been locked up in room 12A for over three months. 'For solitude,' the disgraced former manager had told newspapers, standing up for his somewhat dubious techniques. 'It was a place where they could have the opportunity to think.' Lisa always thought that was the last thing the soldiers would need, to be left alone with their thoughts. She knew how they felt. But this particular soldier had attacked a nurse as she brought in his lunch for him. He had beaten her to death with the metal lunch tray, locked her in this room and escaped into the bush beyond the hotel. He was never seen again.

There was a creak in the far corner of the room by the boarded-up window.

Just the old hotel settling, Lisa told herself for the hundredth time. Shifting to the wall by the door, as far from where she thought she heard the noises. She blinked back visions of a woman in a nurse's uniform, the side of her head caved in.

Then there was another creak in the wall her rigid spine was leaning up against. A jolting movement that made it feel like the hotel was alive. *And it is, isn't it?* Lisa thought. How can a building with so much history not have all that hate, sadness and fear festering in its walls, pulsing, threatening to overrun it and all those in it?

Lisa moved back to the centre of the room, curled up in a ball and waited.

TWENTY-FOUR

Charlie

Saturday morning

CHARLIE LOOKED AT Paige's watch: 6.30 am. This morning, she'd woken up with a slightly clearer head than the last few days. She hadn't eaten since Thursday night and hadn't had a drink since yesterday morning. Her stomach was tight, clenched, and it let out a growl. The hunger she could handle, but she wasn't sure about the thirst. Her mouth was dry and, when she tried to lick her lips, there was no spit in her mouth to moisten them. Her headache was a nagging throb: dehydration, she thought.

She started to question her plan. If she didn't eat or drink, she would only get weaker. What if a time came when she had the opportunity to get out of here? What if she was half dead from dehydration and couldn't fight back when she needed to? She wondered if she had been checked up on as she slept the day away, if the person holding her here had seen that she hadn't done what had been asked. Probably. There had been no lunch or dinner yesterday.

For the first time she entertained the possibility that the person may not come back. Maybe because she hadn't done what they'd asked, they were done with her, moving on. Or what if something happened to them that stopped them coming to feed her? Some kind of accident. She'd be stuck here forever. Charlie got off the stretcher and started pacing, trying to keep the panic at bay.

Who was thinking of her right now? Her dad? Had he given up on her? Probably. How about Jac? Did her sister even know she was missing? Who was thinking about Charlie Morgan right now? The kids at school? Were they wondering where she had disappeared to? Or were they thankful they didn't have to see her face each day? Her teachers? Had they contacted Dad yet, asking about her absence? Then she remembered study leave had started this week. School wouldn't have a clue she was missing, neither would any of the kids there, not that they cared.

She needed to do this. It wasn't caving, it wasn't bowing to their wishes. She had to do what they asked so that whatever was going to happen next could happen.

Over at the drawers, she took the perfume, sprayed it on her wrists and neck, the cloying, sweet smell in the close confines making her dizzy. Looking at the photo, she matched up lipstick and eyeshadow. She mimicked the girl's smile in the mirror, a small up-turn of her lips, no teeth showing, and then turned away, putting the mirror face down on the desk. Looking at the photo once again, taking in the high, slick ponytail and the chunky black velvet headband, she picked up the brush, noticing strands of long blonde hair in it already. Letting out a sob, she started brushing, whispering to herself over and over, 'I am Charlie Morgan. I am Charlie Morgan. I am Charlie Morgan.'

TWENTY-FIVE

Jac

Saturday morning

AT THE DINING room door, Lisa's 'good morning' was curt and Jac figured she still felt embarrassed about having been disturbed in the music room last night. Lisa looked different. Apart from her white shirt, rolled to the elbows, being creased like it had spent a few days on the floor, she wore make-up and her dark blonde hair, which Jac had only ever seen worn in a ponytail, was loose and shaped into soft curls.

Jac was unsure if she would be welcome at breakfast, but as Iris marched past her and into the dining room, her walking stick flailing in the air, barely touching the ground, she said, 'Don't hover, Jac, come in!'

Iris held a stack of papers in her hand, which she placed on the table before taking her seat. She leaned her walking stick against the table, but it slid and clattered onto the floor beside her, where it stayed. Jac noticed that Iris didn't look as put together as she usually did. Her hair, over the last couple of days at least, was always perfectly blow-dried, but this morning it was flat on one side where she appeared to have slept on it. Under her eyes were traces of mascara from the day before. The old woman mumbled to herself as she set about making tea, putting the strainer atop a delicate china cup. Halfway through pouring, she placed the pot down, took a notepad from the pile of papers and started writing.

'Catering!' she yelled out, looking at Jac.

Jac had no idea how to respond and looked to Lisa for help.

'It's okay, Mum. Tama has it all sorted.' Lisa turned to Jac and explained, 'There's a picnic lunch in the orchard during the open day and everyone brings their own, but later on there's an afternoon tea for those who have paid extra—'

'A high tea,' Iris interrupted.

'Yes, a high tea.' Lisa nodded at Iris.

There was silence as Iris stared at Lisa. It continued as Lisa glanced away, looking uncomfortable. Jac waited for another awkward confrontation, or for Iris to lose it again.

'The posters!' Iris exclaimed, hands to her face, which would've looked comical save for the horror in her eyes.

'The posters went up at the high school last week, and they're all around Everly and the surrounding towns. Emails were sent out a couple of weeks ago to those on our list, too.' Lisa's tone was smooth and calm, and Jac admired the way she dealt with Iris's mood and the impending open day.

Iris went back to mumbling to herself. 'I don't have time for this,' she said, taking a last sip of tea and pushing her chair back. 'Nathan! Nathan!' she yelled, grabbing her walking stick from the floor and marching out of the room.

'He'll be outside, Mum,' Lisa called. 'Sorry.' She turned back to Jac. 'Like I said, she gets like this around the time of the open day. Needs it to be a success for...' Lisa took a sip of coffee and didn't finish her sentence. 'After Mum's fall, her head injury, I wondered if she should've cancelled it this year, but she was adamant. And as you've probably learned, nothing much stops Iris once she puts her mind to something.'

Jac nodded, understanding. She grabbed a piece of toast and said, 'I should probably get to work. I've still got the ground floor to do.' She didn't mention to Lisa that she also wanted to go and talk to Michelle Lafferty at the pub later this morning.

'Thanks, Jac,' Lisa said.

She walked through the double doors to get the cleaning equipment from the laundry, wondering if she should leave the Gilmores to their weirdness. But she needed the money, and maybe she would learn something after speaking to Michelle today. She felt it was a long shot but she might get some idea of where Charlie was heading and then maybe she could leave Everly and the Gilmores. Before turning down the tradesmen's hallway she heard voices by the open back door of the hotel. She stood at the back door, Nathan and Iris just a few metres away. Iris's head shot up when she saw Jac. Nathan leaned in and said something to Iris that Jac couldn't hear, a hand on her arm, as if to comfort her, and then walked away. This was the second time Jac had seen the two of them together and she wondered about their relationship. In some ways, Iris looked closer to Nathan than Lisa.

Nathan continued on around the side of the hotel and Iris came back inside, pulling a tissue from her pocket and wiping her nose.

'I was hoping I'd catch you. I was just giving Nathan a list of jobs. Such a busy time!' Iris looked tired and harassed but Jac suspected she wouldn't want to be doing anything else. 'Now, let me give you a quick tour.'

'Oh, Lisa's already shown me—'

'Come.' Iris cut her off and grabbed her by the wrist, squeezing tightly in what Jac assumed was excitement. 'Everything is coming together so nicely for tomorrow.' She seemed like a different person from the one Jac had seen muttering in the dining room fifteen minutes ago.

'As you know, we open a few rooms upstairs for people to look through in the morning and then close off upstairs for visitors. Someone tried to get into my room a few years back, so that was that—we have volunteers on the day standing guard, making sure no one is where they shouldn't be. Look in here.'

They stepped into the main hallway and Iris pulled Jac along. She was going on this tour whether she wanted to or not. They passed the music room on their left and then further along Iris brought her to the threshold of two wooden doors, frosted glass in the upper half, and pushed them open, walking in.

'The ballroom!' she announced.

The parquet floor gleamed under the light of six chandeliers. Tables were set out around the perimeter of the room, covered in white cloths. A woman was in the process of laying out silver cutlery and stark white plates, and voluminous peony arrangements in pale pinks and whites were being set up in the centre of each table by two other women.

Iris looked at Jac, enraptured.

'Beautiful,' Jac said. And it was. They could hold a wedding in here tomorrow if they had to, but Jac couldn't understand the point, the expense, for just an open day.

The three women had looked up, alarmed, when they

had seen Iris enter, but carried on when Iris continued to talk to Jac.

'My mother used to tell me about the wonderful parties my grandparents threw here. They used to hold weddings as well. Paige had her sweet sixteenth here. Pretty much her whole school year attended, and a few friends of mine. Oh, she looked beautiful that night.'

Iris disappeared into her reminiscences again, hands clasped below her chin, a vague smile, tears gathering in her eyes.

For Jac's sixteenth birthday, her dad had dropped a six-pack in her lap that Saturday night and joined her on the couch. 'Best you start off with your parents so we can keep an eye on you.' He'd winked and her mum had joined them. Jac had got drunk that night for the first time on her dad's cheap beer. She had woken up in the middle of the night on the couch in the lounge. Her mum and dad weren't there and Charlie, ten years old, was sound asleep in bed. The next morning, she had tried to get through her hangover with painkillers, water and a greasy breakfast, but nothing helped, and her dad had told her not to worry, that she'd get used to it. She never had, but it hadn't stopped her from drinking.

'Come,' Iris said again, cutting off both of their trips down memory lane.

They walked back out along the hallway, crossing over to a door opposite the music room.

'The library,' Iris said. 'You'll need to clean in here today. This is where I do my talk.'

Jac took in the dark wood-panelled walls and shelves lined with leather-bound classics on one side and a mess of hardcover and paperback novels and non-fiction on the other. A fireplace took up the wall at the end, and overstuffed leather couches and chairs were deposited around the middle of the room.

'These are from when my grandparents opened the hotel in 1910,' Iris explained, pointing to photos set up on a long table, all neatly labelled and dated. One showed the hotel, minus the bush surrounding it now, sitting beneath a white-grey sky, with horses and carts lined up on the crushed stone driveway. Another showed a group of tourists, women in long dresses, hair piled high on top of their heads, and men in suits and flat caps with drooping moustaches.

'My mother and father took over the running of the hotel in 1935 when Mother's parents passed away. They only got to run it for a few years before the war started and made it pointless to keep it going. And it was hard for my mother, a woman on her own when my father left to fight. But she was very strong. My father was killed in 1942. I was one when he left to fight in 1940. I can't remember anything about him. Mother ended up leasing the hotel to the government. The hotel was run as a hospital for almost ten years for returned servicemen, a place where they could rehabilitate, both physically and mentally.' Iris pointed at three photos on display.

Jac took in the vacant, slack faces of the young men sitting in the hotel's lounge in front of the fire. There was another one of the library, back then, looking like it had been set up as a clinic. There was a nurse and a doctor posing in front of a white curtain that had divided the room, bookshelves visible on either side. The third was a photo of four men all with that faraway look in their eyes, present but not, sitting in wheelchairs on the front porch of the hotel. Doctors and nurses were lined up behind them, doing the smiling for the whole group.

'I was five when we moved to Auckland for that time. Mother always told me she missed the hotel, though, so we returned when I was fourteen. I always thought she would run it as a hotel again, but she preferred to live her life in peace. And we did, for the most part. She'd been through a lot and didn't have much support, with her parents and husband dead. My grandparents had left her a multi-millionaire after their deaths. People knew of her wealth around here, knew how important she was. I think she felt the pressure to live up to their expectations. She always very graciously opened the hotel once a year for an open day, and it's always stuck. I'm happy to keep with tradition.'

Jac picked up another photo from the display. It was of a group of young people sitting on picnic rugs down at the domain. From the clothes and hairstyles it looked like it was from the fifties.

'The summer barbecue,' Iris said. 'It was put on for the young people of Everly. There wasn't a lot to do back in those days—although, there still isn't, really, I guess. We'd have a barbecue in the afternoon, with games, and then later that evening we'd have a dance. I remember it being the highlight of my year.' She pointed out herself, standing in the middle of the group.

Jac turned the photo over and scanned the names. 'Francesca Hastings,' she said, recognising this one.

'Yes. Frankie Hastings' mother. Frankie teaches history at the area school now. Do you know her?'

Jac nodded, Iris had obviously forgotten the conversation they had had two nights ago about Ms Hastings possibly being one of Jac's teachers.

Looking back at the photo, Iris said, 'That man there,'

pointing to the man standing next to her, 'Eli Winiata. The love of my life.'

Jac was surprised at the admission. 'What happened?' This was obviously not the ex-husband who Iris had branded a waste of space at breakfast yesterday.

'He wasn't Gilmore material,' Iris said. And she got that look in her eyes again, that glazed stare that showed she was reminiscing about another time. Jac was beginning to get used to it.

'The baby was beautiful, though,' Iris said, not looking at Jac. 'A girl, my mother told me.'

What's she talking about?

'She wasn't in this world for long. I guess it wasn't meant to be.' Iris sniffed once.

Is she talking about Paige?

Iris turned to look at Jac, her smile bright but her eyes slightly unfocused.

Jac picked up a photo of a teenage Iris and her mother. 'You look like her.' It was more than the eyes and the lips; it was the way they stood, their bone structure.

'Mmm,' Iris said. 'She was a good mother. Until she wasn't.' The last few words were muttered and Jac wondered if she'd heard right.

'You enjoy living here?' Jac asked, trying to get the conversation back on track.

'We've all had our part in making this hotel what it is,' Iris said. 'Do you feel it? How solid it is?' Iris tapped the floorboards with her walking stick. 'My mother used to say that everyone who has stayed under this roof— the hotel guests, some happy and content, others arriving with a sadness that couldn't be undone; the soldiers intent on recovery and recuperation, and the soldiers far gone, without hope; the people who have made it their home;

lives that have spanned despair and misery, hope and am-
bition—each one has attached themselves to this place,
putting down roots, anchoring the building to the land.
There's a comfort in that, don't you think? The history
it holds—the stories, even though they aren't all happy.
This place will always be here, and even when I'm gone
it will remember me, just like it remembers my mother,
and all the others before me.'

Jac wasn't sure what to say after Iris's speech but talk
of everyone who had come through these doors, and not
in the happiest of circumstances, chilled her.

'You know what?' Iris whispered, linking her arm into
Jac's like they were best friends sharing their secrets.

Jac waited.

And then Iris said, 'I truly believe this is the year my
Paige will come home.'

TWENTY-SIX

Jac

Saturday morning

FIVE MINUTES LATER, Iris and Jac were back in the hallway, standing outside the library, and Jac was desperately trying to find a way to get away from her. Both turned as the double doors opened from the back hallway.

'Ah!' Iris withdrew her arm from Jac's and waved a hand in the air, beaming. 'Speak of the devil!'

A woman in her early fifties, grey corkscrew curls bobbing, walked towards them, her yellow-and-orange patterned dress swishing around her knees. Smiling at Iris, she held out her hands to her as she approached.

'Morning!' she said, her deep voice loud and cheerful.

Iris accepted a quick hug from her and a kiss on each cheek, then said, 'You live less than half an hour away and I still don't feel I get to see you enough.' She tapped her arm in jest.

'We had dinner last night!' the woman said. 'But you're right. We need to try a bit harder and not wait for the open day to come around each year before we see each other. I have been pretty busy, though. Young minds to mould and all that.' She looked past Iris to Jac.

Iris turned and said, 'Jac, come and say hello to Frankie.'

Miss Hastings still looked the same, just a bit greyer since Jac had seen her last, which would've been a history lesson she was no doubt mucking around in.

'Jac Morgan?' She tried to hide her surprise by grinning even wider, making her apparent happiness at seeing Jac look less than convincing.

Jac gave her a stiff smile in return. She had no idea how to be around her and was surprised the woman had remembered her.

'Hi, Miss Hastings,' Jac said, feeling like a self-conscious teenager again.

'I think you can probably call me Frankie now. How are you?'

'Good. Fine,' Jac said.

She smiled back at Jac, straight, even teeth, open face, kind eyes. Jac had always liked her. She had never given her too much grief for not handing in homework or finishing assignments. Although maybe she'd thought she was a lost cause—most teachers had.

'Actually,' Jac added, 'could I have a word with you?' She glanced at Iris, who was looking at her watch. No doubt she had plans for Frankie. 'I won't be long, I promise.'

'I'll meet you in here, Frankie,' Iris said, turning to the library door. 'I want to go through my talk with you. Don't be too long!' she sang, her words ending on a higher note than where they'd begun. 'We've got so much to do.'

Frankie raised her thin brows and offered a closed-lip smile that suggested she struggled with Iris too. They stood in the hallway, and Jac wondered where to start.

'She's quite excited,' Jac said.

'Yes, a big day for her.' Frankie Hastings tucked a curl behind her ear and it instantly popped back out again.

'You've helped out before?'

'For as long as I can remember. You know history's always been my thing. This place holds a lot of stories,' Frankie said. 'Besides, I have a soft spot for Iris. She knew my mum.'

'I just got the story about that in the library.' This chance meeting of seeing someone from Charlie's school ignited a faint flicker of hope, and Jac asked, 'Do you know my sister Charlie? She goes to the area school.'

'Sure, I've come across her, but she's not one of my students this year. I had her a couple of years ago, I believe,' she said, squinting, trying to remember.

'Right. Well, she's missing.' Every time she said the words, she couldn't quite believe what was happening.

'Missing?'

'Yeah, she was last seen on Monday afternoon.'

'I didn't know. I've been off work the last couple of days. What's being done about it?' She looked concerned, and Jac felt stupidly grateful.

'Constable Dunlop's looking into it. He's talked to a few people, and someone saw her heading out of town on Monday afternoon. I think he's treating it as a runaway.' This was a generous assessment, Jac thought. Dunlop wasn't actually treating it as anything.

'And you don't think she ran away?'

Jac sighed, rubbing a hand over her hair and then smoothing it down. 'I don't know.' She hated admitting that, as much as she cared for Charlie, she really didn't know her sister well enough to tell if this was something Charlie would do.

'I don't know her well,' Frankie said, 'but I do know she's on some teachers' radars. She wasn't hugely popular at school. I believe she prefers to stick to herself. A bit of a loner. Kids can be cruel,' she said. 'The idea she's run away wouldn't surprise me.'

'How do you mean cruel?' Jac asked.

'I…' she hesitated and Jac knew what was coming. 'I understand she gets bullied by kids about your father, and also, the fire. Even after all these years, it still continues.' Her face was apologetic.

Just what Ms Wells had told her yesterday at school. All of a sudden, Jac felt extreme sadness—the thought of Charlie living in that caravan, going to school where she was teased and had no friends—and was mortified that tears were welling up in her eyes.

'Hey, are you okay?' Frankie reached out and briefly touched Jac's arm.

Jac covered her eyes, embarrassed. 'I'm fine.' She wiped her face. 'I just wish I could find her.'

'Look, I'd better get going. Iris will start hunting me down. But if you need anything from me, or the school, let me know, okay?'

Jac swallowed and smiled. 'Thanks.'

'It's good to see you, Jac. Are you well…apart from all this? You left Everly…it must've been difficult…the fire…' She rubbed at her forehead. 'Sorry, I just meant, I hope you're doing okay.'

'Yeah, I'm fine, thanks,' Jac mumbled, feeling no need to get into this with her. 'Go see Iris. I'm fine. It was good to see you too, Miss—Frankie.' She walked away before Frankie could say anything else.

TWENTY-SEVEN

Lisa

Twenty-one years ago

LISA WAS ENJOYING the hum of the hotel. It was getting busier around here, with the open day next weekend. Volunteers were in and out of the house doing everything from cleaning to organising the old photos for the display. It gave her a glimpse of what the hotel would be like next year, with people coming and going. Iris was speaking about it more and more lately, mostly to Paige, who listened without enthusiasm, but Lisa loved hearing about the plans she had for the concerts, the menu and the little touches to the bedrooms.

In the kitchen, Nancy and three other women were huddled in a group, recipe books and pieces of paper strewn across the centre island. There was talk of shopping lists, and different kinds of cakes and slices, and how many they had to make and when. Nancy looked up at her, slightly harassed, her usually neat bun drooping and frizzy. Before Lisa turned to leave, she put a slice of apple shortcake into her hand.

'Every year, I say this open day will be the death of me,' she joked to Lisa, 'and every year, we do it all over again.'

Lisa smiled in return, hoping Nancy would be included in the hotel's new image.

She climbed back up the stairs, her mouth full of tart apple and sweet crumbling shortcake. She clapped the crumbs off her hands and T-shirt, knowing they would soon be vacuumed up. Iris had the cleaner in every day this week, vacuuming and polishing and dusting. Standing at the start of the east wing's hallway she could hear Paige's violin coming from her bedroom. Paige was practising just as hard as usual, even though she had done her audition for the scholarship already. After Paige had told her about the scholarship, Lisa checked with her every day to see if she'd heard back from the university. But there was still no word and Lisa had stopped asking. She got the impression that Paige had missed out. At the beginning, Paige, having thought she had aced it, discussed it often with nervous anticipation, but she had fallen silent on the topic over the last week.

The first door on the right was Iris's bedroom. Lisa turned the brass handle and let herself in. She had been in Iris's room only a handful of times. It always felt a bit cool, sterile, but it gave Lisa the chance to be close to Iris without actually having to be with her. Everything was in its place, making the bedroom look like a showroom in a furniture shop. Iris's dressing gown was draped over the end of the bed. Lisa caressed the soft fabric and then picked it up and put it on. She wrapped her arms around herself, lowered her head, burying her face in it briefly. She closed her eyes for a moment, enjoying the comfort it brought.

She crossed to Iris's dressing table and sat down on the small stool. Bottles of expensive perfume sat on a silver tray in the middle. Lisa dared not spray any of them. She had done that once. Iris had smelled the perfume on her and sent her to the soldiers' hallway for the afternoon, telling her to think about other people's privacy and how she had disrespected her. A heavy hairbrush sat to one side of the dressing table, pots of cream and make-up on the other. Lisa opened the long skinny drawer at the top of the table and ran her fingers along the line-up of jewellery inside. She pulled a ring from its velvet compartment. It was her favourite. An emerald in the centre surrounded by diamonds. Slipping it on, she held out her hand to admire it. Iris had told them it had been her mother's engagement ring. Lisa had never met any of her grandparents. All of them were dead by the time she was born. But ever since she could remember, the portrait of her maternal grandmother on the staircase had always scared her. Helen didn't come across as the warm and cuddly type. A bit like Iris.

She could hear the vacuum cleaner being hauled up the stairs and knew she should leave. Lisa pulled at the ring, but it was stuck. She tried again, the skin around her knuckle puckering.

'Shit,' she muttered. And she tried again. Nervous sweat was making her hands slippery, but it still didn't help the ring off. Shrugging off Iris's dressing gown and leaving it just as she had found it, she tried removing the ring yet again and pulled with such desperate ferocity she heard her knuckle pop. Panicking, she raced from the room and knocked on Paige's door, turning the handle. Locked.

'Paige,' she hissed, then louder as the approaching vacuum cleaner drowned out the sound, 'Paige!' She jiggled the door handle.

The violin stopped and she waited. She knocked again,

fast, sharp taps. The lock clicked and Paige opened the door. 'What?' she asked.

Lisa thought she looked flushed, jittery.

She held up her left hand. 'Help.'

'Is that Iris's?' Paige's eyes widened in alarm.

Lisa nodded, trying to hold back the tears.

'Lise. Come on.' She took Lisa's hand, pulling her into the room and closed the door behind them.

'Why the hell would you go into her bedroom?'

Lisa shrugged, knowing Paige wouldn't understand. She took in the unmade bed and Lisa's violin and flute cases in the corner by her schoolbag.

'Here, let me take a look.' She grabbed Lisa's hand and started pulling. Her finger was red and had started to ache.

'Where's your violin?' Lisa asked, noticing the slight tremor in Paige's hand. What was up with her?

'There.' Paige pointed to the case.

'You were just playing, though. I heard you.'

'I…well, sometimes I put a recording on to make Iris think I'm practising.'

'Iris isn't even here, though. She said she wouldn't be back till late this afternoon.'

'Well, she was here before, and I wanted her to think I was practising—okay?' Paige replied.

'Yeah, all right,' Lisa said, still confused. 'So, what were you doing if you weren't practising?' Lisa knew Paige wasn't telling her something. She was pacing the room, glancing out the window and then to the bed and then to the wardrobe.

'Nothing, Lisa! Bloody hell! I didn't feel like practising today—that's all!'

A noise from the wardrobe could just be heard after

Paige's meltdown. Lisa turned her head. Coat hangers? 'What was that?' she whispered.

'What? I didn't hear anything.' Paige pushed Lisa towards the door. 'Come on. Maybe Nancy will know what to do. And we won't have to worry about her telling Iris.'

Lisa twisted out of Paige's grasp. Grabbing both handles on the double wardrobe, she pulled them open.

'Don't—'

Lisa stared down at Nathan, his six-foot-plus frame hunched over, the hems of Paige's dresses sitting on his back and hanging either side of him.

Paige sighed. 'I guess you can come out now.'

Nathan looked embarrassed as he stumbled out, standing to his full height. He walked over to Paige and stood close beside her.

'Paige?' Lisa was waiting for an explanation.

'Look…' Paige said but didn't speak again.

'Need some help?' Nathan asked. His voice was soft, in contrast to his hulking frame. He nodded towards Lisa's hand.

She held her hand to her chest, the other hand covering it. Taking in Nathan's enormous hands, she was pretty sure he would rip her finger off, if he tried to help.

He grabbed Paige's lip balm off the top of her drawers, inserted a fingernail and dug out a chunk from the small pot.

'Hey,' Paige said in protest.

'Don't worry. I'll buy you a new one.' Nathan grinned at Paige, and she grinned back.

Lisa felt like they had forgotten she was in the room. She held up her finger in front of Nathan to get his attention. He took her hand and smeared the balm all over her knuckle, pushing bits under the band of the ring. Her head bowed, she lifted her eyes to take in his tanned face, his too-long fringe. His front teeth rested on his bottom lip concentrating. He gently wiggled the ring back and forth, and soon it slid effortlessly over her knuckle. His eyes met hers and he smiled, and that's when she understood Paige's attraction to him.

'Thanks,' she said, lowering her head and backing away, busy wiping the balm from the ring.

'You'd better get that back where it belongs,' Paige said.

'And you'd better get him back where he belongs,' Lisa replied.

'Smart arse,' Paige said, but both she and Nathan were smiling.

'Thanks again,' Lisa said to Nathan.

'No problem.' Nathan looked back to Paige. 'I probably shouldn't have come.'

'I know,' Paige said. 'I just wanted to show you my room'

Lisa stood by the door watching the couple. Nathan's hands around Paige's waist looked impossibly big. He was so much taller than her that Paige had to tip her head up to look at him. Lisa watched them whisper and then kiss. She could tell her sister liked him, but she didn't recognise the look in Nathan's eyes, on his face. Love? Lust? It looked like he wanted to devour her.

TWENTY-EIGHT

Jac

Saturday morning

JAC HAD SPENT the last hour in the library, vacuuming and dusting shelves and shelves of books that looked like they hadn't been touched in years, if ever. She should've been cleaning the lounge right now but instead had escaped out the back door of the hotel when Iris was busy with Frankie in the ballroom. She would get the lounge and music room done this afternoon, once she had talked to Michelle Lafferty about seeing Charlie, and to Brian about Nathan. She wasn't sure what more Michelle could say that Dunlop hadn't told her, but the idea of talking to the last person who had seen Charlie made Jac feel somehow better.

Not wanting to attract Iris's attention, she decided against taking the ute and sneaked out the back door. There was evidence of a tidy-up in progress. Weeds and grass had been pulled from the cracks that marred the concrete, small piles dotted around, waiting to be taken away. She walked down the right side of the back of the building and peering into the windows she saw the empty kidney-shaped swimming pool surrounded by wooden decking. She could make out the tall statues in each corner, women with long hair piled on top of their heads, swathes of material slung over their curvaceous bodies. Turning the corner, she made her way round the side of the hotel, careful not to slip on the path, slick as it was with moss, that looked like it was in perpetual shade, either from the hotel or the trees and bush encroaching on her left. There was a row of windows on the second floor, but they were boarded up. Iris obviously didn't care too much about the aesthetics of this side of the hotel. She found the cracked concrete steps that led down into the bush which gave way to a dirt path that eventually came out at the main street of Everly. This was the way Jac and her friends used to come when they used to sneak onto the grounds of the hotel. Stepping off the last step, flax and hydrangeas crowded the path that was criss-crossed with ivy, which ran along the dirt and up into the overhanging ponga trees. Off the path the bush here was thick and half-way down she passed another path with a lichen-covered sign saying it was an easy one kilometre walk to the caves. A few minutes later, she came out onto the main street.

She headed to the cafe first. It was about half full and Jac waited while Brian served a customer.

'Hello again,' he said, giving her a smile. 'What can I get you? Or are you here about Charlie?'

'I just wanted to ask you about when Charlie worked here.' Jac turned around to make sure no one was listening in.

'Sure. Anything to help,' Brian said.

'Do you know Nathan? I'm not sure of his last name. He works up at the old hotel.'

Brain's smile fell away. 'Oh yeah, I know him.'

'And he knew Charlie?' Jac felt like she was on to something.

'Someone's obviously been talking to you,' Brian said.

'Not as much as I wanted them to. Can you tell me what happened?'

'It wasn't really a big deal,' Brian said, using Tama's words. 'But I look after my employees. Nathan was a semi-regular customer. Would call in and grab a pie for lunch or maybe a coffee. At that stage, I knew his face, not his name. He's not very sociable, kinda quiet.'

Get on with it, Jac thought.

'Anyway, there were a few times when he acted a bit inappropriate towards Charlie. I hadn't noticed, to be honest, but she came to me one day saying she felt uncomfortable around him. He used to stare at her, and when she handed over change, he would purposely brush his hand on hers. He'd wait till Charlie was at the counter serving before he came up. Just little things. I ended up talking to him about it.'

'How did he react?' Jac asked.

'Surprisingly gracious, actually. He's the type of guy who looks like he'd knock ya block off. He apologised, and said he wanted to say sorry to Charlie, but I said it was probably best if he just leave it. I got the impression he didn't really realise he had been doing anything wrong, but once I pointed it out, he saw how inappropriate he'd been. Anyway, he hasn't been in on a weekend since then. He seems to have purposely stayed away when Charlie was working. And that was it, really. No more dramas after that.'

Jac nodded, unsure what to think. Nathan had lied to her last night about not knowing Charlie, but was that because he was embarrassed? Or did he have something more to hide?

She thanked Brian and headed to the pub. It was just

before midday and there were a few cars parked in the gravel carpark that stood in the shade of two enormous oak trees. She had spent many an evening in this parking lot, playing with a couple of other kids on the grassy verge. If she was lucky, her mum would've bought her a packet of chips or a Coke. She had only stepped inside once, that she remembered, for her mother's wake. It was a noisy celebration that day; her dad had been drunk before they had left for the funeral service and, arriving at the pub, he had ensconced himself into one of the booths, holding court with friends, telling stories of when he met Isabel. For anyone listening, it was the greatest love story of all time, and not the sometimes explosive, often nagging relationship that Jac had witnessed.

She rested a hand on the tarnished brass handle, taking a moment. This was her father's domain. If alcohol was Eddie Morgan's god, then this was the place he worshipped. Even though he was gone, Jac felt that whoever she came across in here wouldn't be happy to see her. She pushed open the door. It looked the same as it had seven years ago. Same smell of stale alcohol and fried food. Tables were scattered in front of her, and three booths lined the wall on the left. It wasn't busy yet, which made it easier to spot the three men huddled around one of the tables. Her dad's drinking buddies: Des, Tim and Art. She felt her whole body warm as they clocked her journey across the floor to the bar. There was no one behind it at the moment and she picked up a cardboard coaster, turning it in her hands, determined not to turn around, even though she felt three pairs of eyes on her. She smelled him before she saw him.

'Dave said you were back.'

It was Des. He looked about twenty years older, his

face ruddy, his nose tinged purple. He was in his forties but his hair was thinning and almost completely grey. His watery eyes narrowed as he looked Jac up and down.

'You can't possibly be here for Eddie,' he said, straight into it, as though he had just seen her yesterday. 'You go and destroy your own family and you show your face again.' He shook his head. 'Eddie wouldn't want you here.'

Jac fully turned around, stepping back as Des towered over her. 'I'm not here for Eddie. I'm here for Charlie. She's missing.'

'I heard she up and left. It's what you Morgan girls do, huh? Eddie couldn't rely on neither of you.' Des swayed and put a hand on the bar to steady himself.

Jac shook her head.

'What? Nothing to say? You start that fire, kill your mother, ruin your dad's life, then up and leave, just like that.' His voice got louder and spit landed on Jac's cheek. She wiped it away with the palm of her hand in one violent action.

All the whispering and rumours came back to her, not that they were ever far from her mind. The way Everly, or at least Eddie's mates, surrounded him, protected him, shifted blame.

She watched Art and Tim pushing their chairs back, coming to join in. This was a mistake, she realised. She should have stayed away.

As the men advanced towards her, she closed her eyes and whispered, 'Fuck.'

'Hi there, sorry about the wait! Deep-fryer's on the fritz!' A woman burst through the doors that led to the kitchen, stopping Art and Tim in their tracks.

'Jac Morgan?'

Jac tried to remember her name, skin like leather, dull

eyes matching her dyed dark brown hair, which should've been grey by now. She leaned over the bar and touched Jac's arm. 'Sorry to hear about your dad, love.'

She was so earnest and sympathetic that Jac didn't have the heart to say anything flippant, so she just nodded.

'Three more handles, when you're ready, Meg,' Des said, moving away from Jac and back to his table.

'He wasn't giving you any shit, was he?' Meg asked.

Jac didn't answer, happy that Des had gone back to his mates.

With Nathan fresh in her mind, Jac decided to ask about him. 'Meg, do you know Nathan? Works up at the old hotel.'

'Yeah. I know most people here, love. Especially those who like a drink. He comes in often. Never socialises with anyone. Except maybe Tama. You know him?'

Jac nodded. 'Do you remember when Paige Gilmore went missing?'

'Sure do. Threw the whole place into turmoil for a while back then. You were probably too young to remember.'

Jac had worked out she would've been three when it happened.

'A real mystery, that one. I think about her every now and then,' Meg said. 'Poor girl.'

Out of all the stories Jac had heard about the hotel, real and made up, for some reason Paige Gilmore's disappearance didn't register with her. Maybe Paige's story wasn't as captivating to her as the macabre stories about crazy soldiers and murdered nurses.

'Nathan was questioned,' Meg said. 'Quite extensively, if I remember rightly. There were many who thought he did it. Murdered her.'

Jac's heart rate picked up. 'The police cleared him?'

'Yeah. No proof he did anything.'

'What do you think happened?'

'Oh, hun, the year she went missing I heard a hundred and one theories. Her mother killed her. Her mother locked her up inside the hotel to stop her from leaving. Nathan killed her, buried her in the bush or in one of the caves around here. Or she up and left and got herself in some trouble somewhere far away from here. Who knows?' Meg started pouring the three beers Des had ordered. 'So, you here to sort Eddie's funeral, love?'

'Um…yeah.' It was easier to lie than get into why she didn't want anything to do with her father.

'Such a sad thing to happen.' Meg shook her head. 'And I hear Charlie's done a runner.'

Jac pressed her lips together, sick of explaining, but knowing she needed to. 'I'm not sure if she did. Do you have much to do with her? See her around?'

'Nah, not really. Good kid, though, from what Eddie used to say. We all knew he was useless.' She stopped and gave Jac a wry smile. Jac appreciated the honesty. 'But he used to rave about Charlie in here. How well she was doing at school.'

Jac was surprised to feel jealous at Meg's statement. What had her dad really been like these last seven years? Had he turned over a new leaf? She found it hard to believe. Having a yarn to your mates about how great your kid is didn't make you a good parent. He probably thought Charlie was some reflection on him, when Charlie was like she was despite the way she had been brought up. But she was never really going to know what Eddie had been like since she'd left and there was no use wondering. It didn't matter now. Pulling herself back to the present she asked, 'I was wondering if Michelle was here?'

Just then the door behind the bar swung open and a woman in her mid-twenties walked up to stand next to Meg, cloth in hand.

'Someone to see ya, Michelle,' Meg said, loading the three beers on her tray and moving out behind the bar. 'Good to see ya, love.'

Michelle looked at Jac, pushing her black fringe off her face.

'Hi,' Jac said. 'My name's Jac Morgan.' By the look on Michelle's face, she knew who Jac was. 'My sister, Charlie, went missing at the start of the week. I've been talking with Constable Dunlop, and I heard that you were probably the last person to see her.'

Michelle started wiping the bar, looking left and right and anywhere but Jac. 'Yeah, I was on my way here. It was just before four o'clock. I saw her walking out of town, heading towards the main highway.'

'She wasn't with anyone? You didn't see a car stop and maybe pick her up?' Jac asked.

'Nah. That's all I saw, her walking out of town, along the verge towards the main road. That's it.'

Michelle looked up as the main door swung open. Her face went slack, and she moved further away from Jac, as if not wanting to be seen with her.

Jac turned to see that Nathan had just walked in and was seating himself at a booth. He hadn't seen her. She looked back at Michelle, who was eyeing Nathan.

'It's just that I don't think Charlie would've left Everly without letting me know, so—'

'Look,' Michelle leaned closer and hissed at Jac, her

eyes wide, 'I've told you all I know, now please, leave me alone.' She stepped back again.

She was clearly afraid and not telling her something. 'Please,' Jac said. 'This is really important.'

Michelle shook her head. 'Please leave me alone. Just leave it… I have a kid…'

'What do you mean?'

'I don't want to be involved in this, okay? I haven't got anything more to say to you.' She threw the cloth on the bar and walked away.

TWENTY-NINE

Jac

Saturday afternoon

JAC MADE HER way back to the hotel the same way she had come down. She stepped into the gloom of the bush from the main street. She followed the dirt path and stopped before the steps that led up to the hotel. To the right, a few metres in, was a bench seat, and she took in the crude drawings that had been engraved into it, read which girl was 'up for it', who was in love with who, and a variety of swear words from the mild to obscene. The path followed on from this point to the caves. In no rush to get back to the hotel or the people in it, she started walking along it, wondering if Charlie had ever walked here. Jac pushed flax and ferns to the side, her gaze not on the path but on the thick bush, dense with natives, to her left and right. What was she expecting to find? Charlie's body, pale and lifeless, hidden among the undergrowth? Ten minutes later she came out into the open. In front of her was a carpark, half filled with cars and buses. The small ticket booth for the glow worm cave tours was open and there was a line of people waiting to pay. She turned to make her way back to the steps.

Back at the bench seat, Jac sat down, breathing hard. She didn't really understand what had happened with Michelle back at the pub and wondered if she should talk to Dunlop about Nathan. Or was she jumping to conclusions? She didn't know anything about Michelle Lafferty.

'Where are you, Charlie?' she said out loud, then felt like an idiot.

'Hey,' a voice came from the undergrowth.

Jac jumped up. 'Jesus Christ!'

'Sorry, didn't want to frighten ya.'

The boy, in his mid-teens, walked towards her and stubbed out his cigarette on the bench. He was dressed in a pair of old rugby shorts and a singlet, his feet bare. He was the same height as Jac.

'You know Charlie?' he asked. 'I heard you say her name.'

'Yeah,' Jac said. 'She's my sister. What's your name?' she asked, sitting back down.

'Elijah,' he said, joining her on the bench. 'You looking for her?'

'Yeah,' Jac said. 'But I'm not sure if she ran away or not.'

'And Eddie's dead, huh.' Elijah shook his head.

'Yeah,' Jac said again.

'Bit suss, you reckon? Charlie going missing and then your dad drowning in the creek?'

'I don't know.' Jac was struggling to communicate with him. He seemed like a cross between a kid and a fifty-year-old man shooting the breeze. 'Eddie was a drunk. I'm not surprised he ended up drowning in a creek.'

'Ooh.' Elijah covered his mouth, smothering a laugh, his eyes wide. 'You harsh, man. You his daughter.'

'In name only,' Jac mumbled. 'Where do you live?'

'Campground. In one of the vans.'

'So, you and Charlie are neighbours?'

He nodded. 'Not anymore, though, eh? Saw Dickhead Dave clearing the van out yesterday afternoon.'

Jac smiled. She was warming to Elijah. 'Did you see Charlie on Monday? Someone told Constable Dunlop they saw her heading out of town on Monday afternoon, just before four o'clock.'

'Nah, she wasn't heading out of town then.'

'She wasn't?' Jac replied, knowing she shouldn't get her hopes up. Elijah could be talking complete shit.

'Nah, I saw her. We get home from school just after four, on the same bus. I saw her walk into her caravan and then come back out about five minutes later. Had her case with her—whatever musical instrument she plays.'

'The flute,' Jac said.

'Yeah, whatever. And then I saw her walk over the road and up into the bush here.'

'Why would she come up here?'

'She does that lots, plays the flute here, does home-work, right here on this seat.'

'And how do you know that?'

He looked away from Jac, embarrassed. 'Sometimes I spied on her. Not all the time…it wasn't like that. It was just something to do. Anyway,' he said, hurriedly chang-ing the subject, 'on Monday, she didn't stop here, she kept walking up the path.'

'To the hotel?' Jac asked, making sure she had heard him right.

He shrugged and then said, 'Maybe.'

'Why didn't you tell the cops?'

Elijah shrugged again. 'None of my business. Mum says keep out of stuff that has nothing to do with me, es-pecially when the police are asking questions.'

'You need to talk to Dunlop. Tell him you saw Charlie that afternoon.' This made a huge difference to everything. She knew Michelle had been lying.

'Sorry, but that ain't gonna happen.' Elijah shook his head.

'Why not?'

'I'm probably not Dunlop's favourite person. Been in trouble a few times.'

'It doesn't mean you can't say what you saw.'

'He's not gonna believe me. I don't think you get how much he hates me.'

Jac thought he looked proud of the fact. 'What did you do?'

Elijah stopped, as if deciding whether to say anything. 'Just little stuff, being a nuisance, Mum calls it. Ditching school, got caught with a bit of weed last year, parties and drinking, vandalism, that kinda stuff. Best if I stay away from him. I'll only make things worse, I reckon.'

'Do you know Nathan? He's the gardener up there at the old hotel.'

'Kinda. They're all weird up there.'

'What do you mean?'

'I dunno. That old lady's crazy.'

'What do you mean?' Jac asked again, getting frustrated.

'I dunno,' he muttered again.

She grabbed his arm. 'Do you think Charlie could've gone up there, to the hotel that afternoon? Do you think Iris or Nathan could've done something to her?'

Elijah pulled his arm from her grasp, his cheeky grin disappearing. Jac could see he was scared of her.

'I dunno. I better go.' He backed away from her. 'Hope ya find ya sister.' And then he was off, jogging back down the path.

'Shit,' she said. She had totally fucked that up.

If Elijah was right, Charlie never left town. But why had Michelle told Dunlop she had seen Charlie leaving? Was it a mistake or had she deliberately lied to him?

Could Charlie have gone to the hotel that afternoon? It was so close. From this bench to the back door of the hotel would've been no more than three hundred metres, Jac thought. Could something have happened to her up there? She could have had an accident. There were tomo all around the farmland here, sinkholes where water had dissolved the underlying rock. Jac looked around her. This stretch of bush was nowhere near big enough to get lost in.

And the alternative, her subconscious prodded. *Nathan? Iris?*

THIRTY

Jac

Saturday afternoon

THE STAFF ACCOMMODATION at the back of the hotel was a single-storey building and looked more rundown than the hotel, white paint peeling from the weatherboards and large patches of grey lichen covering the red corrugated iron roof. Jac knew Nathan was at the pub. Maybe she could have a quick look around inside.

'Jac!' Iris shouted from the back door of the hotel. 'I've been looking everywhere for you.'

Jac stopped and turned towards Iris.

'How have you got on?' the old woman asked. It sounded like she hadn't realised Jac had been gone for the last hour.

'Good,' Jac said, covering her tracks 'I've just got the lounge and music room to go. I'm heading to the lounge now.' She looked back at Nathan's accommodation. Was it locked? Would she be able to get in for a look around before he got back?

'Do you know where Nathan is?' she asked Iris, as they headed back inside.

'He's running a few errands for me. He should be back around two. Why?'

'No reason,' Jac said.

'Come on then,' Iris said. 'There's still so much to do.'

They stopped inside the back entrance hallway. 'Iris, how well do you know Nathan?'

'Very well. He's worked for me for over twenty years.'

'And he was here when Paige disappeared?' Jac asked, trying to confirm what Meg had already told her.

Iris stopped and stared at Jac. 'How do you know about Paige?'

'I… Lisa told me about her, and you mentioned her in the library this morning.'

'Yes, yes of course.'

'So, Nathan was here when Paige disappeared?'

'Yes, he was. He's been very good to me. So helpful with…everything. I guess I've always had a soft spot for him. He'd do anything for me. I like that kind of loyalty. It means a lot.'

Jac nodded.

'Excuse me, I'll let you get on. I need to talk to Tama about the food for tomorrow.'

Iris went into the kitchen and Jac headed through the double doors and down the main hallway to the lounge. Frankie came in a minute later holding two vases crammed with flowers. 'Take one of these, would you, Jac—they weigh a tonne.' Jac took one of the vases from Frankie and put it down on one of the many side tables. There were already four vases in here and there was an overwhelming scent from the lilies, freesias and roses. She rubbed her nose in reaction to the assault.

'I'm glad you turned up. Iris was on the warpath,' Frankie said.

'What do you mean?'

'She's been looking for you. Starting to stress about

the rooms not being done. Both Lisa and I reminded her you had more pressing things to attend to.'

'Is everything almost ready?' Jac asked. 'Am I the only slacker?'

Frankie smiled. 'It's really the same set-up each year. Getting out the same photos, regurgitating the same stories. I'm impressed Iris does it every year, actually. It's a lot of work for someone her age, and for someone as private as she is. It's not like she's getting anything out of it. It does seem to get more and more popular each year, though. People from all around the district come and make a day of it. The weather's usually great. I guess it kind of kicks off the start of summer.'

'Lisa gave me the impression she does it all for Paige… with the expectation she'll come back,' Jac suggested, wondering how much Frankie knew and what she thought.

Frankie nodded. 'She's said as much to me over the last couple of years. During this time, she seems to drift away from us a bit and goes back to the weekend Paige disappeared. She almost tries to relive that day moment by moment, as if she can undo what happened. Sad, really.'

'Did you know Paige? Were you here when it happened?'

'Yes, unfortunately. It was my first year helping with the open day. Actually, it was Paige who convinced me to help out—she was one of my students—and she thought my knowledge of the area would be useful, and Iris seemed happy I offered. We did a bit more research into the hotel, when it briefly became a rehabilitation facility for soldiers returning from the war.'

'I didn't know much about that, until I saw the photos in the library today,' Jac said.

'This place has a lot of ghosts,' Frankie said, looking

at a photo of Paige on the mantel and then turning back to Jac.

'Do you have a theory about what happened to Paige?' Jac asked.

'I don't know... She was a very talented girl. She had a few good friends but I think the other kids at school were a bit wary of her.'

'How do you mean?' Jac asked.

'She wasn't overly friendly. She obviously came from a very wealthy family. Most girls either worshipped her and wanted to be friends with her, or hated her, unable to get over their envy, and the boys—well you can guess what the boys wanted. She and Lisa were very close, though. And I know Paige's disappearance really affected her. I taught Lisa that final year of high school. She was a polite, sweet kid but when Paige disappeared, she kind of did too. She worked hard but didn't offer up much else. She lost the few friends she had.' Frankie glanced at the door. Lowering her voice, she added, 'I think she just wanted to get through that year and get away from Iris.'

'So, you think Paige just ran away? Or...'

'Possibly. I know Paige had plans. She wanted to go to uni, study music. But I'm not sure how keen Iris was on that.'

'I heard the police looked at Nathan as a possible suspect in her disappearance. Could he have had something to do with it, do you think?' Jac was talking about Paige but was thinking of Charlie.

'Look, I don't know. I always thought he was a bit...' Frankie paused, fiddling with the flowers. 'I didn't know him back then, still don't, really. But there were rumours he and Paige were involved.'

'What?'

'Nathan and Paige. Apparently, they were an item.'

In the kitchen last night, Nathan had said he didn't know Paige that well, and Meg hadn't mentioned anything, either. Maybe she had forgotten. Jac was starting to look at Charlie and Paige as one. Nathan seemed to be the common denominator in this. She thought back to Michelle and her reaction when she saw Nathan this morning. Had he made her say something to Dunlop to make everyone think Charlie had left, when he had actually taken her?

'Sorry, Frankie, I just need to pop out for a sec.' Jac ran along the hallway and outside. There was no one around as she walked over to the staff quarters. The front door was locked, so she made her way around the back of the building, along a cracked concrete path, shaded by trees. The back door was unlocked. She stepped into the dim, uncarpeted hallway. She tried the door on the left and it opened. If Nathan had something to hide, wouldn't he lock his door? Crouching low, she made her way throughout the long, skinny room. There were abandoned newspapers, magazines and clothes spread across the floor. The bed was unmade and there were a few dirty dishes in the sink. In the fridge was milk and a six-pack of beer. The wardrobe was pretty much empty, apart from a pair of work boots and a few worn shirts hanging up. On the top shelf were folded jeans and sweatshirts. The bathroom at the back was small and smelled of damp. There were two towels lying on the floor and the shower had dark lines of mould around the seals. There was nothing here. For someone who had lived in the same place for over twenty years, Nathan had remarkably few possessions. Jac thought of her room back in Sydney, where she had lived for the past two years. She had lived in Auckland for eighteen months before leaving for Australia where she had lived a nomadic life, travelling around the country, picking up work in hotels or bars until she had decided to settle in Sydney. Everything she owned fitted into a backpack.

She stood listening. There was a muffled thump, scratching. She walked slowly to the door, her ears straining. Was he back? She came out into the hallway, listening again. The sound was coming from the room opposite. She turned the handle. It was stiff with age; she leaned into it, ramming her shoulder against the door. It screeched open and she peered into the mess. The room was packed full of old dining room chairs and couches, plus outdoor furniture and canvas umbrellas marred with mould, leaning up against the window, blocking the light. Precarious towers of boxes lined one wall. Jac squinted.

'Charlie?' she whispered, her heart belting in her chest.

There was the noise again. She crept into the room, moving around boxes. Three bookcases stood in the centre of the space and she made her way around them, and the further she got in the darker it got. She heard the rustling again and looked up. Two golden eyes peered down at her and she stumbled backwards, tripping and landing awkwardly, her hip scraping against an old bedside table.

'Shit,' she said.

The possum stood staring at her as she ran from the room.

She made her way out of the staff quarters and back to the hotel, heart pumping. Was she getting desperate, forcing pieces of a puzzle together that didn't belong? She felt like she'd jumped to conclusions after her conversations with Michelle and then Elijah. Was she making something out of nothing? But Nathan had lied to her—twice.

He knew who Charlie was when he said he didn't. He had been in a relationship with Paige when he said he barely knew her. Jac looked up at the hotel. It was so big. Was Charlie here? Did Nathan have her? Jac couldn't help but think it was the perfect place to hide someone.

THIRTY-ONE

Lisa

Twenty-one years ago

LISA ADJUSTED HER position against the apple tree in the orchard. She had her back to the hotel and was surrounded by trees and lush long grass. She could see the creek snaking through the back of the property and, beyond that, thick bush that led to neighbouring farms. It was blissfully quiet out here, with an occasional bird calling from a tree. So much better than the hotel that was constantly shifting and moving. She thought a building of that age should've settled, established itself more firmly on its foundations. But it often sounded unsettled, unhappy with its location. A bit like Paige, she thought. Paige and Iris were in the music room, rehearsing for the open day in five days. Lisa wasn't needed and knew it was best to keep out of the way. Iris was getting more and more worked up about it, expecting perfection from everyone involved.

She heard the rustle of grass and turned to see Nathan walking towards her, a pruning saw in his hand. She scrambled to her feet and he stopped in his tracks.

'Sorry, didn't see you there,' he said.

She smiled at him, feeling her cheeks burn. Ever since

he had helped her get Iris's ring off her finger a few days ago, she had started looking at him differently. She was coming to understand Paige's attraction more and more. Not that he would ever look at her like he looked at Paige.

'How's the finger?' he asked.

She held it up, showing off a small red mark.

'Sorry, didn't mean to hurt you.' His eyes flitted from her finger to somewhere over her shoulder, as if he couldn't make eye contact with her.

Lisa realised she still hadn't spoken and was staring at him, hand in the air. 'It's fine. Really. Thanks for your help.'

'No worries.' He ran a hand across the stubble on his face, looking at the ground.

She couldn't think of anything else to say for a moment, and then, as he was about to move on, she blurted, 'Did you know that Paige has applied for a scholarship? She wants to go to uni next year.'

From the look on Nathan's face, brows raised, she could tell it was news to him.

Shit. She probably shouldn't have said anything. How was she supposed to know Paige hadn't said anything to him?

'You didn't know?' Lisa asked.

He shook his head. He ran a hand through his hair, the long fringe flopping back into place.

'She always told me she would stay here,' Lisa said. 'That we'd run this place together. But now she's desperate to go to uni and win this scholarship.'

'She never said anything to me.'

'Well, she hasn't got the scholarship yet,' Lisa said.

'Do you think she'll get it?'

Lisa shrugged. 'I hope not.'

'Me too,' he said, his smile sad.

'So, are you guys girlfriend and boyfriend?'

He hesitated. Lisa thought he looked embarrassed.

'I guess so,' he said. 'Paige doesn't really like that label. Not sure why. Says she doesn't want it to be anything serious.' He paused. 'Now I guess I know why.'

'You won't say I said anything, will you? She'd kill me. She hasn't told anyone about applying for the scholarship, not even Iris.'

He nodded, and Lisa wondered how much of their lives she had shared with Nathan. Did he know about the soldiers' hallway? She found herself flushing with embarrassment at the thought of him knowing how Iris treated her.

'She's talked about wanting to get out of here before,' Nathan said. 'Says she feels suffocated. I just thought she was all talk. Like most people her age. Wanting to get away from home as soon as possible. I didn't realise she had such a firm plan—that didn't involve me.'

They stood in silence for a few more seconds. Lisa liked the idea that he appeared to be as devastated as she was.

'Right, I'd better get on,' Nathan said, raising the pruning saw in his hand.

'Maybe if she mentions it—wanting to leave—you could try and talk her round to staying?' Lisa asked, hopeful that there was someone else who could convince Paige to stay.

'Of course,' he said. 'I'm with you. I don't want her going anywhere.'

THIRTY-TWO

Jac

Saturday afternoon

IT WAS NEARING four o'clock by the time Jac got to the music room. She felt more frustrated and confused than ever. She had no idea what was going on and the longer she stayed in this hotel, the more certain she was that someone here had something to do with Charlie's disappearance. Nathan. Or Iris. But then, five minutes later, she would tell herself she was clutching at straws. And around and around she went, as she arranged the chairs in the music room into neat rows, facing the small stage. The grand piano, at the back of the room, was her last task. She tugged on the off-white cover and it fell to the ground. The dark wood was already gleaming and so she quickly ran a soft cloth over it. Bending down to retrieve the cover, her hand brushed a piece of paper. She picked it up. Sheet music. There was handwriting at the top, in pencil, and she read the few words written in neat printing.

Charlie, this one's a bit more challenging, but have a go—Ms Wallace

What the hell is this? Jac had heard of Ms Wallace. She was Charlie's music tutor at school. What was the sheet music doing here? Jac looked around the room, as if trying to find something else, forgetting that she had just cleaned the place. There was nothing else. But this meant Charlie had been at the hotel. Why had nobody said anything? *Because they didn't want you to know.*

Jac started shaking, from anger or fear, she wasn't sure. She marched out of the music room looking for Iris or Lisa, or even Frankie. She found Iris in the lounge standing by the table full of framed photos in which she and Paige were the stars.

'Charlie was here,' Jac said, waving the piece of paper in front of Iris.

'What?' Iris placed a hand on the stitches on her forehead, all of a sudden looking like she was a hundred. Her face was pale and drawn. 'Who's Charlie?'

'My sister! She's missing. I showed you a photo a couple of days ago. You said you didn't know her. Lisa said she had never seen her. Same with Nathan—and that was all lies. But this is hers! She's been here. There's no other reason for it!' Jac was yelling now and didn't care that Iris was shrinking back from her.

'What's going on?' Lisa came into the lounge, placing a protective arm around Iris's shoulder and frowning at Jac.

Jac pushed the piece of paper into Lisa's hand. 'Charlie was here.' She took a deep breath, calming herself, and lowered her voice. 'This is hers. I was just asking Iris about it.' She turned to Iris again. 'Did you see Charlie?'

'I did,' Iris said. Her face brightened. 'She was in the music room. She was playing the flute and—' She looked to Jac and then to Lisa, confused.

'Mum, I'm not sure if you're remembering right,' Lisa

said. Turning to Jac, she handed her back the sheet music and added in a whisper, 'Charlie *does* look a bit like Paige. Maybe she's getting confused?'

'I am remembering right!' Iris said, pouting like a petulant child.

'When was this?' Jac asked, ignoring Lisa, wanting to grab on to whatever Iris could give her.

Iris looked up, as if the answer was hiding in the chandelier.

'This week?' Jac asked, prompting. 'A few days ago? She was last seen on Monday. I met someone today who told me they saw Charlie coming up here, through the path from the main street. You told me you didn't know who Charlie was when I asked you.' Jac rattled off each statement, getting herself more and more worked up, even though she could see it wasn't helping Iris.

'Maybe...a week ago?'

'And what was she doing here?' Jac asked.

'She was visiting me... I guess. She told me how beautiful the hotel was looking. She played me my favourite song on her flute—*Dance of the Blessed Spirits*. It was a lovely time. And then she had to go.'

Jac was alarmed to see tears in Iris's eyes.

'Where did she go?' Jac asked. 'Did she say where she was going? Back to the campground? That's where she lived. Or was she going somewhere else?' She felt like shaking the old woman.

'My beautiful Paige,' Iris said, touching her cheek and inspecting her hand as if surprised to find tears.

'Mum,' Lisa said, a hand on Iris's elbow. 'Why don't you have a lie down. I've got everything under control here.' Lisa put her arm around her mother's shoulder. The action seemed to jolt Iris back from wherever she had been.

'Don't touch me!' she yelled at Lisa, who took a step back. 'Why are you here? I don't need you here!'

Lisa glanced at Jac, a mixture of embarrassment and hurt on her face, which made Jac look away.

'Sorry… She's not well.'

'Not well! How dare you! She should be here—not you! Not you! Not you!'

Iris grabbed a photo frame and swung it at Lisa's head. The corner caught Lisa's cheek, making Jac wince and Lisa gasp. Iris swung again but Lisa stepped out of the way. Then Iris lost her footing and stumbled but righted herself by holding on to the table. Jac, inching back from the two women, watched them, waiting with trepidation for whatever was going to happen next.

Iris calmed down just as quickly as she had exploded. Ignoring Jac, she glared at Lisa and walked out of the room, muttering below her breath.

Lisa, covering up the thin, bloody scratch on her cheek and blinking back tears, followed her mother out of the room.

THIRTY-THREE

Charlie

Saturday afternoon

CHARLIE TRIED TO open her eyes. She was groggy, her limbs
heavy, as usual. Her fingers had found the scar on her
elbow, the one she'd got climbing the corrugated iron fence
at their old house. The scar was long and jagged and bumpy
because, when it had happened, her parents had been at
the pub and, when they got home, they'd been too drunk to
take her to see the doctor. Jac had done the best she could,
splashing it with antiseptic, dabbing at the gaping wound
with a tea towel, using four plasters to cover it. It had eventually scabbed over, after constantly reopening. Charlie felt
that familiar fog stealing her memories, images of Jac appearing and disappearing like smoke. She was facing the
wall of her prison and now realised something had woken
her up. But trying to open her eyes seemed fruitless, when
they insisted on sealing shut tight like a ten-year-old scar.

She heard it again, the rattle of the cage, and prised her
eyes open. She turned around on the stretcher, eyes wide
in the half-light of the lanterns, and then squinted. She
could see someone, a shadow on the other side of the wire
cage. They stepped further back, into the darkness, disappearing altogether.

'Help me,' she said, her voice barely a whisper. Clearing her throat, she tried again. 'Who's there? Please, help me. What am I doing here?' She sat up, trying to ignore the pounding in her head that made it sound like her voice was coming from far away. There was no answer. They weren't here to help.

She stood, closing her eyes for a second as the cage swam in front of her. The harder she tried to focus on finding the figure, the more her head ached. Even though she couldn't see them, she could feel them. There was a minute change in the air. The feeling of someone sharing the space with her.

Charlie adjusted the thick headband on her head, and pressed her lips together, hands fluttering towards the studs in her ears, which still throbbed. For a moment she hoped she looked how the person expected her to, and then admonished herself—she had done what they had asked but it didn't mean she liked it. She dropped her arms to her side.

In front of her, right inside the door to the cage, there was a music stand. The sight of the sheet music, something so boringly familiar, made her want to cry, made her yearn for the stupid, tiny caravan, and even for school. She ran her eyes over the piece—*Dance of the Blessed Spirits*. She was vaguely aware of it. A classical piece, different from the normal folk music she played.

'Play,' the person whispered.

The voice was husky, scratchy; Charlie's ears were playing tricks on her after hearing nothing but her own ragged voice and breathing for days.

She took up the flute. It was heavier than her school-issue nickel flute. Was it Paige's? A shiver ran up her spine. She brought the instrument to her mouth and scanned the sheet music one more time, taking in the tempo and dynamics, the crescendos and long slurs. The flute, even though heavy, felt comfortable in her hands. For the first time in two days, she felt like she was in control. She began, slowly, hesitantly. It was by no means the best she had ever played; she knew the piece was too advanced for her. When she was finished, there was silence.

'Please,' Charlie said. 'Please, I'll do anything. Just get me out of here.' She felt the hysteria rising, a rush of blood to her head, her breathing coming too quick. Once she had calmed herself, telling herself to listen for more commands, she realised the person was gone.

They had left behind food and Charlie stuffed two spoonfuls of gluggy mac and cheese into her mouth. She hadn't eaten since Thursday night. It stuck in her throat, making her gag. She needed water. And then, just before she picked up the water bottle that was sitting in front of the lantern, she saw it. She screwed her eyes shut, and opened them again, wondering if the dim light was playing tricks on her eyes. She examined the seal of the water bottle. It was full but the seal had been broken, the plastic ring separated from the lid. She tipped the bottle over and then righted it, placing it down in front of the lantern again. She watched a very fine powder start to fall, like snowflakes in a snow globe, to the bottom of the bottle. She had been so preoccupied with the bump on the back of her head she hadn't thought for a second that she was being drugged. All those times they had entered the cage, undressing her, dressing her, piercing her ears, leaving her food and water. This was how they'd been able to do it. She picked up the water bottle and threw it across the room, where it rebounded off the door to the cage. Walking over to it, she wondered how much she could drink without it having an effect. But she couldn't drink any. She needed her wits about her.

Kneeling down she picked up the water bottle. She had to be seen to be drinking, and she didn't want them to know she had found out what they had been doing. Undoing the cap of the bottle, she pulled the edge of the carpet back, and emptied the water onto the compacted dirt. She hesitated, a whisper of a plan forming. Sweeping the damp dirt with her fingers, she then poked, making a small indent. She started scraping the dirt, enjoying the feeling of it packed under her nails. Standing up she took the spoon from the food tray, never having been given a knife or a fork, or anything to fight back with. Then she started digging. It wouldn't take much, she thought, maybe a foot to clear a hole under the cage so she could crawl out.

And what then? I'm obviously locked in some kind of room.

She could hide further down, past the door, and when they walked towards the cage, she could run through the door.

Charlie smiled for the first time in days. She would keep going. She wasn't sure if they'd come back today, but if she heard them come back—and she would now, since she wasn't drugged, a door unlocking, footsteps—she'd stop and cover up any progress she'd made with the carpet. She had a plan. She was going to get out.

THIRTY-FOUR

Jac

Saturday evening

JAC DEBATED ABOUT going down for dinner that evening.
She was pretty sure she wouldn't be welcome, and realised,
maybe too late, that if she was going to find out what happened with Charlie, and if it had anything to do with Iris
or Nathan, she needed to tread more lightly.

At the bottom of the stairs, she looked along the main
hallway and could see the back of Lisa and someone else
standing by the front door. She walked down, stopping
halfway at the library door, listening in to the conversation.

'Thank you for coming on a Saturday, Doctor Lee,'
Lisa said. 'She was determined to have the stitches out
before the open day tomorrow.'

'The cut's healing well,' Doctor Lee replied. 'There's no
problem there. I'm a little bit worried about the concussion
and her recovery. She appears to be confused. The way she
was talking just now—about Paige.'

'I know. She often acts like this around this time. It's
the anniversary of my sister's disappearance this weekend. It's always hard for her.'

Silence, and then Doctor Lee said, 'Let's make an ap-

pointment for next week. It might just be the side effects
of the concussion, which can be ongoing, but we can also
run a few tests for Alzheimer's.'

'You really think it could be that?' Lisa asked.

Jac could hear the worry in her voice.

'It could be, but let's just wait and see. You're doing a
wonderful job caring for your mum. I know it must be hard.'

Understatement of the century, Jac thought.

'It's fine. She's a bit challenging sometimes…'

'I can imagine. When you get a chance, ring the sur-
gery and we'll take a look at how we'll progress from
there. Good luck for the open day. I hope Iris enjoys herself. I could see she was a bit stressed, but maybe once the
weekend's over it'll help how she feels overall.'

Jac made her way back towards the stairs, deciding
against joining them for dinner and, back in her room,
she sat on her bed staring at the piece of sheet music she
had found in the music room. It was her one, tenuous con-
nection to Charlie. Lying back on the bed, her stomach
grumbled. She had missed lunch and had been too busy
cleaning this afternoon to get anything to eat. She wondered what the others were talking about around the dinner table downstairs. Were they talking about her? About
Charlie? Were Iris and Lisa regretting inviting her into
their home? Wondering when she was going to leave?
Or maybe they didn't care at all and were chatting about
tomorrow, glad she wasn't there, accusing and questioning them.

There was a tap on the door and she got up to answer it.

It was Tama, and he stood there with a covered tray
in his hands.

'Lisa said you weren't feeling well, and that you might
like your dinner in your room,' he said.

'Oh right…thanks,' Jac replied, opening the door wide.

Tama set the tray down on the bed and turned to her. 'Everything okay?'

Jac stood by the door, staring at the tray. She had only talked to Tama once. Knew nothing about him, apart from him standing up for Nathan after he had lied to her about not knowing Charlie.

'Yeah,' Jac answered. 'Actually—no. I'm worried about my sister, worried that she's still missing and I have a feeling…' She didn't know how much she should say. 'I don't know.' She was suddenly exhausted. 'I get the feeling the hotel has something to do with her disappearance.'

Tama raised his eyebrows. 'The hotel or the people in it?'

'What do you mean by that?' Jac answered his question with one of her own.

'I heard you guys before—in the lounge,' Tama said sympathetically. 'You asking if Ms Gilmore had seen your sister here.'

Jac felt as if Tama was on her side, or at least not completely loyal to the Gilmores. 'Do you know anything about Iris, about when her daughter Paige disappeared?'

He shook his head. 'Way before my time, sorry.'

'You haven't heard any rumours? About maybe Iris harming Paige?'

'Nah…nothing like that. Iris speaks of Paige a lot. Misses her still.'

Jac nodded.

'Sorry I can't be of more help. Enjoy your dinner. Just leave the tray outside your door and I'll grab it later.'

As hungry as Jac was, she only picked at the lasagne and salad. She thought about how Iris had reacted to seeing the sheet music this afternoon. Was she hiding something, or was she really just a forgetful old lady? Either way, Jac was no closer to discovering why Charlie's sheet music had been in Iris's music room.

She knew Iris was down at dinner. This was her chance to look around. She picked up her tray and left it outside her door, then made her way through the smoke doors and into the east wing hallway. She crossed to Iris's room, wincing as the floorboards beneath the plush carpet creaked. She stopped, looking down the staircase, but all she could hear was the faint occasional scrape of cutlery on plates in the dining room below. The hotel seemed to be constantly moving, complaining, making life difficult for whoever was in it. Nothing could be done quietly; on opening a door or window, it was broadcast throughout the hotel, and creaking floorboards constantly announced someone's arrival.

Iris's bedroom door was ajar and, pushing it open, Jac walked in.

There were no similarities between the room Jac was staying in now and Iris's. It was bigger, brighter, lighter. The king-sized bed was covered with a heavy white brocade bedspread shot through with silver. The walls were painted a fresh white, and plush carpet was soft beneath her bare feet. But, breathing in, Jac could still smell the underlying mustiness that pervaded the whole hotel; it seemed no amount of new furniture or paint or the open French doors could rid even the renovated rooms of it. She poked her head into the ensuite. In here, there were a few signs of wear: the clawfoot bathtub, which spanned the back of the wall, had a crack in its enamel, and the tiles, an intricate geometric pattern in dark grey, green and white, had dulled with time, some chipped at the corners. There were sleek glass bottles of bubble bath and body wash and a round container filled with pale pink bath salts. Next to two neatly folded towels on the vanity were pill canisters, various plasters and bandages, a small bowl and cotton pads. On a silver hook behind the door hung a thick white robe. The small room smelled of Iris's floral perfume, with an underlying hint of antiseptic.

Jac opened the large double wardrobe, which was crammed full of clothes, and ran a hand along the expensive items: cashmere cardigans, silk shirts, woollen suits. The shelf above held a few old shoeboxes. As she looked around the room, she saw that most surfaces— drawers, bedside tables and the dressing table—held at least a couple of photos. And they were all of Paige, or Iris and Paige together. She sat down at the white dressing table opposite the ensuite door, next to the French doors that led out onto a balcony. She opened the long, slim drawer of the dressing table. There was a jaw-dropping display of jewellery in front of her. Earrings and rings set with diamonds or sapphires or rubies sat in lined, lidless boxes, along with several thick gold bracelets. She was sure there was no costume jewellery here. She brushed a finger along a gold necklace that was studded at intervals with diamonds. Peering into the back left corner she saw a photograph. She grabbed at it, her short nails struggling for purchase. It had been ripped into six pieces but then had been Sellotaped back together again, some time ago, she thought, as tiny fragments of stiff tape drifted to the carpet.

It looked like it had been taken on the same day as the photo Jac had seen downstairs in the library this morning, of the annual picnic Iris had told her about. This one was of Iris and Eli Winiata—'the love of my life', she had called him. In the photo, Iris wore a pale green full skirt and a white short-sleeved shirt. She only looked fifteen or sixteen. Jac slipped the photo back where she had found it. At the back in the opposite corner she pulled out two keys. One was small, only about two centimetres in length; the other was a normal-sized key with a circular gold keyring attached to it, embossed with the number 12A—it looked like an old hotel key. Jac made sure everything was put back in its rightful place and closed the drawer. She sat on Iris's bed. This bedroom wasn't going to give up any secrets, at least not any that were going to help her find Charlie.

She got up, smoothed the bedspread and cast her eye around the room, making sure everything was as she had found it. As she was leaving, pulling the door back into the right position, she saw a glint of gold, something wedged tight into the carpet by the frame of the door. A ring. Bending down, she picked it up. The large stone and most of the gold band had been embedded in the plush carpet like it had been dropped and trodden into the pile. She held it up to the light. The ring was heavy in her hand. Its emerald, set in a circle of diamonds, was the size of a pea. It would've been worth tens of thousands of dollars. Imagine having so much money, Jac thought, that a ring this size could be left lying on the floor, one vacuum cleaner suck from disappearing. She eyed the ring in her palm again and slipped it into her jeans pocket.

Turning right out of Iris's room, she walked past two other doors to the end of the hallway. There was another hallway, if it could be called that, small and unlit. It only stretched a few metres off to the right and at the end there was a door, almost invisible in the darkness. Jac turned to the wall in front of her. The navy and floral wallpaper here was beautiful, if a bit worn. She ran her hand over the embossed print, stopping when she felt her hand catch on something. She leaned down. At waist height, she could see a lock, the tarnished brass camouflaged by the busy wallpaper pattern. She ran her hand over the lock and then, looking up and along, using her hands, she found it—the outline of a door. It had obviously been hidden on purpose. But why?

'They don't like you snooping.'

Jac jumped and turned, her hand to her heart. 'Jesus Christ, you scared me!'

'Sorry,' Tama said, her dinner tray in his hands. 'Thought I'd better warn you. The cleaner before Tui got fired because she tried to get in.'

'What's behind there?' Jac asked, turning back to the wall.

'Nothing, I don't think. Well, no, that's not right. There's a whole hallway back there, with rooms, but I don't think it's been used in years. They call it the soldiers' hallway. Used to keep the patients back there who were a bit more out of it than the others.'

Jac remembered the drawn faces of the soldiers in the photos Iris had shown her this morning. She and Tama stood for a moment in silence, both looking at the door.

'I'd better go,' he said. 'Be careful.'

Back in her room, with Tama's casual warning buzzing in her head, Jac put Iris's ring under her pillow. Not liking that hiding place, she put it in her pack instead, in a pair of socks, then decided against that and put it in the coin compartment of her wallet, which seemed just as bad. In the end, the ring ended up where it had started—in her pocket.

She spent the rest of the night sitting in front of the open window, which overlooked the back of the hotel: the staff quarters and orchard to the left, the expanse of bush directly in front of her and to the right, leading down to Everly. She placed her hand on the front pocket of her jeans, feeling the ring, wondering about the absence of guilt she felt. It made her think about her dad. The times he had come home with a new stereo or TV, telling her and Charlie it had 'fallen off the back of a truck'. It wasn't until she was in her teens that she found out what that actually meant. The phrase 'like father, like daughter' spun around in her head until she shut it down. She was nothing like him. She did what she had to do to survive. He was a lazy, selfish prick, only ever out for himself.

It was close to eleven o'clock when Jac pulled the stubborn window closed. She felt wired. Like she should be doing something but didn't know what. She stepped out of her room, looking right, down the pitch-black hallway of the west wing, and then left, seeing the dull light from sconces in the east wing hallway shining through the glass of the smoke doors. Going through the doors, she stopped when she heard talking. She wasn't sure where it was coming from. By the time she was halfway along the east wing hallway, she worked out the voice was coming from the far end. She walked towards it. Turning right into the small hallway she'd seen earlier. The door was now slightly ajar and she pulled it open, closing her eyes and gritting her teeth as the hinges whined. In front of her was a staircase with half a dozen steps leading upwards. Thinking about where she was in the hotel, she realised these led up to the turret. Jac placed a foot on the first tread and stopped again as her weight sent a cracking noise up the stairs. She stood still. Listening. And figured out that it was Lisa she could hear speaking.

'God, I can't wait till tomorrow's over,' she said. 'Everything will go back to normal then. I'm sure of it.'

Jac strained to hear another voice. Who was she talking to? Was she on the phone? Or talking to herself?

'This place could really be something, Paige. It *will* be something, one day. Remember how we talked about it? I've been going through all the photos. She still goes on about all the happy times we had. She had no idea then and she has no idea now. There was nothing about this place that was happy, really, was there Paige?'

Jac raised her brows. Lisa was talking to Paige?

'No, that's not fair. We did have some good times, didn't we?' Jac heard Lisa say, answering her own question.

There was a creak behind Jac and she turned. Iris was looming over her and Jac gasped. With her white hair and face devoid of make-up, and wearing a long white floor-length nightgown, she looked exactly like the kind of ghost Jac and her friends had conjured up in their heads all those years ago.

'What are you doing? I need Lisa. You're not Lisa! Where is she?' Iris's voice got louder and louder with each sentence, her head whipping left and right. Jac edged away from the door, back along the hallway. She didn't want Lisa to know she had been spying on her.

Lisa came down the steps, the shock visible on her face.

'Sorry,' Jac said, hoping her lie would be believable: 'I was on my way downstairs to get a drink and saw Iris walking down here. I followed her and when I asked her if she was okay, she just started shouting.'

Ignoring Jac, Lisa closed the door behind her and snapped a small padlock into place. She walked over to Iris. 'It's okay, Mum. You're okay. Bad dream?' she asked as she guided Iris back to her room.

Iris muttered something Jac didn't catch.

'You're okay,' Lisa said again. 'It'll just be a bit of stress about tomorrow. But you know it's all planned and it's going to be wonderful.' Her voice faded as they entered Iris's room and she closed the door behind them.

THIRTY-FIVE

Charlie

Early Sunday morning

CHARLIE OPENED HER EYES. She hadn't planned on sleeping, she had only meant to lie on the stretcher for a moment and revise her plan. She had started digging late in the afternoon yesterday, or at least had tried, but had given up soon after when the ground had proved too hard to break. She had laid down on her stretcher; the familiar tiredness had overtaken her even without the drugs. She looked at her watch now. Two am. What else was there to do but dig? She got off the stretcher and, with something resembling energy, she now started digging in earnest.

Two hours later, her nails black and some broken, she placed her misshapen spoon at her side, bending and stretching her cramped fingers. She had managed to tunnel out a small hole, right up against the cage. The job was so much bigger and harder than she'd thought it would be. The dirt was like concrete in places. There were small pebbles and even rocks that she had to dig around and dislodge. She had dug down about twenty centimetres but still had a while to go before she had any hope of fitting under the cage. Picking up her spoon, she started digging again and as it plunged into the hole, she felt contact with yet another rock. Throwing the spoon to the side she clawed at the packed dirt around it. This one was bigger than the others she had come across, the colour a dull white. She kept digging and soon the dirt loosened. Charlie brushed the dirt from around it, but it was only when she paused again, sitting back, that she noticed how strangely smooth it was. She brought the lantern closer. And then inhaled sharply, choking on the dusty air. It wasn't a rock. She dug away the last of the dirt and raised the lamp to her discovery. A skull. She backed away, a hand covering her mouth.

She shuffled back against her stretcher, the sweat cooling on her skin, making her shiver. She let out a sob, which echoed around her. The skull glowed a stark white in the lamplight.

What the hell was this? She got back on her feet and started pacing the room but the shock of the discovery made her dizzy and she had to sit back down, her head between her knees, feeling like she was going to throw up. This wasn't happening. This couldn't be happening. She felt like she'd hit a wall. She knew she should continue digging, but she was tired and wanted all of this to be over. Tears rolled down her cheeks and dripped onto the floor. She needed to move. She couldn't just sit here. If she didn't do something about getting out of here she was going to be next. She was going to die down here.

Ignoring the skull as best she could, she kept going, scraping at the dirt under the cage, refusing to give in to her heavy limbs and thumping head; refusing to look at the watch on the drawers. Time was slowly creeping towards morning. They would be bringing breakfast soon, and she didn't intend to be here. She couldn't be here.

THIRTY-SIX

Lisa

Twenty-one years ago

LISA STOOD AT the side of the hotel, looking across the front lawn. She licked her lips, feeling Paige's waxy lipstick. Nathan was mowing out there. To Lisa, the lawn didn't look like it needed it but, with the open day tomorrow, Iris wanted everything perfect. Nathan looked up briefly, and she stood up straight, patting her hair quickly, jutting a hip out and then standing up straight again. Had he seen her? She didn't think so. Her shoulders slumped.

'Hey!' Paige came up behind her, digging her fingers into her sides and making her jump.

'You scared me.'

'What are you doing over here?'

'Nothing.' She pressed her lips together, and her eyes darted to Nathan and back without even meaning to.

Paige looked over to Nathan, and smirked. 'Come on, Lise. What are you doing?'

Lisa knew that Paige knew, and she felt a flush crawl up her neck and cover her face.

'Are you wearing my lipstick?'

'No.'

Paige looked back over to Nathan, who had stopped to remove his shirt. Paige's eyebrows danced up and down and she gave him a wave. He looked around before he waved back.

'Nice try, Lise,' Paige said, as she walked away.

Lisa wasn't sure what she was referring to—the lie about the lipstick, or her pitiful attempt at flirting with Nathan.

IT WAS A couple of hours before dinner, and Lisa stood in her bedroom in front of the mirror. She had just spent the last half an hour applying fake tan to her naked body. She had bought it at the mini mart yesterday. She had always envied Paige her complexion, never quite getting over the fact her sister was blessed with olive skin, when she'd been pale and freckly, and she thought maybe this would help improve the way she looked. Her skin felt sticky to the touch and smelled of oily coconut. She slipped into a dress, one of two she owned, a simple black A-line that fell to her knees, and brushed her hair. Iris hadn't cut it for over three months and it was the longest it had been in years. It sat on her shoulders, and she could pull it into a ponytail, which she did now. She grabbed the head-band of Paige's, which she'd taken from her room, and put it on. She took Paige's lipstick and applied a fresh coat. She closed the curtains, darkening the room slightly, and went back to the mirror, happy with the effect. She turned from left to right and smiled at herself, then ad-justed the smile, closed her mouth, let her lips turn up just a touch—that was it—a smile that looked like it held a se-cret. She squinted her eyes, which made the transforma-tion complete. Imagining Nathan behind her, she leaned back slightly, feeling his hard body pressed against hers, strong arms encircling her waist.

A sharp knock interrupted her daydream. She ripped the headband off, wiped her mouth and threw open the curtains.

'Lise! Open up.'

She walked over to the door and let Paige in.

'Jesus Christ! What the hell did you do to yourself!' Paige covered her mouth but couldn't keep the giggle from escaping.

'What? What do you mean?' Lisa touched her hair and her lips.

'Your skin! What did you do?'

Lisa turned to look in the mirror. She blinked hard, twice, and stepped closer. With the curtains closed her skin had looked bronzed but she could see it had gradually darkened over the last half an hour and was now more of a deep orange.

'I… I tried some fake tan. Oh my god, look at me! I can't go downstairs looking like this!' She turned to Paige in a panic.

Paige recovered from her laughing fit and dragged her out of her room and down to her own. She started running a bath. Lisa didn't have one in her bathroom.

'Strip,' Paige demanded.

Lisa stood there, unsure.

'Lise, come on. I'm helping. You can't let Iris see you like this—she'll have a fit.'

Lisa started stripping, while Paige left the room, coming back a moment later with baby oil. Wrapped in a towel, Lisa watched as Paige covered her in the stuff, massaging it into her legs, her arms, her neck and face.

'In you hop,' Paige said, indicating the bath.

Lisa did as she was told, and the sting from Paige having laughed at her gradually fell away as the colour leached from her skin into the water, muddying it.

'You don't need that stuff,' Paige said. 'Why did you even bother with it?'

I'm so pale, I feel invisible, Lisa thought. *If I had a tan, I'd look more like you.* She realised how shallow that sounded and only shrugged in reply. An admission would be an embarrassment. Paige wouldn't understand.

'Get yourself dressed. Dinner will be ready soon.' Paige turned and left.

Back in her room, Lisa put her black dress back on and shoved the lipstick and headband into her desk drawer. She looked in the mirror again. Apart from darker patches on her knees and elbows and the palms of her hands, her skin was back to normal: pale, and all freckles present and accounted for.

She found Paige in the lounge, standing by the French doors, peering out through the filmy curtains to the driveway. 'What are you doing?' Lisa asked, joining her.

'Waiting for Miss Hastings. Iris said to keep an eye out for her and to open the door and greet her when she arrives. She told me, "Don't make her have to knock." What the hell does that even mean?'

Miss Hastings' old blue car edged its way up towards the hotel, stopping halfway around the circular drive.

DINNER WITH MISS HASTINGS could have been awkward. But she was young and fun, considerably closer in age to Paige and Lisa than she was to Iris, and she didn't act at all like a teacher as they sat at the table talking about the open day. She talked with passion about the hotel and its history, the architecture and the first tourists that visited.

Lisa found her own smile faltering when Miss Hastings started talking about the soldiers' hallway, though. How tragic it was that soldiers had been locked up in there.

'I was telling your mum we should open the hallway up for visitors this year.'

Lisa wanted her to stop talking about it but didn't have the courage to change the subject. She looked over at Iris, who was smiling at Miss Hastings. Lisa identified the frostiness behind that smile. Miss Hastings didn't.

'And I told Miss Hastings it was a mess back there. There's no way we could get it up to scratch for people to look through.'

'They'll just have to make do with the photos,' Miss Hastings said. 'Maybe next year, though?'

Iris smiled again and moved the conversation away from the soldiers' hallway and on to Paige and all her accomplishments.

Lisa kept her eyes on her dinner, shaking her head almost imperceptibly as Miss Hastings tried to satisfy Iris's need for praise of her eldest daughter, while at the same time glancing now and again across at Lisa, no doubt wondering why the youngest Gilmore was being ignored.

'Are you all ready for tomorrow?' Miss Hastings asked, clearly wanting to change the subject.

'Yes.' Iris sighed. 'I think so. I actually don't know why I do this every year.'

Because you love the attention, Lisa thought.

'Well, I'm glad you do. It's always been such a great community day and a wonderful way to fundraise for the school,' Miss Hastings said. 'Everyone really appreciates how hard you work to make it a success.'

Iris nodded, accepting the compliment. She raised her wine glass, looking at Paige and Miss Hastings, who did the same with their glasses. 'Here's to tomorrow and yet another successful open day.'

Lisa raised her own glass, not that she was included in the toast.

After dinner, Iris invited Miss Hastings into the lounge for coffee. The four of them stood at the main staircase outside the dining room. 'Paige, you need to do a bit of practice. Off you go. And an early night, please. It's a big day tomorrow.'

Lisa and Paige both said goodnight to Miss Hastings. Lisa started making her way up the stairs but Paige didn't move. When Iris and Miss Hastings had disappeared into the lounge further along the hallway, Paige headed for the back of the hotel.

'Where are you going?' Lisa asked, coming back down the stairs.

Paige raised her brows and smiled, then said, 'I haven't spoken to him for almost a week.'

Lisa waited until Paige had disappeared through the double doors to the back entrance, and then followed her. If she hadn't spoken to Nathan for a while, it meant he hadn't got the opportunity to speak to Paige about leaving. Lisa felt sick with expectation, regretting telling Nathan about Paige's plans, but also wondering if he could convince her to stay. Lisa thought if Paige wouldn't stay for her, maybe she would stay for someone like Nathan.

The light was on in the staff quarters. Lisa stood with her back to the wall, listening at the open window, every now and then sneaking a look at what was happening inside.

Paige and Nathan were standing by his bed. She could hear murmuring. Lisa thought they were talking about tomorrow. Then Nathan said, 'I hear you might be getting out of here.' His tone sounded casual, but Lisa knew better.

'What do you mean?' Paige asked.

Lisa looked through the window. Paige was running her hand through Nathan's hair.

'Lisa told me you've applied for a scholarship for next year. That you're going to go to uni.'

Paige's hand dropped.

'You didn't tell me about any of that. Were you going to?' Nathan asked.

'Of course I was. Nothing's settled yet. I haven't heard back about the scholarship.' Her voice was getting higher and higher. 'I probably didn't even get it and I'll end up having to stay here.'

'That wouldn't be a bad thing,' Nathan said.

'Yeah, it would,' Paige replied. 'I want out, Nathan. And the scholarship's going to do that for me.'

'So…what about us?'

'Can we stop talking about this now?' Paige asked, dodging the question.

Lisa watched Paige leading Nathan to the bed. He sat and she straddled his lap.

'I haven't seen you in ages,' she said.

'I just want you to know how much you mean to me.' Nathan wrapped his arms around Paige's waist. 'I'd hate it if you left. Really hate it.'

'I know,' Paige said.

'Do you?' Nathan asked. 'I wonder if you mean more to me than I do to you.' His voice sounded sad, not angry. 'I love you, Paige.'

There was no answer from Paige; instead, she kissed him.

Lisa backed away from the window. Nathan had been

her one hope of making Paige stay. She had been depending on the fact Paige cared about him, wouldn't want to leave him and what they had, but from what Lisa had just heard, he hadn't persuaded Paige at all.

THIRTY-SEVEN

Jac

Sunday morning

WITH ALL HER relentless questions circling, Jac woke, showered and dressed for the day, throwing on the same pair of jeans she had worn since she arrived. Going through her bag, she picked up a T-shirt and sniffed under the armpits, screwing up her face as she pushed it to the bottom of her pack and found another one.

Jac was uncertain about joining Iris and Lisa for breakfast and thought she could go down to the kitchen instead, get a cup of coffee and a piece of toast. Leaving her room and pushing the smoke doors open, she was just in time to see Iris unlocking the door to the soldiers' hallway at the other end. Iris pulled the invisible door open that was covered with the same navy and floral wallpaper as the wall surrounding it and stepped inside. Jac looked over the banister down the main staircase, wondering where Lisa was, and then made her way down the east wing hallway to the door Iris had just gone through.

Walking into the dim hallway, she was amazed at how big it was. Looking left and right, she counted five doors. She watched torchlight dance around inside an open door almost opposite where she stood and heard the scrape of wood, a muffled thump. She poked her head inside the room, noting the number attached to the door in small brass letters: 12A.

Iris was kneeling in the centre of the room. Even more oddly, there were two short boards on one side of her, which had clearly been pulled up from the floor, and three white lilies on her other side.

Jac squinted in the dim light of Iris's torch, trying to make out the room. It was small, much smaller than the one she was staying in; the window boarded over, torn wallpaper on the walls.

Iris looked up when Jac stepped into the room. 'What are you doing here?' she asked, shifting back on her heels. She looked worried, her eyes wide. 'I thought everyone was down at breakfast. You mustn't say anything. No one knows. I just come here sometimes, to leave her a little something.' Her voice became higher and more hurried as she spoke.

Paige? Is she talking about Paige? Jac thought, her stomach sinking as she took a couple of hesitant steps over to the space in the floor. Peering in, keeping her face impassive, she saw clumps of lilies and roses, all in various stages of decay, surrounding a small skeleton that at some point looked like it had been shrouded in an off-white material, but had been eaten away and now fell in pieces around the collection of bones.

Jac stepped back. It wasn't Paige. Too small. She remembered her conversation with Iris in the library yesterday. She'd mentioned a baby, that she wasn't in the world for long.

Why was this baby hidden away under floorboards in this disused hallway? 'Wh—what happened?' Jac asked.

'There was nothing right about it,' Iris said, gazing into the space. 'That's what Mother said. I was only seventeen. Mother said Eli wasn't the right man. So the baby wasn't right.' Iris picked up the fresh flowers at her side and lay them down next to the bones. 'Mother told me she didn't survive. And that it was all for the best. It just shows that it wasn't meant to be.' Iris smiled down at the skeleton. 'But when the time was right, I got my Paige. Mother was dead by then. She wouldn't have agreed with my affair with Eli, starting that forbidden relationship again—she always said it would've ruined her, and me, ruin the Gilmore name. But I got Paige out of it. She was perfect. Eli didn't stick around. Had a wife to go back to, and I had Andrew.' Her mouth turned down like she had smelled something rotten. 'Not even Eli knew about Paige in the end.'

Iris looked up at Jac, confused, alarmed. 'You shouldn't be in here.' She reached into the space and gently ran her fingers along the chalky white skull.

Jac was torn: should she go to Iris, offer her comfort, or leave her be? She tried to work out the circumstances Iris had been in, thinking of the photo she had seen of Eli Winiata and Iris at the picnic when they were teenagers. Helen had disapproved of Eli. Iris had got pregnant to him. The baby had died, or... Jac didn't want to think of the alternative, the reason why the baby was here, instead of in a cemetery. And then there was Paige. Eli and Iris had had an affair years later. Is that what she had said?

Iris started returning the floorboards, slotting them into place, and Jac backed out of the room.

Walking back through the east wing's hallway Jac gazed ahead, trying to make sense of what she had just seen and how she felt. There was a sickening mix of com-

passion for Iris and revulsion for what she had just seen.
Coming down the main stairs, and turning at the landing, she saw Frankie and Lisa standing together outside
the dining room, talking.

'Any sign of Mum up there?' Lisa asked. She looked
tired, her make-up barely covering the rings under her eyes,
and her mouth was tight, even as she tried to smile at Jac.

'I think she's on her way down,' Jac said, not wanting
Lisa to check up on Iris. From what Iris had said, there
was no indication Lisa would know about what her mother
was hiding in the soldiers' hallway. She had never felt so
strongly the need to get out of this place than right now.
Charlie's sheet music she'd found in the music room was
the only thing stopping her.

'There you are,' Lisa said as Iris appeared at the landing.

Jac was afraid to meet Iris's eye, but as Iris slowly made
her way down the last few stairs, she walked over to Jac
and stood right in front of her. 'You,' she said, pointing her
finger in Jac's face, who had to look up at her. Gone was
the vacant, confused look Jac had just witnessed a few
minutes ago. This Iris was fuming.

'My ring,' Iris said, looking at Jac. 'My ring's missing.
My emerald and diamond one.'

'Why are you looking at me?' Jac asked, concentrating on keeping her face impassive, her voice calm, even
though her heartbeat increased.

'You took it.'

'No, I didn't.' Jac felt three pairs of eyes on her, knowing as long as she denied it, Iris couldn't prove anything.

'Yes, you did!' Iris screamed, advancing on Jac.

Jac stepped back and over Iris's shoulder she saw Nathan and Tama come through the doors from the back of

the hotel and stop behind Frankie and Lisa. *Great. An audience*.

'Mum,' Lisa said. 'I'm sure Jac didn't take your ring.'

'What would you know!' Iris glared at Lisa.

Jac watched as Lisa took a deep breath and then exhaled slowly. 'Mum, you've probably just misplaced it.'

'I haven't *misplaced* it, you stupid girl. *She's* taken it.'

Lisa turned to Jac. 'Sorry. She gets like this. The open day.' She lowered her voice. 'Although this year seems even worse. Maybe it's the fall.'

'Has she seen the doctor recently?' Frankie asked.

'I don't need a doctor.' All emotion had gone from Iris's voice. 'I need my ring back.'

Jac looked away, scared that her face would give her up.

'I wear it every year,' Iris said.

'Mum, why don't you wear another one? You have so many beautiful pieces to choose from.'

'You know why it has to be the emerald,' she said, accusing, her head whipping from Jac to Lisa.

'She was wearing it the day Paige disappeared,' Lisa murmured, explaining to whoever wanted to know.

'Stop whispering about me!'

Lisa stepped towards Iris, arms out, ready to comfort her, but Iris turned away, her bottom lip protruding.

'Nathan?' Iris said.

Nathan stepped forward, looking embarrassed to be called on in front of everyone but still coming to Iris's side. She reached out to him and gripped onto his forearm like she was clinging to a life raft. They walked through the double swing doors, towards the back door of the hotel, Nathan leaning his head towards her as Iris spoke to him. Where were they going? Jac watched them until they disappeared, Nathan obviously having a calming effect on Iris as they went.

'She's not well,' Lisa said to Jac. Three words that were supposed to explain and excuse all at the same time.

No kidding, Jac thought.

Frankie's eyebrows pulled together in worry as she and Lisa walked into the dining room. Jac followed, but Lisa stopped her at the dining room door. 'I've been meaning to say thank you for helping out the last couple of days, especially with everything that's been going on. I'm well aware Iris probably pressured you into it. Feel free to enjoy the open day today. I'll make sure I get your payment sorted and then you can get on. I think Iris is going to need a bit of quiet time after today.'

Jac nodded. She had outstayed her welcome. She had the day to find out what the hell was happening in this place. The first thing she wanted to do was find out what Nathan and Iris were doing right now.

THIRTY-EIGHT

Lisa

Twenty-one years ago

'Up! Come on. *Get up!*'

Lisa was roused from a deep sleep by Iris's voice and the screech of the curtains as they were thrown open.

'Paige has been up for at least an hour helping me. Maybe you could think about someone other than yourself for once.'

Iris stormed from the room and Lisa slid out of bed, already wishing for the day to be over. She put on jeans and a T-shirt, for now. Iris would expect her to wear a dress for the high tea this afternoon. She brushed her hair and pulled it into a ponytail. Glancing at herself in the mirror, she thought that would have to do. Who would be looking at her anyway?

She could hear Iris downstairs, heeled shoes beating a staccato rhythm along the main ground floor hallway, her sharp tones ordering people around. Lisa took the stairs slowly, stopping on each one, listening as Iris yelled out, 'Nancy!' and the sound of her footsteps retreated through the doors from the main hallway in the direction of the kitchen.

Knowing Paige, she would be as far from Iris as possible, so Lisa left through the front door and stepped outside to look for her. They couldn't have hoped for a better day. It was spring at its best. There wasn't a cloud in the sky and there was a cool breeze, which meant that, even if the sun continued to shine, no one would overheat. Lisa walked out to the circular lawn in the middle of the driveway, a hand brushing a rose. Half a dozen rose petals, dark pink, fell onto the neatly cut grass. She looked around for Iris and scooped them up. On her way around the back of the hotel, she threw them into a lavender bush.

She spotted Paige and Nathan by the staff quarters. If Iris happened to step out the back door, she would be able to see them. Lisa thought Paige was getting more and more brazen with her relationship with Nathan. Iris wouldn't like it. Nathan was a hardworking employee but he was just that. An employee. Not someone for Iris Gilmore's sainted daughter to be involved with.

Standing at the back of the hotel Lisa could see the piece of paper in her hand and was holding it up to Nathan. Lisa couldn't hear what Paige said, but from Nathan's face she guessed it was nothing good. Paige bowed her head, her hand falling to her side. She looked up again at Nathan, her voice pleading. She put a hand to his face, but he turned away, avoiding contact. Paige grabbed his forearm and pulled him towards her, but he pulled away again.

'You can't!' he said, his voice travelling across the concrete. 'We need to talk about this. Please, don't decide anything else.'

'Lisa! Where are you!' Iris's shrill voice came from inside the hotel somewhere.

Lisa glanced at Nathan and Paige, who had obviously also heard Iris. They stepped away from each other, Nathan disappearing around the side of the staff quarters and Paige walking around to the front of the hotel.

'Lisa!' Iris came out the back door. 'What are you doing? Are you trying to be difficult? Get in here right now!'

AN HOUR LATER, the doors to the Gilmore Hotel were open and people started making their way in. Iris's voice, a special one put on for the crowds today—loud and authoritative but also friendly and chirpy—could be heard throughout the hotel welcoming people. 'Please come in, come in. Hello, Jane, how are you? Yes, yes beautiful day.' Lisa found Iris's fake friendliness disconcerting.

She stood back, halfway down the main hallway, as volunteers readied themselves to take small groups around the hotel. She had only seen Paige in passing, as Iris had put everyone to work before the doors opened. She wanted to talk to her, ask her what was happening with Nathan, but she hadn't got a chance yet.

'Lisa, darling,' Iris said and Lisa flinched at the unfamiliar term. 'Can you show these children outside?' Iris bent down to their level. 'Lisa's going to take you outside to play a few games, okay?' The four children nodded, looking eagerly at Lisa.

She spent the next hour taking kids through the old-fashioned games that had been set up on the mown grass just before the orchard. They threw horseshoes and played cornhole. There were sack races and egg-and-spoon races. Lisa attempted to supervise the games, pay attention to the kids, of who more were arriving as the minutes passed, and looked for Paige at the same time. Where was she? She had seen Nathan walking around, sticking to the perimeter of the action. Iris expected him to be available for questions about the gardens, but he didn't look willing.

Miss Hastings approached, followed by two students from Lisa's school.

'Lisa,' she said, 'I thought you could do with some help here.'

'Yeah, sure,' she said, trying to summon a smile.

'Off you go girls.' Miss Hastings pointed towards the group of kids gathering around the empty sacks. 'Thanks for your help.'

'Yeah, thanks,' Lisa mumbled to the two students' retreating backs.

'Is Paige here? I haven't seen her?' Miss Hastings asked, looking around.

'She's here somewhere,' Lisa said. 'I might go look for her, if you don't mind taking over here?'

Lisa made her way through the increasingly busy grounds and saw Nathan again. 'Where's Paige?' she called out.

He shrugged his shoulders, walking past her without stopping. She grabbed his arm as he passed, but he easily shrugged out of her grip.

'I saw you guys talking before. I heard you say something about her leaving.'

'Nathan!' They both looked up at Iris, who was walking towards them. 'Can you show this group the rose garden out the front, please?'

'No problem, Ms G.' An accommodating smile replaced the look of worry on his face. 'I think you need to talk to Paige. She won't listen to me,' he said to Lisa, as he walked away.

THIRTY-NINE

Jac

Sunday morning

LEAVING FRANKIE AND Lisa to their cosy breakfast, Jac walked out to the back of the hotel. Iris and Nathan were standing over by the staff quarters. They were deep in conversation and didn't see her. Iris was wringing her hands. She looked upset. Was she crying? Was this about the ring? Or what happened in the soldiers' hallway before? Did it have anything to do with Charlie? Nathan held a hand to Iris's arm, comforting her. He nodded once and set off towards the orchard, while Iris made her way back towards the hotel. When she passed Jac, she said, 'I think it's probably time you left.' She didn't wait for a response and Jac didn't give her one.

She could see Nathan crossing the orchard, his orange shirt bright against the green trees.

Follow him.

There wasn't a lot of cover, so she waited and watched him. He stopped at an old shed about three hundred metres away which was hugging the boundary fence, a row of tall pine trees behind it, and saw him go inside. She made her way through the damp grass, stopping and watching, hiding, crouched in the long grass behind overgrown fruit trees. Pulse racing, she sprinted to the shed and stood at the side of it, listening.

Could Charlie be here? She couldn't hear any talking, just Nathan moving around inside, something being dragged and, a few minutes later, a thump, like something being closed. And then the door was flung open and she watched Nathan head across the orchard away from the hotel. Giving him some space she started to follow. If he turned around, she would easily be spotted even among the fruit trees. The orchard gave way to a grassy paddock, and he veered left, down to the creek. Hopping from one protruding rock to another, he was across in five long strides. To the left was farmland; straight ahead was bush, a lot thicker than the small area in which she had met Elijah yesterday. The towering pines and natives stretched up and out before her. Nathan disappeared into the gloom and she ran to the creek. Her short legs hopped to the first rock, then the second and third, but in her hurry she ended up slipping off the fourth one. Her legs plunged knee-deep into the water. She waded to the other side and kept going, scared she was going to lose Nathan, and just as scared he would notice her following. With soaking wet shoes and jeans, she sprinted into the trees. She stopped, listening. She heard flowing water, but nothing else. She started jogging, her eyes struggling to make out shapes in the thick bush. There was no track here and Jac didn't even know if she was heading in the right direction. But then she saw a flash of his orange shirt. He wasn't moving fast. He was maybe twenty metres ahead. He stopped and Jac ducked down, ferns tickling her face. He looked around, and then he disappeared.

'What the fuck?' Jac whispered.

She got up and, crouching low, she kept her eye on the

spot where she had last seen him. Had he fallen? When she got to the spot, she could see where he had gone. She was standing in front of the yawning entrance to a limestone cave. She peered inside. From what she could see, it sloped down for a metre or two but then there was nothing. It was too dark for her to see. She reached into her back pocket.

'Fuck,' she whispered. She'd left her phone charging on the bedside table in her room.

She edged forward, almost slipping on the slimy mud underfoot. She had walked maybe five metres and she couldn't see her hand in front of her face, but up ahead— or was it down?—she saw a torchlight's arc, just before it disappeared too. She couldn't go any further but she was desperate. She edged forward again, one arm in front of her and the other on the limestone wall, using it to aid her progress. And then she completely lost her footing. There was a scrabble of pebbles and she felt the uneven ground below her vanish. She braced herself for a plummeting fall. But she landed a second later. A metre-drop at the most, she thought. She yelped in pain as she felt her ankle twist and tried to get up, blindly reaching out to find the wall. She turned around in a slow circle and felt nothing but cool, damp air.

'What are you doing?' The torchlight was bright in her eyes and she couldn't see anything beyond it.

'What are *you* doing?' she replied.

'Going for a walk.' Nathan's tone was teasing, amused.

'You're doing more than that.' Jac struggled to get up and Nathan walked closer, dropping the light towards the ground.

'So what if I am?'

He shone the torch above her head and she looked up. She could see the small ledge where she had slipped.

'Need a hand to get back up?' he asked.

'No,' she said. She limped to the ledge and pushed herself up.

Nathan followed behind.

Was Charlie down there? What other reason would he have to come here?

'Charlie!' she yelled. 'Charlie!' She listened. Nothing but the distant sound of rushing water.

Nathan looked at her briefly before he carried on walking, out the entrance, then skirted the cave, going further into the bush.

'You've taken my sister.' Jac tried to sound forceful, but fear left her voice meek and shaking.

He stopped and turned to her. 'No, I haven't.'

'I don't believe you.'

'I don't care what you think.'

'You and Iris. I know the story about Paige. I've seen how similar Charlie is to her. Charlie was at the hotel—Iris told me. I don't think she was supposed to. She got confused and let it slip. And people around here have told me all about you.'

'Is that right?' He didn't look concerned or worried and it made Jac angry.

'Where is she?!' she yelled.

'I don't know where your sister is. I can't help you.'

'What are you doing out here then? You and Iris, I've seen the way you talk together, always whispering. I don't take Iris for being the kind of person who's matey with the help.'

Nathan raised his brows at that. 'We're just two people who cared very much for the same person who's no longer here. That kind of thing brings people together.' He turned away and carried on into the bush.

'What the hell is that supposed to mean!' Jac yelled. He didn't stop. 'I'm going to the cops,' she yelled again, and Nathan stopped this time but didn't turn. Jac's stomach dropped in fear. She started backing away, but then, after a moment, he continued walking away from her.

She couldn't follow him. Her ankle ached and when she looked down she could see some slight swelling at the top of her canvas shoe. Having no torch, she couldn't go back into the cave and see for herself why he'd gone down there, so she limped back the way she had come, annoyed she couldn't do anything more. She would go and see Dunlop right now. She could tell him about the sheet music and that Elijah had seen Charlie heading up to the hotel on Monday afternoon, not heading out of town. He'd have to question the people here. He'd have no choice.

She retraced her way back across the orchard, the pain in her ankle a dull ache. She came to the shed. There wasn't much to it. Wooden planks, a corrugated iron roof. She pulled the door open. Inside, it was dark and gaps in the walls let in the insipid morning light. There was a workbench that ran the length of the back wall. On top were various gardening implements and tools. On the left were sacks of fertiliser and mulch. On the right was an old steamer chest, the dull silver metal overlaid with wooden slats. It looked totally out of place in the shed and Jac took three long strides across the dirt floor to open it. She thought it might be locked, but the buckles easily unlatched. She lifted the lid. On one side were old sheets, two of them. They were dark pink and folded in neat rectangles. On the other side was an empty Fanta bottle. Jac lifted it up, noting the lipstick stain at the top.

There was a pot of lip balm, half used, a pile of sheet music for the piano and violin and, Jac noted with dread, the flute. There was a small pile of newspaper articles, neatly cut out, maybe ten in all, from both the local paper and the national one, reporting on the disappearance of Paige Gilmore. Pushed down the side, tight up against the sheets, was a piece of pale blue material. Jac lifted it up and shook it out. She identified it straight away—she'd worn the same one seven years ago. It was a school uniform polo shirt. The words 'Everly Area School' were written around a crest with an oak tree surrounded by five stars on the pocket. 'Charlie,' she whispered. She held the shirt close to her. She was right. She knew Michelle Lafferty had been hiding something from her. So what had happened? Had Charlie come up here on Monday? Did Iris lure her here for Nathan? Obviously, Iris and Nathan were close. Jac had seen them together enough over the last few days, and she now recalled Iris describing Nathan as having been loyal to her over the years.

Jac closed the lid to the chest, keeping hold of the shirt. She needed help. Would Dunlop help, though? He hadn't believed her when she told him Charlie was missing. But she had so much more now. This would make a difference. It had to.

FORTY

Jac

Sunday morning

JAC RAN BACK to the hotel, shots of pain radiating from her ankle, which she ignored. She was deliberating driving straight down to Everly to find Dunlop, but he wouldn't be at the station on a Sunday and she had no idea where he lived. She needed her phone.

'Jac! Over here,' Frankie called out from the back of the hotel as Jac ran in from the orchard.

Jac came to a standstill. Frankie. Could she help? Could she be trusted? Jac took a deep breath, looking around for Nathan. He would still be out in the bush. She had to be calm, do this right. She walked over to Frankie.

'Would you mind helping me in the music room?' Frankie asked. 'Iris doesn't like the way the chairs have been arranged.'

The last thing Jac wanted to do was go back inside the hotel, but she needed her phone. and she'd have the chance to talk to Frankie in private.

They walked through the rear entrance and through the door, into the main hallway. Jac glanced in the dining room on her right. It was empty. As they passed the main staircase she looked up to the landing. There was no sign of anyone. In the music room, Jac slid the double doors closed so she wouldn't be overheard.

'What have you done to yourself?' Frankie asked as Jac limped over to her.

'Nothing. I'm fine. Just rolled my ankle.'

'Oh, I'm sorry. If you've hurt yourself you should keep off it. I can do this,' said Frankie, as she started dragging the chairs out of their tidy rows. 'I think they look fine as they are. But Iris said a semi-circle looks more welcoming.' She stopped. 'Are you sure you're okay? You look a little flushed.'

'I think Nathan's taken Charlie. Or Nathan and Iris. I'm not sure...'

'What?' Frankie's forehead creased. 'What are you talking about?' Frankie stopped what she was doing and moved over to Jac.

'It's Nathan. He's got Charlie.' Jac bent over for second. She was out of breath and the room started spinning as she tried to convey to Frankie what had happened. 'I followed him... I hurt my ankle. He said he didn't have her but I don't believe him. He was on his way into the bush. I followed him into a cave. I don't know what he was doing in there... I found this in the shed down by the orchard.' Jac held the shirt out to Frankie. 'I need to call the police.'

'Hey, Jac, calm down.' Frankie took the shirt from Jac. She held it up in front of her. 'This isn't Charlie's,' she said.

'What? How do you know?'

'This is the school's old uniform. They changed it... oh, five years ago now. The new uniform shirt is slightly darker and a different material.'

Jac sat down on one of the chairs. Frankie handed her

the shirt back. Then she realised something. 'It's Paige's,' she said, remembering what else was in the box.

'I don't know about that.' Frankie sat down beside Jac, placing the shirt on the chair next to her.

'It doesn't mean he doesn't have Charlie, though. He was in the bush. He was going somewhere. I should've kept following him. I need to call Dunlop. He needs to know about Michelle…and Elijah…'

Frankie rested a hand on Jac's knee, trying to calm her. 'Take some deep breaths. That's it. Jac, you should know that this time each year Nathan often heads out into the bush—he does it for Iris, but for himself too.'

'What are you talking about?' Jac asked. Frankie's calm disposition was starting to annoy her.

'Nathan always thought it was possible Paige was taken by someone, possibly murdered, her body dumped. Over the years, he's traipsed the bush all over Everly, covered every inch and most of the caves as well. I think he knows now she's not there, but each year he does it, and now it's just become something he does for Iris on the anniversary, I think. They are very close. I always feel a bit sorry for Lisa. She makes the effort to come home many times a year. She spends her whole six-week Christmas break with Iris but each year I see her at the open day and Iris still treats her as if she's the hired help.' She shook her head.

'Look, you're going through a tough time,' Frankie said. 'It's understandable you're feeling a little bit confused, what with your sister and your dad.'

Jac slowed her breathing. 'Do you blame me for being confused? At first Nathan told me he didn't know Charlie, but he does. Iris told me from the very beginning she didn't know who Charlie was, and then yesterday she tells me Charlie was in this damn room with her! For all I know, Lisa probably knows her as well.'

'Well, Lisa does know Charlie,' Frankie said.

'What? She told me she didn't.'

'Are you sure?'

Of course I'm bloody sure, Jac felt like yelling, but instead she nodded and, keeping her voice calm, she asked, 'How does Lisa know Charlie?'

'When Lisa came home a few months back, the school was in desperate need of a relief music teacher for a couple of weeks. Lisa filled in for us on very short notice.'

Fuck, Jac thought, her mind racing, trying to reorganise the jigsaw puzzle in her head. 'My first night here we talked about Lisa being a teacher. She and Iris didn't say anything about Lisa teaching at Charlie's school.'

Frankie shrugged. 'I'm not sure why Lisa wouldn't mention it.'

Because she had something to do with Charlie going missing, Jac thought.

'And it probably slipped Iris's mind,' Frankie said.

'And Lisa taught Charlie?' Jac asked, her mind spinning at this new piece of information.

Frankie nodded. 'I remember Lisa being impressed with Charlie's talent. We talked about it. I believe Charlie's in the quartet that Lisa would've taken for lunchtime practice a few times over those two weeks she taught at the school. Lisa's also very good at the flute. Maybe not quite as good as Paige was, but still very accomplished.'

She lied about knowing Charlie, Jac thought. *Lisa had so many chances to tell me she had met her, talked to her, but instead, she lied.*

FORTY-ONE

Lisa

Twenty-one years ago

After looking for Paige outside and on the ground floor, Lisa wound her way through the hordes of people going in and coming out of the various rooms then took the stairs two at a time and raced up the main staircase. She ran along the hallway and barged into Paige's room.

Her sister was sitting in a chair looking out the window, a piece of paper in her hand. She turned and looked at Lisa, a dreamy smile on her face.

'I've been looking for you everywhere,' Lisa said, closing the door behind her. 'What are you doing?'

'I got the scholarship.' She held the piece of paper in the air. 'I'm getting out of here. Mrs Pratchett dropped the letter off in the mailbox this morning.'

'Scholarship?' Lisa replied. 'You got it?' Lisa had started to think—hope—that maybe Paige had missed out on it.

'Yeah. My three-year degree paid for, plus living costs. Depends on my exam results, of course, but I'm not worried.'

'I… You can't leave without me. Iris said you weren't allowed.' She threw in the last remark in desperation.

Paige sniffed, turning back towards the window, the smile dropping from her face. 'Nathan doesn't want me to go, either. Keeps trying to talk me out of it. I thought at least he and you would be happy for me.'

'I want you to stay—I *need* you to stay.' Lisa couldn't figure out if she was upset or angry with her sister. Was she really going to leave? She couldn't. She wouldn't.

Paige got up, obviously not wanting to carry on the conversation. Lisa followed Paige out of her room and down the stairs. There was no one left inside and, from the back door, they could see a few stragglers heading to the orchard, picnic baskets and blankets in their arms. Lisa could smell the barbecue that was cooking up sausages for everyone. Paige walked out the back door and then stopped. Nathan was coming up from the orchard, empty boxes in hand. When he saw Paige, he placed the boxes down and walked towards them.

'Lise, I'm not talking to him. He's so bloody desperate for me to stay. I don't want to see him!' She took a few steps back towards the hotel.

Lisa sighed. 'Come on then.'

They both turned. Paige took the first door to their right. The tradesmen's hallway, seldom used, was dimly lit. Towards the end there were doors leading to the kitchen, laundry and basement and Nancy's small office at the end that she rarely used. Paige sprinted towards Nancy's office, but Lisa called her back.

'In here,' Lisa hissed as they heard Nathan enter the hotel, his hurried footsteps disappearing in the direction of the main hallway. Lisa stopped at the door halfway down the hallway and turned the handle, ramming her shoulder into it and pushing when it wouldn't open. She ushered Paige through, yanked the rusty key from the lock and closed the door behind them, pulling the cord to light up the stairwell. Lisa pushed the key into the lock and turned it. With some effort the mechanism scraped and clunked into place.

They stood panting in the ghostly glow, the naked bulb at the bottom of the concrete steps illuminating the stairs and strings of gossamer spiderwebs. Lisa walked down and opened another door, which led into the hotel's basement. Any sounds of the hotel were swallowed up by the concrete walls.

'God, we haven't been down here in years!' Paige said, squinting into the darkness.

Lisa didn't think anyone had. There were large masses hunched in the darkened corners, old furniture and boxes, where the bulb's light didn't reach.

'This place is creepy,' Paige said, her voice shaking.

They both sat down on the bottom step, resting their feet on an old rug that stretched a metre out in front of them. It still felt soft, even though the blue and green pattern was faded. Another one of Iris's rejects. The air was damp and cool. Even their voices sounded dull and flat.

'I don't understand,' Lisa said, desperately wanting Paige to realise that her place was here, at the hotel, at least for now. Couldn't uni wait? 'I know you want to get away. I just didn't think...'

'Didn't think I'd actually do it?'

'You can do anything,' Lisa said. 'I just didn't think you'd leave.'

'I'm so excited, Lise,' Paige said. 'And, hey, we've still got Christmas and New Year's and the whole summer ahead of us. I promise I'll make it a special one.'

They sat in silence, Lisa enjoying the closeness of Paige, the side of her body pushed up against her own.

Paige being close by always made her feel more than what she was; stronger, braver. Paige couldn't leave.

'Please don't go,' she whispered, leaning into Paige. She could still talk her around.

'I have to, Lise.' Paige sounded determined.

'But we have plans. Iris has plans. The hotel reopening… And you know it's not just that. What's going to happen when it's just me and Iris?' The thought frightened her. Iris could keep her in the soldiers' hallway for days if she wanted to, without Paige here to ask after her.

Paige didn't answer.

For all her talk over the years. She doesn't care about me.

'Lise…' Paige stood, disconnecting them, and Lisa felt the rush of air on her bare skin. 'You've only got one more year here, then you can do anything you want.'

Paige's flippant statement made Lisa's anger spike. She made it sound so easy, even when she knew that wouldn't be the case. 'So, what about Nathan?' Lisa asked. 'You're going to leave him?'

'It was never anything serious.'

'Does he know that?'

'Of course.'

That was a lie. She'd seen the way Nathan looked at her sister.

'He loves you. Aren't we enough for you to stay? Nathan and me?' She sounded whiny and pitiful, even to her own ears, and she heard Paige sigh in frustration.

'Lise,' Paige grabbed her hands and pulled her up off the step, 'you need to realise that this is going to happen. I can't stay just for you. I need to live my life. Start living my life. It's about bloody time.'

Lisa shook her head. 'Iris isn't going to let you go.' She had images of Iris locking Paige in the soldiers' hallway.

The thought should've made her feel bad, but it didn't. Maybe it's what Paige needed in order to see sense. That she belonged with them, here, at the hotel. 'She's not going to let you go,' Lisa said it again, feeling comfort in the statement because it was one hundred per cent accurate.

'It's not a matter of letting me, Lise. I'm going, whether you or Iris or Nathan like it or not.' Paige dropped Lisa's hands; she turned and walked up the stairs.

Lisa pushed past her. This conversation was not over. This needed to be sorted. Now. She stood in front of Paige, looking down at her from the top step.

'I'll tell Iris. I'll go and tell her right now.'

'No. I'll tell her when I'm ready. Anyway, you wouldn't do that to me. Land me in it with Poison Iris.'

Something in Paige's voice, the certainty, caught Lisa off guard, even when it shouldn't have. Paige was fobbing her off, like she knew exactly what Lisa was capable of, which wasn't much.

Lisa grabbed Paige's arms in desperation. 'You can't leave. You know what it's like for me, Paige. You can't leave me here with her!'

'Lise, calm down. I promise you, it's not going to be that bad.'

'You actually have no idea,' Lisa muttered, realisation dawning.

'What?'

'You don't, do you? You have no idea what I go through. You sympathise, say all the right things, but you don't care. You only care about yourself. You're just like her.'

'That's bullshit, Lisa. I'm nothing like Mum.'

Lisa could see it now. Wondered why she never had before. The selfishness, the need for control. 'You're going to leave me here, and I'll be the one who pays. She'll find a way to blame all of this on me and she'll punish me.' Lisa could see it playing out all so clearly. '*You can't go.*'

'I can, Lise. I'm sorry, but you can't stop me.' Paige's tone had turned hard.

Lisa dug her nails into Paige's bare arms. Paige tried to pull away but Lisa wouldn't let her. 'Lise, that hurts— let go.'

Lisa didn't care that it hurt. She dug her nails in deeper, held on tighter. Paige needed to feel this, feel what she felt, day in, day out. Pain. Fear. Confusion. Paige squirmed but still Lisa held on. She looked into Paige's eyes, enjoying that her sister was hurting and that, for a change, it wasn't her. Before she had even thought through what would happen next, Lisa pushed Paige as hard as she could, releasing her from her grip. She registered the shock on Paige's face; the sharp intake of breath; her grasping hands, trying to regain her balance; the whisper of a touch as Paige's fingertips brushed her shoulder the instant before she fell backwards down the stairs. Lisa heard the crack as Paige's head connected with one of the concrete steps. She landed awkwardly at the bottom, legs and arms splayed, her face turned away, looking blindly into the darkness.

FORTY-TWO

Jac

Sunday morning

JAC RAN FROM the music room, along the hallway, dodging a few unfamiliar people who were arriving to help with the open day. She had no idea where Lisa was but hoped she wasn't upstairs. She ignored the pain in her ankle as she ran up the main staircase. She barged into her room and grabbed her phone from the bedside table. She turned the phone on, but nothing happened. She held the button down on the side again for a moment longer, waiting for the screen to light up. Nothing. It was flat. She looked down and saw the charger plug was only half inserted into the electrical socket. *How could I have been so stupid?*

'Goddamit!' she cried out. She needed to get out of here and find Dunlop, but she didn't know how to convince him she was certain that the Gilmores had something to do with Charlie's disappearance. What if Lisa or Iris or even Nathan knew she was onto them? If Jac left the hotel they could take Charlie from wherever she was and hide her somewhere else, unless… Jac didn't want to think about the alternative. She plugged her phone in properly but knew being able to turn it on and charge it enough to make a phone call would take time.

Leaving her room, she came out into the east wing hall-way, she slowed to a limp and, as she came to Lisa's bed-room, opposite Iris's, she tried the door handle. Locked, of course. She carried on along the hallway. At the end on the right was the turret room, where Lisa had been last night. If she had something to hide, would she hide it in there?

There was a silver latch screwed into the door with a padlock hanging through its loop. The latch and padlock looked new. The latch plate had been attached to the old door with screws and was slightly crooked. Jac jiggled it in frustration, giving it a useless yank. Could she unlock it somehow? Remembering the toolbox in her bathroom, she ran back along the hallway, grabbed the hammer out of it and ran back to the door. She had no idea what she was doing or if she was strong enough to break the padlock. It was worth a shot, though. Whatever Lisa had in there, it was important enough that she kept the room locked. Jac realised, too, that if she did get through the door, there was going to be no explaining away or covering up what she had done.

'Fuck it,' she mumbled to herself and grabbed the pad-lock, pulling it towards her. She inserted a finger into the shackle and started hitting the side of the padlock, but it didn't work. The latch, however, screwed into the wall beside the door, didn't look that strong. With the hammer heavy in her hand, Jac took aim, swinging down with all her strength—mostly missing the latch and gouging the door. She tried again. This time she made contact and the latch was ripped from its screws. She hit it once more and, with the padlock attached, it fell to the floor with a *thunk*. She hoped no one could hear what she was doing. Ignor-ing the mess she had made of the door, she wrenched the door open. She raced up the short flight of uncarpeted steps and out into a small bright space with a panoramic view of Everly and beyond. Turning from the view, she started looking inside boxes that were stacked along the back wall opposite the windows. They were full of an assortment of old glasses, mugs and kettles. She looked behind the old armchairs in the room too, and underneath them. Nothing. There were multiple rugs covering the wooden floors, overlapping, curling up in the corners. Jac kneeled down and lifted each of them up, exposing the floorboards, looking for a notch in the wood or some kind of imperfection to show there was a hiding space underneath, like the one in the soldiers' hallway. She couldn't find anything. She stood up, looking around her. There had to be something in here. She lifted the heavy velvet curtains of each of the three windows, enveloping herself in a cloud of dust, looking underneath the swathes of material. When she got to the last window she found a small, recessed shelf hidden behind the curtain.

Jac peered inside the shelf. It wasn't very deep and, taped to the back of it, were photos. They looked like they had been cut from newspapers or some type of magazine. Some were black and white, others colour images. Jac pushed the curtain along the track, covering the window, to move it out of the way. She peered in at the photos again. All girls. All very similar in looks. Blonde hair. Full lips. Late teens, as far as she could tell. Jac reached in and tore each of them off the back of the shelf. There were eight in total. She stopped at the last one. Charlie. Jac knew the photo. Charlie had texted it to her earlier in the year. The school quartet had gone up to play a concert in Auckland and the local newspaper had written an article on them, and included a photo of the quartet along with a separate photo of each girl. The other photos looked like they had been cut from school magazines, the paper glossy and thick. Where were these girls now? Were they alive? Had Lisa done something to them? Jac's foot nudged something, and she moved the curtain further along. She looked down at the rectangular case, knowing in her gut what it was before she even picked it up. She put the photos back on the shelf and picked up the case. Opening it she saw a silver flute, nestled in black velvet. There was a label glued onto the inner top of the case *Property of Everly Area School*. It had to be Charlie's. Jac closed the lid and put the case on the ground.

Did Nathan have anything to do with any of this? Iris? Was it all Lisa? Obsessed with girls who looked similar to her missing sister?

'There you are.'

Jac gasped and spun around. Lisa was standing in front of her, smiling.

'Just thought I'd come and check on you.' Lisa's tone was light, but her cheeks were flushed, her eyes darting from Jac to the shelf, and to the flute case on the ground, then back to Jac again. Calculating. 'Frankie told me she mentioned something to you about me knowing Charlie and that you got very upset. And now I find you here. It must've taken some effort to break in. You made a real mess, and right before the open day starts.'

The way she spoke, it was as if they were having a casual conversation. But the look in her eyes told Jac she was furious. Jac didn't know what to do, how to approach Lisa with what she had found.

'I don't understand,' Jac said.

'You don't have to understand,' Lisa said. 'This has nothing to do with you.' Her voice remained friendly. 'I had a feeling you were getting closer, or, even if you weren't, I could see you weren't going to leave Everly until you had your answers. You showing up was completely unexpected. Your dad's accident was a happy coincidence. Got him out of the picture. I honestly didn't think he'd go to the cops, but Dunlop didn't do anything about it anyway. Eddie Morgan was such a loser, couldn't be taken seriously.'

'You have Charlie?' Jac asked, wanting to be sure.

Lisa raised her brows but didn't answer. Her lips turned up into a smile.

'All those girls.' Jac turned her head to the photos on the shelf. 'They look a bit like Paige.'

'How observant of you.'

'So, what's your plan? You thought it would be a great idea to abduct an innocent girl to play the role of your missing sister?' Jac needed to get out of this room. There were people downstairs who could help her.

'It's going to make it better.' Lisa sounded determined. She sounded crazy.

'Make what better?' Jac asked.

Lisa shrugged. 'It's for Mum. For me. Paige was my life. I miss her. It's all wrong without Paige. She should be here. She belongs at this hotel. She belongs here, with her family. It'll make Mum happy.' Her voice was small, pitiful, and just for a second, Jac felt sorry for her.

'Why now? Why Charlie?' Jac edged her way forward. Lisa shifted in front of the doorway.

'I've always seen girls who remind me of Paige. When I started uni, there were girls in my class who bore a resemblance to her. When I used to go out at night with my friends and drink too much, I always thought I saw her across crowded dancefloors, or ahead of me as we lined up to get into clubs. It always hurts. With teaching, there were girls, like Paige, the same age as when she…

disappeared. I tried to get to know them. I got close to some, kept their photos from the school magazines. I always wanted to bring them home in the school holidays, introduce them to Mum. I imagined how happy it would make her, but—'

'You wanted to abduct them,' Jac said. 'Call it what it is, at least.'

Lisa ignored Jac and carried on. 'When I arrived home a few months back and taught at Charlie's school, I met her, got to know her, her circumstances. We got on well. We talked a lot about her home life. She reminded me so much of Paige. After I finished at the school, I couldn't stop thinking about her. Now is the perfect time. I'm no longer teaching as I need to look after Mum. I'll be here at the hotel for good now, and I think I can give her a better life.'

Jac took another step forward, wincing as she put weight on her sprained ankle. Lisa looked down at Jac's feet and took a step towards her.

'You abducted her,' Jac said. 'You think Charlie can take the place of Paige. You're crazy. You're not going to get away with this.'

Lisa shook her head and muttered, 'I will get away this. I've put too much work into it for it not to happen.'

'And Michelle Lafferty?' Jac asked, trying to buy time so she could figure out how to make a break for it. Could she push Lisa out of the way? Or down the stairs?

'She's a young single mother who values her job and is scared of the power of the Gilmore name. I gave her money to lie if Dunlop or anyone else came around asking about Charlie Morgan, but also told her that if she told anyone about our deal, I knew someone who would hurt her and her son. Nathan knows nothing about it. But he's a useful name to throw about. Lived here for all these years but too much of a loner. People don't like that. Don't trust it.'

Jac didn't need to hear any more. She needed the cops. Nothing was going to make Lisa give up where Charlie was. She took a step back and launched herself forward, but Lisa was ready for her. When Jac pushed past her, Lisa kicked out at her injured ankle. Tripping and falling out the doorway, Jac saw the stairs rushing up to meet her. She landed at the bottom, her left wrist taking the impact and eclipsing the pain in her ankle. And Lisa was on her in seconds.

'When Frankie told me about your conversation in the music room just now, I had a feeling I needed to be prepared,' she said, taking a thin length of rope from her back pocket.

Jac started yelling, trying to get up, kicking out, but they were in such an enclosed space, she couldn't do much damage. Lisa punched her once, and Jac felt her tooth cut into her lip, tasted blood. Lisa grabbed her arms, looping the rope around her wrists. Half dragging her out into the east wing's hallway, Lisa pulled a key from her pocket. Jac scrambled to her knees, a lightning bolt of pain shot through her wrist as she tried to use her tied hands to get up.

'Help!' she called out. 'Hel—' Lisa turned and pushed her over, kicking her in the stomach, taking her voice and breath with it.

She dragged Jac inside the soldiers' hallway and picked up the torch lying on the carpet before slamming the door and plunging them into darkness. With some effort, Jac stood. It hurt to breathe and she wondered if one of her ribs was cracked. Lisa turned on the torch, its muddy yellow beam lighting the dank hallway.

'Is this where Charlie is?' she asked Lisa. 'Charlie!' she started shouting. 'Charlie!'

Lisa didn't respond to her question; instead, she pushed Jac into a room. It was the same one she had found Iris in that morning. Lisa shone the torch on the number on the door.

'Twelve A,' she said. 'You know why they do that? Thirteen's unlucky. I spent a hell of a lot of time in here and I can tell you that it was still pretty damn unlucky.'

'What are you going to do with me?' Jac asked.

'I need you out of the way. You're going to ruin everything.'

'You can't leave me in here!' Jac said.

She rushed towards Lisa, knocking her off balance and into the wall, crying out at the same time as her wrist and ribs protested with burning pain. But Lisa recovered quickly and within seconds she had pulled the door closed on Jac.

'Let me out! Help! Help!' Jac kicked at the door. And then she was silent, listening, trying to catch her breath.

'No one's going to come looking for you, Jac,' Lisa said behind the door.

The lock clicked into place and a few seconds later she heard the door to the hallway close as well. Jac sat down, taking deep breaths, the panic threatening to overtake any sensible thoughts she had.

Who knew she was staying at the hotel? Had she told anyone? Frankie knew she was here, and Tama. Nathan too, and she didn't think he had anything to do with all this now. But none of these people cared about her. Lisa could tell them she had left and that would be it. They wouldn't think about her again. No reason to. Lisa was right. No one was going to come looking for her.

FORTY-THREE

Lisa

Twenty-one years ago

LISA STOOD AT the top of the steps. 'Paige?' she whispered, leaning forward, one hand on the concrete wall. The form at the bottom of the stairs was still. 'Paige?' Lisa said again.

Her legs started shaking, and she sat down heavily on the step. But then she stood up again immediately and hurried down the steps.

'Paige…come on,' Lisa said. She crouched by her sister. She touched her arm, rubbed it. She moved up to look at Paige's head. Paige's eyes were wide open, staring into the dim basement. '*No.*'

Lisa touched Paige's face, ran the back of her hand over Paige's forehead, and down the other side.

'Paige?' She slapped her lightly. Nothing. Laying her head down on Paige's chest, she prayed for some kind of movement. The pumping of a heartbeat. A small intake of breath. Nothing. She ran her hand over Paige's hair, stopping by her ear when it reached something warm and sticky. The blood on her hand looked brown in the darkened space. She rubbed her hand on the rug, over and over, and then rubbed her hands together, eventually rubbing them both on her jeans.

It was a stupid accident.
Was it?
I didn't mean to push her.
Didn't you?

Lisa replayed the last minute. She could still feel the heat of her anger on her skin, deep in her bones.

She wasn't sure how long she had been sitting in the basement when a muted beep dragged her out of her stupor. She looked around and then down at Paige's wrist. Grabbing the clasp of Paige's watch with shaking hands, she pulled it off, silencing the alarm. It was one o'clock. Everyone would be out in the orchard now, eating lunch. Lisa looked up the stairs, then back at Paige's body, a sob escaping her lips. She wanted to scream. Instead, she put her hands tight over her mouth and let out a guttural growl that made her throat burn.

Her head played through what would surely happen next. She would go upstairs, tell Iris what had happened. Iris would go to pieces. Iris's life would be over. And so would Lisa's. She knew Iris wouldn't protect her—and why should she? Lisa had just killed her sister. She was seventeen. Would she go to prison for the rest of her life? She had a feeling Iris would make sure she would. But this couldn't be the end. She had so much she wanted to do.

So did Paige, Lisa said to herself.

She drew in a shuddering breath. Paige was supposed to be putting on a concert in a couple of hours, at the high tea.

What am I going to do?

Lisa got up and walked into the darkness of the basement. As she got closer, she could just make out the rusted gardening implements leaning against the wall in the far corner that looked like they'd disintegrate at the touch.

There was a hoe and a rake and a couple of shovels. Lisa reached for a shovel; rust peeled off the handle and stuck to her palms. She walked around the basement, prodding at the earth. Some parts felt like concrete, jarring her arms. Towards the back wall, the dirt felt damp and slightly spongy. She took a tentative stab there and a slice came away. She glanced at Paige, then walked back to her body. Kneeling down, and avoiding the vacant stare, Lisa placed a hand over her sister's eyes, closing them.

It took more than an hour to dig the shallow grave and, by the end of it, her jeans and T-shirt were stained with dirt. She leaned the shovel against the wall, and then dragged Paige's body into the hole. She tried not to think about what she was doing, keeping her gaze on the far wall, so she couldn't see her sister's blood-stained, matted hair from the injury that killed her. As she shovelled the dirt on top of Paige, she looked straight ahead, into the darkness of the basement, at her father's stuff, clothes and boxes of old records, things that he hadn't needed to take with him when he'd abandoned them. When he'd abandoned *her*. If Paige hadn't bothered with the scholarship, this never would have happened. If Iris had given Paige just a little bit of freedom, this never would have happened. If Nathan had helped more at the start to persuade Paige not to go, this never would have happened. If Paige had thought of someone other than herself for a change, this never would have happened.

But it did happen, and it's all my fault.

When she was finished, she wiped the tears and snot from her face with the bottom of her T-shirt and put the shovel back where she'd found it. She dragged boxes and suitcases and furniture from the side of the room near the door and rearranged them in the far corner, making sure the stuff covered over the site of the hole she had filled in.

Numb and exhausted, she left, first rolling up the rug and putting it onto her shoulder, pulling the door closed behind her and walking up the narrow stairs. At the top, when she opened the door to the hallway, she couldn't see anyone around, but could hear faint movement in the kitchen ten metres away. She pulled the rusty key from the back of the door and locked it from the outside, struggling as the mechanism strained into place.

She made her way to the main hallway and up the stairs without anyone seeing her. She had no idea what she would've said if someone asked her what she was doing carrying a rug around. She hurried into Paige's room, stopping for a moment to take it in: the flute case, a dress thrown on the floor, her unmade bed, the chair she had been sitting in a couple of hours before, dreaming about life away from the hotel. Lisa carefully closed the door behind her and took Paige's rucksack from the wardrobe. Into it she stuffed clothes, underwear, Paige's wallet, make-up, perfume and her flute. She carried the rucksack across to her own bedroom and pushed it into the back of her wardrobe, along with Paige's watch, the rug and the dirty clothes Lisa was wearing.

In the shower, she washed her hair and removed the dirt from her nails, scrubbing at her body until it stung. Her guilt, anger and sadness couldn't be washed off, though, and she got out of the shower feeling no better. On her left hand, on one of her knuckles, she noticed a small dirt-filled scratch, and on the other knuckles, a streak of dark reddish brown she'd missed. Her stomach lurched and she wiped her thumb across her knuckles, harder and harder until the smudge disappeared, but so hard the scratch started bleeding. She ran her hand under the tap in the bathroom and inspected it. Better. She dried her hair, brushed it and then slipped on the dress Iris had told her to wear today, the navy one with small white polka dots.

The grief came then. Hitting her so hard she crumpled onto the floor.

No more Paige.

She was going to leave me anyway.

Lisa didn't want to think about what the next few hours, days, weeks, years would bring. She would take it as it came. She choked on a sob and pressed her lips shut. She got up and looked at herself in the mirror.

I haven't seen Paige since this morning.

Yes, it looks like some of her clothes are missing...and her perfume and make-up.

No, I'm not sure where her flute is. It's usually by her music stand. She never goes anywhere without it.

Lisa nodded. That's the way the story would go. Paige had run away. The talented, beautiful daughter of a demanding and possessive mother was finally free.

FORTY-FOUR

Charlie

Sunday afternoon

CHARLIE LOOKED AT the digital watch as it beeped midday. No one had come down this morning, and she didn't know if that was a good sign or a bad sign. At first there was relief. Then there was the thought that had been buried just below the surface since she had been locked up in this place: *They're going to leave me here to die.*

Sitting on the dirt floor, her stomach grumbled, even though food was the last thing on her mind. She leaned her aching back against the stretcher. It was no use. She had dug as deep as she could and she was still at least an inch off being able to crawl under the wire cage. The ground had got rockier the deeper she went, which made it impossible to dig any further.

She glanced over at the skull, steadying her breathing, wondering how long it had been there. How did they die? Charlie crawled over to it and looked into the hollow pits where its eyes had been.

Tell me your story. Did the same person do to you what they're doing to me? Did they keep you here? Did you die down here?

Charlie swallowed. Her future seemed clearer. If she could call it that. She knew now that, at some stage, she was going to die down here. Futile as it might have been, she grabbed her spoon and began to dig again.

As she was attacking the dirt, she heard the snap of the lock, the groan of a door being opened. She looked up, peering through the cage and into the darkness. There were footsteps approaching, scuffing on the dirt. She waited, backing up towards her stretcher, but when the figure finally presented itself in the insipid light of the lantern, Charlie thought she must be seeing things. Her mind, maybe still blurry from the drugs, was offering up an image that couldn't be right. She shut her eyes tight, then opened them again, but the image remained.

'Miss Gilmore?' she said, her heartbeat quickening in excitement. 'Why are you here? How did you find me?' She ran up to the side of the cage, avoiding the hole to her left. A sob escaped and the tears that came were of intense relief.

Miss Gilmore smiled and Charlie thought it was the most wonderful thing she had ever seen. She felt the tension, anxiety and fear melt away.

'Can you let me out?' She linked her fingers around the wire mesh of the cage and rattled it. 'They might be back soon. We need to be quick.' Her voice was croaky from disuse. She held a hand to her thumping head.

'Your sore head,' she said. 'It's a combination of sleeping pills and you knocking your head when you passed out in the music room,' Miss Gilmore said.

'What? What are you talking about?' Charlie replied, confused.

But Miss Gilmore was now looking down at the mess

of dug-up dirt and rocks inside the cage, her eyes widened and her mouth opened.

'I know, it's terrible… I don't know who it is,' Charlie said, looking down at the skull, clearing her throat so she could be heard. 'I… I was trying to escape. I was trying to dig under the cage… Please, help me.' She realised now that Miss Gilmore hadn't uttered a single comforting word, and didn't look relieved that she had found Charlie.

'What have you done?' Miss Gilmore whispered.

Charlie knew then, from her reaction, that something wasn't right. It was like Miss Gilmore didn't even know who she was. She had hardly even looked at Charlie.

Miss Gilmore didn't seem surprised she was down here or relieved she had been found. Right now, she was backing away from the cage, not unlocking it, her eyes on the unearthed skull in the hole by Charlie's foot. Then Miss Gilmore moved forward again and finally unlocked the cage door. She stepped inside and stood over the skull, making a whimpering noise and covering her face. She breathed in deeply once, exhaled and then walked towards Charlie, backing her into the darkest corner.

'Clean it up. Cover her up. Fill in the hole.' Her voice was low and quiet.

'I don't understand any of this,' Charlie said. 'What are you doing?'

Miss Gilmore didn't answer her.

'My dad will be looking for me, you know.' Charlie had no idea if this was true or not, but Miss Gilmore didn't know that. 'You're not going to get away with this.'

'You need to forget about your dad. You belong here now, okay?' Miss Gilmore's voice had lost the sharp edge. 'Forget about that other life you lived. You're going to be so happy here. It's going to go back to the way it was always meant to be. I'll be back at seven tonight. Make sure you're ready. Put these on.' She threw her a long floaty skirt with square front pockets and a black silky short-sleeved shirt. 'Do the make-up, like the photo. Remember the perfume.'

Charlie didn't answer.

'Got it?' Miss Gilmore grabbed Charlie's face in her hands and squeezed. 'I can't have you messing this up.'

Charlie nodded and Miss Gilmore released her grasp, caressing her cheek instead. 'This is going to be perfect.' She turned and stopped at the skull, bending down and brushing a hand along the side of it. 'Paige,' she whispered.

The wire cage slammed shut and Miss Gilmore locked it. Charlie edged forward.

'Fill in the hole,' Miss Gilmore said. 'She doesn't deserve to be dug up like that. This is her resting place. You need to leave her in peace.' Then she disappeared into the shadows and Charlie heard the door slam and lock.

She couldn't believe it. Miss Gilmore had been her teacher, if only for a short time. She had taken an interest in her. Praised her, complimented her on her flute playing. She eased herself onto her knees. Miss Gilmore was right about one thing, this was Paige's resting place, for better or worse, and so she pushed the piles of dirt into the small trench, covering up the skull. Covering Paige. What had happened to her all those years ago? Miss Gilmore obviously knew Paige. Even cared about her. As Charlie pushed the last bit of dirt over Paige's skull, she whispered, 'I'm sorry this happened to you.'

She looked at Paige in the photo Miss Gilmore had obviously given her. She had given her exactly the same outfit that Paige was wearing that day. Charlie hadn't studied much else in the photo over the last few days; mostly she had looked at Paige's face, noticing the similarities between this girl and herself. But now she looked at the background. The photo was taken outside, and Paige was standing on a grassy area, rose bushes to her left. Out of focus, behind her right shoulder, a two-storey building loomed. It was bright white with a red roof, a turret in the far corner.

She knew that place.

'Gilmore Hotel,' she whispered. And that's when it came back to her. That little spark she needed to ignite a memory that had refused to make itself clear. She reached into the corners of her brain that had been foggy for so long. Little bits came together, started connecting. Miss Gilmore had taught her a few months ago at school. She remembered that, of course, but there was something else. An invitation to come up to the hotel. Walking through the bush with her flute case. Miss Gilmore meeting her at the back of the hotel, ushering her into the music room and closing the door.

Charlie closed her eyes, the memory fading in and out, like clouds passing over the sun. Old Mrs Gilmore had come in while she was playing the flute with Miss Gilmore. That was it, nothing else. She felt the back of her head, still tender, remembering Miss Gilmore's words a few minutes ago, 'You knocked your head when you passed out in the music room'. Miss Gilmore offering a drink after she had played. She remembered feeling light-headed. The last thing she remembered was Miss Gilmore rushing towards her but she mustn't have been quick enough.

She knew of old Mrs Gilmore. Most kids were scared of her, said she was a hermit. A bit crazy. She knew Jac and her friends used to sneak up to the hotel when they had been drinking. Dared each other to go inside. Jac had told her she had made it inside once. She vaguely remembered hearing about a girl going missing years ago. Was that Paige? Old Mrs Gilmore's daughter? So, would that mean Miss Gilmore was Paige's sister?

Charlie looked around the darkened room as if it could give her some clue. She was at the Gilmore Hotel. All this time she had only been five hundred metres from home. For what seemed like the hundredth time she wondered where her dad was. What was he doing? Had he told Jac? Charlie was sure people would be out looking for her. That's the way this kind of thing went. A teenage girl goes missing and people start searching. The newspapers get involved. Was everyone out looking for her? Had they looked for her at the hotel? Had they walked the grounds shouting her name? Come inside? Searched? It was a big place. Had they questioned the Gilmores? And how about that gardener who worked here? She shuddered thinking about the way he looked at her when he came into the cafe, the way his fingers purposely touched hers as she gave him his change.

She took a deep breath and let out a long scream, and then she started yelling, 'Help me! Help! I'm in here!' Even though it felt like her skull was going to split in two.

There would be someone out there putting all of this together. They would be here soon. She had to believe it.

FORTY-FIVE

Lisa

Twenty-one years ago

LISA WAS IN PAIN. Actual physical pain. Her skin felt like it was covered in small stinging paper cuts. Her stomach cramped intermittently, causing her to draw her legs up and cocoon herself in her bed. It had started last night, late, after everyone had left, casting sympathetic looks as they went and making promises that only Lisa knew they couldn't keep. The police officer had said they would resume the search first thing. Iris had trudged up to bed, muttering, refusing to accept the worst.

All night Lisa had replayed over and over in her head what had happened. What she had done. She wanted to take it back, of course she did. She had never wanted anything so badly in her life as to see Paige sneak into her room right now, climb into her bed, and talk about the open day. Instead she was alone, the guilt and sadness tearing her up from the inside out. And she deserved it. She deserved to be in pain for the rest of her life.

When Paige hadn't turned up for the high tea recital, at first, Iris had been livid. She walked around the music room, talking to people, laughing, but every time she came across Lisa, she would hiss in her ear, 'Where is she? Find her!'

Lisa put up the pretence of looking for her. Asking Miss Hastings and some of the volunteers. Walking the grounds and searching the rooms on shaking legs a high-pitched buzzing in her ears. By the time the open day was finished and the spring day had clouded over, Lisa saw Iris's temper waning and a new emotion cross her face: worry. At eight pm, on Miss Hastings' advice, Iris called the police. Word spread and the hotel and grounds were searched and, when Paige wasn't found, the whispers started. Who had taken her? Had there been an accident? Did she run away?

Lisa looked at the clock on her bedside table: seven am. She hauled her aching body out of bed and pulled on shorts and a T-shirt. As she adjusted her T-shirt, she glanced at the knuckles on her left hand; the scratch was barely visible now, but she could see the reddish-brown hue she had seen the afternoon before, when she'd got out of the shower. She licked her thumb and pushed it across her knuckles harder and harder with no success. She flung open the curtains, holding her hand to the light. Apart from aggravating the small scratch again, her knuckles were clean. Satisfied, she made her way downstairs, which, even at this time, was already a flurry of activity. The front door was open and she could see a group of people outside, at least thirty of them, being instructed by Constable Johnston, Everly's sole police officer. Lisa turned and walked through the doors to the back entrance hallway and into the kitchen, where she found Nancy making sandwiches.

The woman placed the knife on the bench and rushed over to her. 'Oh, my darling.' She drew Lisa into a hug and Lisa burst into tears. 'It's okay, pet. It's all going to

be okay. They'll start looking again today. We'll find her.'
She patted Lisa's back, then blew her nose into a tissue
and continued buttering bread.

Lisa wanted to shout out that, no, it wasn't going to be
okay, but she stayed quiet.

All morning the volunteers searched every inch of the
orchard, the creek where she and Paige swam and the
thick bush at the back of the property. Abseiling gear was
supplied by one of the caving companies and some of the
larger caves in the area were searched.

Just before lunch, Lisa watched Iris produce a key for
the door to the basement. She didn't know Iris had one.
Constable Johnston flicked on the light and made his way
down, while Lisa, her heart in her throat, stood beside Iris
at the top of the stairs, hoping she didn't notice the rug
was missing. But how often did her mother go into the
basement? He was down there for less than thirty seconds; he called Paige's name, waved a torch around and
then reappeared, shaking his head.

'Well, of course she's not down there,' Iris sniffed.

'We have to search everywhere, Ms Gilmore. We can't
assume.' His eyes were kind but his voice was firm.

After lunch, Constable Johnston sat in an armchair
in the lounge. Iris sat on a couch and Lisa sat in another
armchair, as far away from Iris as possible. They both
needed comfort but weren't seeking it from each other.
Constable Johnston looked at them both in turn, with a
sympathetic smile. The stubble covering the lower half
of his face was the same colour as his greying hair. Lisa
thought he looked friendly, like a local policeman should.

'Just a few questions,' he said to Iris, 'so we know
we're doing everything we can to get Paige home. Okay?'

Iris didn't say anything. Today, she seemed to be either

dazed and in another world, or trawling the rooms and grounds, directing the search parties, even though they were being led by Constable Johnston.

'Do you know if Paige was in a relationship with anyone?'

Iris and Lisa were both quiet. Did Iris know about Nathan and Paige? Lisa wondered.

'Yes. With Nathan,' Lisa said, making Nathan a prime suspect with those three words. She turned to Iris but she didn't look shocked.

'It was nothing serious,' Iris said.

How would you know? Lisa thought.

'And what's that got to do with anything?' Iris added.

Constable Johnston ignored Iris's question and looked at the notebook in front of him. 'Nathan Thomson? He works here?'

Iris nodded.

'He's been very involved in the search so far,' Johnston said. 'I'll be talking to him this morning.'

'Nathan wouldn't have hurt Paige,' Iris said.

Johnston scribbled something down and asked, 'Do you know if she had—has—any enemies? Possibly someone who would want to cause her harm?'

'Paige?' Iris exclaimed, in disbelief. 'Everyone loved her.'

'You've both checked her bedroom, like I asked. Have you noticed anything missing?' A pencil hovered over his pad.

Iris and Lisa both nodded.

'Can you let me know what you noticed was missing?'

Iris didn't speak, gazing out the windows instead.

Lisa took a deep breath, ignoring the buzzing in her head that took her back to yesterday as she stuffed Paige's belongings into a rucksack that was now sitting in her wardrobe along with the blood-stained rug. 'Clothes, her perfume and make-up, her wallet and her flute.'

'Is it possible Paige may have run away?' he asked.

'No,' Iris said. 'She would never do that to me.' Iris blinked rapidly, as if she was confused by such a suggestion.

'Okay. We'll continue the search, of course. We'll stay in contact with you. As you know, there were a lot of people here yesterday and we need to speak to everyone. Everyone's been very cooperative so far.'

Johnston stood, flipping through his notepad. 'If you'll excuse me, I need to speak to… Nancy McGowan. Please, don't get up,' he said to Iris. 'I'll let you know of any developments. Just…sit tight.'

'Sit tight,' Iris muttered 'Where is she? Where can she be?' Iris didn't look at Lisa. They hadn't talked directly to each other all day.

Lisa felt the lounge room closing in on her. The air felt stale, suffocating. She ran from the hotel, down the dirt path, only stopping at the creek. She could see a line of people disappearing into the thick bush on the other side. Nathan was one of them, stooped shoulders, eyes on the ground in front of him. She wished this could all be over. But she didn't know what *over* meant. Was *over* when the search party gave up? Was *over* Constable Johnston saying there was nothing more they could do? Was *over* everyone going back to normal—school and work? For Lisa, it would never be over.

FORTY-SIX

Charlie

Sunday evening

CHARLIE SPRAYED THE perfume onto her bare wrists and then dabbed them against her neck. She looked at the digital watch: 6.45 pm. It was almost time. Whatever was going to happen, it was about to start. She looked around her prison. She had filled in the hole like Miss Gilmore had asked, covered Paige back up and then rolled the carpet back into place. Covering up the mystery of Paige Gilmore. She wondered if anyone would ever find out what had happened to her. But maybe, she thought again, those closest to her already knew.

She paced the room, pressing her lips together, feeling the unfamiliar sheen of lipstick—Paige's lipstick, then stopped when she heard the key in the lock.

She heard footsteps and Miss Gilmore appeared, standing in front of the cage, scanning the floor. She nodded. The cage slid open and she stepped inside. Charlie edged her way back, past the stretcher, so her back was jammed against the wall.

'Hello, Paige,' Miss Gilmore said, avoiding eye contact, her eyes flitting to Charlie's mouth or chin, or up and over her shoulder.

Miss Gilmore walked towards her. She looked friendly, like the Miss Gilmore who had taught her, who had told her how talented she was—different from a few hours before, when she had threatened Charlie, telling her to be ready, to clean up the mess she had made.

It's because I'm not Charlie anymore, she reminded herself. *I'm Paige.*

Miss Gilmore stopped in front of her and enveloped Charlie into a hug. She buried her face in Charlie's neck and inhaled. Charlie tensed. 'I've missed you,' Miss Gilmore whispered. 'So, so much.'

Who was Lisa to Paige? Was she her sister? Did she put Paige in the ground?

'You look beautiful,' Miss Gilmore said. 'This is going to make everything better.' She leaned forward and kissed Charlie's cheek. 'With you back again, everything will be better.' She stepped away from Charlie, taking in her outfit.

'Miss Gilmore, please, I don't understand what's—'

'My name's Lisa,' she said. 'You call me Lisa. Now, we need to get upstairs.'

Upstairs? Charlie thought. *I'm getting out?*

If she could get out of this cage and up those stairs, maybe she had a better chance of getting away. She didn't know the inside of the Gilmore Hotel at all, but once she was outside, she was positive she could orient herself— and even if she couldn't, who cared? She just needed to get away from this place.

'Right.' Lisa clapped her hands together, unable to hide her excitement, her eyes bright. 'Let's go.'

Charlie, following Lisa, stepped out into the darkness across the dirt floor, to a door and up some concrete steps. Immediately, she felt light-headed and her legs wobbled just from the effort of climbing the stairs. She was weak and wondered if she would have the strength to fight or run when she got the chance. Lisa opened a second door out onto a narrow hallway. Charlie squinted, the lights hurting her eyes. She followed Lisa through yet another door. To the left a few metres away looked like an exterior door, but they turned right and went through a set of double swinging doors and stepped into a wide hallway, the polished wooden floors so clean she could make out her blurry reflection. There was not a single sound apart from their footsteps on the floor. She could see the front door, and possible freedom, at the very end, and closed doors on either side along the hallway. To her left was the staircase leading to the second floor. The place felt like a maze and her head swam. She stumbled and Lisa caught her arm, whispering, 'You're okay.' Charlie lowered her head. She had traded one prison for another and, right now, she felt her basement room might be preferable to whatever was coming next.

FORTY-SEVEN

Lisa

Twenty-one years ago

LISA HAD NEVER felt so alone in the days and weeks that followed the open day. Nathan was closely questioned after Paige's disappearance. From what Lisa picked up, he cooperated completely, admitted they were in a relationship. He told the police about her scholarship, too, which they questioned both Iris and Lisa about.

Lisa saw the look of shock on Iris's face and the quick recovery. Iris told the police that, yes, of course she was aware of the scholarship. The police asked her if she had given Paige permission to take it up next year, and again she said yes. In the end, the scholarship became just another sad detail in Paige Gilmore's disappearance.

When the police finally finished with Nathan, they found he had always been with someone the day of the open day, doing tours, answering questions about the garden, always in view. Lisa wasn't questioned too closely. She had told the police she had helped with the games and answered questions from visitors inside the hotel. She said she had been in the orchard at lunchtime, that she hadn't seen Paige there. Iris couldn't refute the fact Lisa had been in the orchard because Iris never cared or noted where Lisa was. No one ever suspected she had anything to do with her beloved sister's disappearance. No one. Not a single person. It didn't make her feel any better.

Nathan left for a month soon after. With Iris's blessing, he went in search of Paige. Lisa didn't know where he went, where he thought Paige may have gone, but when he returned, he looked wrecked. He and Iris grew closer. Lisa often saw them talking together. Paige's disappearance had created a bond between them. Every weekend, he left the hotel early in the morning to search the bushland around Everly, which had already been scoured multiple times.

One afternoon, she heard someone in Paige's room and found Nathan going through her drawers. Some of her clothes and the sheets from her bed were haphazardly folded in his arms. 'I just don't want to forget her. And her smell.' Lisa understood but still wanted him out of her sister's room. He didn't belong here inside the hotel. It wasn't his place.

Ultimately, due to the fact that some of Paige's clothes were missing, plus her wallet and flute, and absolutely no evidence of any kind of accident or foul play, Paige Gilmore was officially a missing person. Some people in Everly had come to the theory that Paige had been under her mother's thumb too long, that she had finally had enough and broken free. And there was the other gossip, people wanting more from the hotel on the hill, for it to live up to its past. Some thought Iris had killed Paige after she found out about Paige's plans to leave. Some thought it was Nathan, young love gone wrong. Some spoke about a man, not a local, who was seen at the open day, staring at Paige, and they suspected him of having led her off into the bush. But these were just rumours, shared between families sitting around the dinner table, or groups of friends at the pub. People always had an opinion when asked, 'What do you think happened to Paige Gilmore?'

Lisa finished up the school year in a daze. She was excused from final assessments and only attended school because she couldn't bear to be at the hotel with Iris and her grief, which filled every room. Some of Lisa's teachers had taken her aside, talked to her in low tones about her loss, but really they just wanted the inside scoop. Miss Hastings, Lisa thought, had taken it hard. She often sought out Lisa in the music room, where she hid at lunchtime, offering her comfort, a chance to talk. Lisa appreciated it but never said anything. When school had broken up for the summer holidays a few weeks later, Miss Hastings came up to the hotel every week to sit with Iris. She seemed to be the only person who could bring Iris out of her haze of bereavement. But Lisa never stuck around when Miss Hastings was there. She had a way of looking at her that made Lisa think she knew something.

It's called a guilty conscience, she told herself.

The doctor who had come to check on Iris in the days after Paige's disappearance told Lisa there was nothing physically wrong with her and gave her sedatives to help her sleep. When Iris hadn't got any better a month later, he told Lisa she was grieving and needed time.

'Try and be there for her, to listen, or just to sit with her.'

So, they would sit in the lounge after dinner. One evening, Lisa moved over to the couch where Iris was sitting, taking the spot where Paige had normally sat. Iris looked at her, her face lighting up for just a moment, before she realised it was Lisa and not Paige.

The doctor had told Iris she was only supposed to take

the sedatives at night to help her sleep. But Lisa knew she took them more than that, and she didn't mind. They made Iris a bit softer around the edges. Every now and then, she would speak to Lisa, as a mother would to her teenage daughter. From the chaise longue by the windows, she would call out to Lisa when she got home from school, asking her how her day was. Her speech was often slurred, her eyes hooded, but Lisa would ignore that and bathe in the attention, words falling from her mouth in excitement, ignoring the blank, faraway look on Iris's face that would eventually follow. Then the frown would come. Iris would look around. Look at Lisa and then, everything clicking into place, she would sigh and turn away. During these times, Lisa wanted to tell Iris so much more than just how her day at school was. She wanted her to know that she liked school but loved music, maybe even more than Paige had done, but she knew by now not to mention her sister's name. She wanted Iris to know she would like to be a teacher, that she found the boys at school silly and immature, and that she missed Paige more than anything.

Christmas passed by like any other day. There was no tree, no presents. Iris took herself off to bed on New Year's Eve at eight o'clock. Lisa had been invited to a party. Her popularity had increased since Paige's disappearance, but Lisa wasn't dumb enough to think it meant anything. The kids at school only wanted a bit of gossip, wanted, somehow, to be attached to the sister of the girl who went missing. So instead, Lisa went up to the turret, a bottle of expensive wine in her hand, and saw the new year in by herself. Shedding tears for her sister, three floors below, and for herself, unable to see how life was going to get any better.

Four months on, with summer over, life without Paige

was exactly how Lisa thought it would be. Like a light had gone out and her days were filled with darkness.

It was the Friday evening of the final week in March. The weekend loomed in front of Lisa, never-ending. Monday seemed impossibly far away. Nancy had left for the weekend. 'You just ring if you need anything, pet, okay?' she had whispered to Lisa on her way out the back door, relief plastered over her face. Iris was never easy to work for and, since Paige's disappearance, Nancy had had to put up with Iris's terrible mood swings. Lisa wondered how much longer poor Nancy would last at the hotel.

Lisa now edged closer to Iris, joining her on the sofa in front of the unlit fire. Her mother looked far older than her fifty-eight years. She had stopped wearing make-up and her greying hair fell limp around her face. Iris prided herself on her appearance but for months she had drifted around the hotel, walking from room to room, in one or other of the three dressing gowns she owned.

Sitting next to Iris, Lisa wasn't sure what to say, so she placed a hand on top of hers. Iris looked up. Lisa knew she wasn't really looking at her, more through her.

'Paige…' Iris said.

Lisa didn't say anything. She didn't want to break the spell. Iris held her arms open. Lisa hesitated, and then sunk into her mother's embrace, the feeling at once comfortable and foreign. She was still as Iris rubbed her hand up and down her back. She buried her face in Lisa's hair, breathed in, and then stopped. Iris sat back, her eyes coming into focus, the spell broken.

'I'm sorry,' Lisa whispered. She didn't know what she was apologising for: Paige's death or tricking Iris into showing affection.

She sometimes thought confessing would ease the burden, and the words often sat on her tongue, ready to fall out in a jumble. When she felt like this, it made her nervous, like she was unable to control herself, and she bit the inside of her cheek to stop the confession.

'What are you sorry for?' Iris turned to Lisa, her eyes vacant again.

'I'm sorry...' *Be careful.* 'I'm sorry that Paige isn't here.'

Iris shrugged, her gaze shifting around the room. 'Nothing you can do about it.'

'I'm here,' Lisa said, with hope, grabbing Iris's hand, wanting that contact again. Her palm felt warm and clammy.

Iris looked down at their hands. 'Yes, you are here.' She pulled her hand from Lisa's grasp and stood. 'It should have been you,' Iris said, her mouth slack.

'What?' Lisa had heard perfectly, but the shock had made her question Iris.

'It should've been you.'

Iris walked from the room, her slippered feet shuffling across the floor. Lisa watched her leave, Iris's words stinging like she had been slapped.

Once Iris had made her way up the stairs, Lisa took herself off to the library. On the top shelf, only able to be reached by a ladder, she removed the copy of *War and Peace*, and retrieved the rusted key she kept hidden there, taped on the back inside cover. As for Iris's spare basement key, Lisa had found an opportunity to steal it after Johnston's inspection and had hidden it with Paige's things in her wardrobe. As far as she knew, Iris didn't even know it was missing.

Downstairs in the basement, she unlocked the door and turned on the light. She came down here often, at least once a week, the smell and feel of this place took her back to that day and what had happened. She always had to wait a few seconds, steadying herself, before she could walk down the steps. Hating having the blood-stained rug in her wardrobe and not knowing what else to do, she had brought it down one night and added it to the collection of junk, jamming it into a corner. She had shifted all the boxes and furniture that she used to cover Paige's resting place that day back against the wall. She wanted access to the ground, to be close to her. Lying down on the damp, compacted dirt, she ran a hand over the earth.

'Hi,' she said, her voice a whisper. She cleared her throat. 'It's hard. So hard. You know how sorry I am, don't you, Paige? You know it was an accident... Iris isn't well. I want to make things better. I want to be there for her. I want her to know that, even though one daughter's gone, she still has another one. Maybe it's just going to take some time.' She nodded to herself in the dark. 'Time is all we need.'

She knew she was kidding herself. She knew that what Iris needed to get better was Paige. Iris needed Paige in her life, just like Lisa needed her. Paige was the one who held their dysfunctional unit together and now she was gone. What was Lisa supposed to do about this? She wasn't sure yet. But she would make it better, somehow.

FORTY-EIGHT

Jac

Sunday evening

JAC HAD SCREAMED and yelled and banged on all four walls of her prison. There were hundreds of people in and around Gilmore Hotel—someone had to be able to hear her. There was a thin rectangle of light coming through the window that had been boarded up. She had already tried to prise off the board but, in the process, a splinter had lodged under one of her fingernails. With her teeth, she had tried to undo the rope that bound her wrists, but she couldn't get anywhere apart from slightly fraying it. She paced out the room, hands out in front of her in the dark. It was five long strides by five. When she managed to calm down, resting her voice for now, she sat in the middle of the room, almost every part of her aching, from her twisted ankle and wrist, her ribs, her swollen lip. She ran her fingers over the floorboards, stopping and pulling away when she felt a notch in one of them. She scooted back against the wall, as far away as possible, knowing who she was sharing the room with. What had happened all those years ago? A young Iris had had a baby out of wedlock with someone Helen disapproved of. Had she kept Iris in here? Was this where Iris gave birth to her baby? Jac shivered, thinking about what Iris would have gone through.

Don't feel sorry for her. Don't feel sorry for any of them.

Jac had never been afraid of the dark, even when she was a child. She had always liked being alone, away from her noisy and most often drunk parents, the blaring TV. Bedtime, to her, was solitary comfort. She leaned back against the wall. Her throat ached from yelling. How long had she been here? It felt like hours but she couldn't make out the hands on her watch.

Was this all just Lisa? Did Iris and Nathan really have nothing to do with it? She was still struggling to put the puzzle together. As her mind spun, she tried to ignore the one thought that was vying for attention above everything else.

What if they leave me here? What if no one comes?

Is that what Charlie was thinking too? Where was she? Was she close by?

Jac felt completely hopeless but she didn't cry. She had learned from an early age that it was pointless, didn't get you anywhere or anything.

It may have been minutes later, or hours, when she heard a key in the door. She got up from the floor, favouring her right leg, and prepared herself, ready to run or attack, whatever option presented itself first. She was expecting Lisa, but when the door opened she saw the outline of Iris, carrying a torch.

'Jac!' Iris stepped back in shock. 'My goodness! What are you doing in here?' She didn't wait for an answer and continued talking. 'A visitor mentioned to one of the volunteers this morning that they heard some kind of commotion upstairs. I was only just told—thought I'd better come and investigate.'

Jac limped out into the hallway, the light from Iris's torch and the east wing's hallway lighting the space.

'What were you doing in there?' the old woman asked again.

'Iris, I know this sounds…bad…but I think Lisa may have taken Charlie.'

'Charlie?' Iris echoed, eyes squinting, trying to pull up a memory.

'My sister!' Jac yelled, unsure if Iris was putting on an act. 'Charlie's my sister and she's been missing for a week. I think she's somewhere in the hotel.'

'I know everything that goes on under this roof and there's no one being hidden anywhere, dear.'

Iris's calm manner was infuriating Jac. 'Check these other rooms for me, please.'

Iris looked alarmed, her eyes widening, the set of keys jiggling in her hands. When she didn't do anything, Jac grabbed them and went to the first door.

'Your hands,' Iris said. 'Why are you tied up?'

She sounded genuinely confused and Jac ignored her as, with some difficulty, she forced the key into the old lock, only to realise that it wasn't locked. She rammed a shoulder into the door and it opened. She did the same with the other four rooms along the abandoned hallway. Each time, she was met with a musty, mouldy smell. There was nothing in any of the rooms. Nothing that suggested anyone had been in them for years.

'Nothing but ghosts and past mistakes in there,' Iris muttered.

'She must be somewhere else,' Jac said. 'Where else could Lisa hide her?' Jac was assuming that Charlie had been abducted and hidden away, and tried not to think about the other, more violent and final alternative.

Iris adjusted the long cardigan she was wearing, pulling it around her body, looking at Jac like she was mad.

'Iris, could you please untie me?' Jac held up her hands.

But Iris only took the keys Jac was still holding.

'Iris? Could you please untie me and then I think we need to call the police?' Jac was starting to shake, the fear that this old woman wasn't going to help her becoming more and more real.

'The police? I don't think that's necessary, is it?'

'What? Of course it's necessary.' But Jac could see she wasn't getting through to her.

'Come on. I don't like it here,' Iris said.

They walked out into the east wing's hallway, where Iris stopped and turned to Jac. 'Your lip...' she said.

Jac probed her swollen lip with her tongue.

'How did you end up locked in that room?' Iris asked.

'Lisa,' Jac said, waiting for her reaction. 'She did this to me as well.' She raised her bound hands to indicate her lip.

'Oh, no, surely not.' Iris chuckled as if Jac had told a faintly amusing joke. She stopped at her room and Jac watched her go in and put the keys back in her drawer.

'Iris, if you could please untie me. Then we can call the police.'

Iris stopped at the top of the stairs. She looked at Jac, her eyes narrowing. 'You seem very angry. I don't like all this talk of the police and the way you're accusing the people who live here.'

'Mum? Are you there?' Lisa's voice came from downstairs.

'You need to forget all this nonsense. Or perhaps you should just leave,' Iris said, taking the stairs slowly, one at a time, hand grasped around the banister.

Jac knew she should leave, make a run for it. But what

would happen to Charlie in the time it took her to contact the cops and for them to arrive?

Jac stuck close to Iris. Lisa wasn't expecting to see her, and she didn't know how she was going to react.

Lisa's voice rang out again. 'Mum, we're in the dining room.'

'Yes, yes, coming.' Iris's tone was clipped.

Jac walked into the dining room behind Iris, concealing herself as much as possible. The heavy curtains had already been pulled closed. Jac glanced down at her watch: seven pm. She had been locked up for most of the day. She squinted, her eyes adjusting to the light in the dining room. All the chandeliers were off, and only a dim glow came from the wall sconces. Candles ran the length of the long table, their flickering flames casting dancing shadows on the off-white lace tablecloth.

Lisa was standing at the head of the table, and the smile fell from her face when she saw Jac.

Lisa turned her gaze to the far end of the long table, causing Iris and Jac to both turn and look. And everything else was forgotten as, at the same time, Iris said, 'Paige?' and Jac breathed out in a sigh of relief, 'Charlie.'

FORTY-NINE

Jac

Sunday evening

JAC WATCHED IRIS make her way down the table to where Charlie was seated at the end, each chair she passed used as a crutch. Lisa came to Iris's side and took her hand, leading her to Charlie. Charlie's gaze hadn't left Jac's since she had walked into the room.

I see you, Jac wanted to shout. *I'm here. I'm not going anywhere*.

Jac thought of the various escape routes. No doubt the front and back doors would be locked, considering what was going on now. Lisa wouldn't have wanted anyone wandering in—or breaking out. Would it just be a matter of turning a deadbolt or would she need a key? There were the French doors in the lounge, that opened out onto the front of the hotel—how fiddly would it be to open them? She tried to think of the latches on them but hadn't noticed when she had been in there over the past few days. Maybe her best hope was upstairs. She could grab her phone and call the police. Where was Tama? He obviously wasn't here with this charade going on. Was Nathan only a few metres away in the staff quarters? There were too many questions and no obvious way she could get Charlie away from these people. At the moment, all she could do was watch the weird show that was playing out in front of her.

Iris released her hand from Lisa's, stepping away from her, then bent down and drew Charlie into a hug. Charlie's head pushed into Iris's breast. 'I knew it! I knew it!' Iris said, tears in her eyes. 'Didn't I say,' she turned to Lisa, who was now standing on the other side of Charlie. 'Didn't I always say she'd be back.'

Lisa nodded, the smile on her face telling Jac she believed all of this. But while Lisa was beaming at Iris, Jac watched as her thumb rubbed across her knuckles, back and forth.

Iris crouched down beside Charlie. 'Oh, my beautiful, beautiful girl. Where have you been all this time? No—no, don't say anything. Just let me look at you.' Iris held Charlie's face in her hands, kissed each cheek and sat down beside her, moving her chair closer so there was no room between them.

Charlie's gaze wandered back to Jac's, pleading. 'Jac,' she could see her mouth move but couldn't hear her across the room.

Run, Jac mouthed to her. *Get up. Run.*

Charlie shook her head. Was she too scared? What had Lisa done to her over the last few days?

'Dinner's organised,' Lisa said. 'We can all sit down and have a lovely meal.'

'Of course, of course.' Iris pulled a plate and knife and fork over for herself, so she could stay sitting right beside Charlie.

'Tama has arranged everything for us,' Lisa said. 'Unfortunately, he won't be working here anymore. He had his last day here today. And the same with Nathan. He's just left too.' Lisa looked at Jac as she said this. She was telling her there was no help.

'Both gone?' Iris asked.

Lisa nodded, and Jac waited for Iris to kick off—surely she would have something to say about that. But instead, she turned back to Charlie. It was Charlie and Jac against Lisa and Iris. Jac knew they could do this. They at least needed to get out of the dining room together and Jac somehow needed to get her hands untied. Jac looked at Charlie, then nodded. She could tell Charlie was terrified, her face pale and eyes wide. As Iris put her hand on Charlie's, she whipped it away like she'd been burned. Iris either didn't notice or pretended not to.

Jac braced herself and said, 'Run, Charlie!' And then she turned and ran from the dining room, hoping that Lisa would come for her, and that Charlie could push Iris aside and follow. Jac ran up the staircase and heard hurried footsteps behind her. She ignored the pain from various parts of her body and propelled herself up but then a hand grabbed her ankle and she fell, knocking her head on the corner of the wall at the top of the stairs. She blinked hard twice, the pain in her head overriding all her other injuries, and watched, helpless, as Lisa towered above her.

FIFTY

Charlie

Sunday evening

CHARLIE SAT UP straight in her chair, the wooden back digging into her shoulder blades. The old woman, Iris, put her hand on hers again and Charlie snatched it away, the contact of her slightly damp and warm skin making Charlie shudder.

'Goodness me, such drama,' Iris said, after Lisa had rushed from the room. 'Lisa can take care of that. That woman shouldn't really be here. Now, darling,' Iris said, 'have a drink, you must be parched. You would've had such a long day.'

Where does she think I've been? Where does she think Paige has been?

The fire in the grate behind her was sending out waves of heat, making her lean towards the table, trying to escape it. In front of her, she felt the heat from the candles, too, which forced her to move back again. She watched the tapered candles flickering, lighting one half of the old woman's face and leaving the other half in shadow.

Iris didn't seem to care that Charlie hadn't spoken a word to her yet and continued speaking. 'Remember when we bought that skirt?' She ran her hand along Charlie's thigh, feeling the material, making Charlie squirm away from her touch. 'You'd been wanting it for ages. You look so beautiful. Although, what you must think of me…' She patted her perfectly coiffed hair, then held a hand to her cheek, while the other moved down to smooth her stomach as she sat up straight, making her slight paunch appear smaller, as if all of this could take the decades off. She reached forward for one of the two photo albums in front of them, which Lisa had laid out before Iris had arrived. The tablecloth pulled with it and Charlie watched the candles in their holders wobble slightly and then right themselves. She placed her hands on the table as if she could make them stop moving, the flames flickering violently in the dimness.

Iris opened the stiff black cover of the first album and started turning the thin black pages, the photos held in place with small, triangular self-adhesive corners.

'Oh, look here, your first swim in the creek! Look at those chubby little thighs.'

Charlie looked at the muted tones of the coloured photos. A two-year-old Paige was dressed in a pair of pink swimming togs, standing in front of Iris, both arms up above her head, holding onto her mother's hands, showing off a toothy grin.

Iris continued flicking through the album, and Charlie recognised the similarity between her and Paige at around age thirteen. She looked closer, looked past the early nineties fashion, and saw herself.

'I'm not Paige,' Charlie said. She cleared her throat and tried again, speaking over Iris's reminiscing. 'I'm not Paige. My name is Charlie Morgan. Jac is my sister.'

Charlie noticed the spark of recognition when she said

her and Jac's names but then Iris, clearly determined to stay in this fantasy world, said, 'Nonsense, you're just confused, my darling.' Iris turned the next page of the album. 'Oh, here you are with your new flute! How you loved that flute. Look at you all dressed up. I think that was our New Year's party. Remember?'

'I don't remember because I'm not Paige.' Charlie's anger surged, energising her. She could feel herself growing stronger every time she denied she was Paige. This woman was crazy and Charlie needed to get out of here. With Lisa gone, this was her best chance to escape. She could easily take on this old woman, and then get herself and Jac out of here. It sounded like she had run up the stairs when she'd run out of the dining room, but for now she just needed to focus on getting away from Iris before Lisa came back.

'Look, and here's one of the open days,' Iris said, ignoring Charlie's denial.

While Iris continued talking, flicking through the pages of the album, Charlie, inch by inch, leaned down towards the floor. She felt the rope tight around her bare ankles, grabbing at the knot, trying to loosen it.

'What are you doing?' Iris asked. 'Sit up straight, please, Paige. You know I don't like slouching.'

Charlie reached forward and pointed at a photo of Iris and Paige and a small group of people standing in the orchard. She needed to take Iris's attention away from her. 'When was this taken?'

Iris leaned forward, engrossed in the photo, pulling the album to her, scanning the faces, and then rattling off names.

Charlie grasped the bottom of the tablecloth in her hands. Her breathing was coming quicker and she felt sick.

She didn't know if it was going to work, but she needed to do something to distract Iris for long enough to get her legs untied. She swallowed, remembering her father shaking her awake the night of the fire, picking her up in his arms while she was still half asleep. She remembered the coolness of her bedroom and then the sudden, painful heat as her father ran with her down the hallway and into the lounge to the front door. The black smoke curling up to the ceiling with nowhere to go, the flames jumping from chairs to coffee table, slithering along the carpet. She thought it was a nightmare. She thought, somehow, she had ended up in hell.

Would her idea work? Would she have enough time to untie herself before the flames reached her? The longer she thought about it, the more likely it was that she would stay here, a prisoner. So she yanked the tablecloth towards her. There were at least ten candles running the length of the table and they all toppled over. Some extinguished, landing on crockery, but others fell and caught the old lace tablecloth. Charlie's eyes widened at the small fires almost instantly dotting the table, eating away at the lace like it was tissue paper, slowly spreading. She grabbed the closest candle, fear making her grasp it so tight the solid wax snapped in her palm, and she held it to the photo album.

'No!' Iris yelled. 'Paige, what are you doing?!'

The first album caught easily, the thin, dry paper eaten by the solitary flame. She did the same to the second one, grabbing the corner and pushing it towards the old woman.

Iris yelled again, pushing her chair back from the table and the steadily burning albums, flames licking at parts of the tablecloth that hadn't caught yet.

Charlie's fingers were clumsy as she undid the knots

at her ankles, untying one rope and then the other. She stood but then stumbled back, her legs unwilling to hold her up. The whole table was now ablaze, sending smoke up towards the ceiling. She covered her mouth and stood again, backing away from the table. Iris was throwing a jug of water at the flames, but they were out of control.

Charlie darted past her and ran for the door where she bumped into Lisa. For a second they looked at each other, Lisa's eyes wide with shock. With all her strength, hate and desperation coursing through every muscle, Charlie pushed her to the floor, taking a moment's enjoyment as Lisa's head banged against the wall, and then sprinted to the stairs without looking back. Lisa would have to choose, either come after Charlie or take care of the fire and her mother. Charlie prayed it was the latter, and that Jac was somewhere up these stairs.

FIFTY-ONE

Jac

Sunday evening

JAC LAY IN the soldiers' hallway, assessing her injuries. When Lisa had tripped her and she had knocked her head against the wall, she hadn't blacked out, but she was definitely stunned and, with some difficulty, Lisa had dragged her in here and locked her up in the hallway, not in one of the rooms, anxious to get back to Iris and Charlie, no doubt. Jac had tried to struggle but her ankle, wrist, ribs and head flared in pain. Lying on her back by the door, she tried to think of a way out but there was none. Unless Charlie could help her. Had she been able to get away? Jac hoped so.

She started screaming, thumping on the door with her bound hands. She remembered the way the door to the soldiers' hallway was camouflaged and looked like part of the wall. She had to make as much noise as she could or Charlie would miss the door altogether. She continued screaming, her throat raw and burning. She kicked at the door, over and over, until she heard thumping in return. She stopped.

'Charlie?' she yelled. 'Charlie!' *God, please be Charlie.*

'Jac! It's me. Shit, how do I get to you? How do I get you out?'

Jac grabbed at their best hope. 'There's a key. Room...' *What was Iris's room number?* 'Room number sixteen! On your left. There's a set of keys in the dressing table drawer. Go!'

Jac heard Charlie's receding footfalls and she lay her hands on the door, eyes closed. *Please, please, please.*

It was taking too long. *Come on, Charlie.*

And then the relief of the scrape of the key in the lock and Charlie's panicked face in front of her.

'Come on,' Jac said. She led Charlie down the hallway, through the smoke doors and into her room. Slamming the door behind them and locking it, she turned to Charlie, holding up her hands.

'I can hardly see,' Charlie said, working at the knot. She turned to flick on the light, it fizzed, flickered and then went out.

'Typical,' Jac said. 'Come over here by the window.'

Charlie untied her with shaking hands, and Jac drew her into a quick hug. 'I don't know how we're going to get out of here. It'll be all locked up downstairs. And I don't know where Lisa is,' Jac said, glancing at the locked door.

'The dining room's on fire,' Charlie said, her eyes wide.

'What? How?'

'I knocked over the candles, set alight the table and photo albums... The old woman was freaking out. So that's probably keeping Lisa busy.' A small hysterical giggle escaped from Charlie's painted lips.

'Good,' Jac said, rubbing Charlie's back. Jac picked up her small shoulder bag and shoved the ute keys and her phone into it. 'Fuck, what are we going to do?'

'Call the police,' Charlie said desperately.

All Jac wanted to do was to get out of this place, but she grabbed her phone back out of her bag and held down the button to turn it on. Nothing. It hadn't charged. She knew she'd plugged it in this morning after having not done it properly. She looked down at the wall socket. 'Fuck this place!' Jac screamed.

'It's okay, don't worry about it,' Charlie said. 'Let's just get out of here.'

'The window,' Jac said, thinking of the drop. Could they jump? Of course they couldn't, it was too high. She shook her head and then remembered. 'The fire escape! We can use the fire escape.'

Jac crossed the room and jerked the stubborn window up. The sun was just setting, disappearing behind the tall oaks and pines, the light growing dim. The fire escape looked every bit as old as the hotel. Jac could see the ladder had come loose from the wall on one side.

'Will it hold us?' Charlie asked.

'It's going to have to. Come on, we need to get moving. You go first.' She looked over her shoulder, expecting Lisa at any moment.

Charlie climbed out the window onto a narrow gangway and shuffled two metres along to the ladder. The whole structure screeched under her weight. The ladder wobbled in her grasp but, once she was on, it appeared to hold. She made her way down, the loose bolts rattling. Jac dared not get on until Charlie was off. With both of them on the ladder, there was a good chance it wouldn't hold. As soon as Charlie was off, Jac eased her way out the window and along. With the first step down, the ladder groaned and there was a pinging sound as a bolt from one side of the ladder dislodged. She closed her eyes, hanging on as the ladder tilted to the right.

'Come on, Jac, quick!' Charlie shouted up to her.

Jac looked down to the concrete below, thinking what

the fall would do to her already broken body. Her injured wrist and ankle felt weak, and she struggled to gain purchase on the footholds, her fingers uncooperative. The ladder screeched against the building with every move Jac made, no doubt broadcasting to Lisa exactly where they were. With a couple of metres to go, the ladder jolted once and the whole thing came away from the wall. Jac jumped free, landing on the concrete, on her side, the ladder just missing her as it came down too. She closed her eyes for a second, panting.

'Jac! Are you okay?' Charlie rushed over to her.

'I'm fine. Help me up.'

Jac groaned at the effort, but she didn't seem to have any extra injuries.

They ran down the side of the hotel, past the dining room, the windows dark, curtains pulled. Jac had no idea if Charlie's fire had spread or if Lisa had managed to put it out. They made their way around to the front of the hotel, Charlie's arm around Jac, as she ran-limped to the ute that was parked away from the hotel at the start of the driveway.

'Get in,' Jac said, ignoring Charlie's questioning glance at seeing their dad's ute.

Jac shoved the key into the ignition. The engine coughed and rumbled and then died. She tried again. 'Shit!' She turned to look at the hotel, expecting Lisa to come charging out the front door any second. Should they get out and make a run for it? She tried again. Nothing. 'Come on, you piece of shit!' she yelled, trying one last time. The engine fired into life. Jac shifted it into gear, pressed her foot to the floor, did a U-turn and sped down the driveway and away from the hotel.

Jac turned right onto the main street and headed out

of town. 'Dad?' Charlie asked, gazing back towards the campground.

Jac shook her head, wondering how she was going to find the words.

'What?' Charlie asked as they drove out of Everly.

'He's not there.' Jac didn't want to say it. Charlie had been through too much already.

'*What?*' Charlie asked again. 'Jac?'

'He…died. Dad's dead.'

'What? How…' Charlie looked confused more than anything. 'When?'

'It was a day or two after you were taken. He was drunk…fell in the creek.'

Charlie was silent, brushing away tears. 'She kept me in the basement,' she said, her voice barely a whisper.

Jac gulped, holding back tears. Charlie had been so close for the past few days—in the same building—and she didn't even know it.

'When I was down there, I wondered if he cared enough to notice I was missing, if he would do anything about it. I wasn't sure. I honestly didn't know.'

'He did notice you were gone,' Jac said, happy that she could give Charlie that. 'He went to the cops, but…' Jac didn't want to tell Charlie that between their drunken dad and Michelle Lafferty's false statement no one had looked for Charlie, except her. 'Lisa had a plan. She made sure no one would be looking for you. But Dad texted me before he died. He was worried about you.'

Charlie cranked the old window down, flooding the cab of the ute with fresh air. 'He wasn't all bad, you know,' she said.

Jac gripped the wheel.

'I know you don't agree,' Charlie said.

She could tell Charlie the truth, right now, set the record straight about what happened the night of the fire. She didn't remember a lot of specific stuff from when she was younger, day-to-day life, how she was treated. Although that wasn't entirely true, she *chose* not to remember. Memories were like that. If you didn't take them out every now and then, stretch their legs, breathe life into them, they curled up and died. Other memories, though, had a life of their own, couldn't be ignored. They had legs. They jumped up and down, shouted to make themselves known, whether you wanted them to or not.

Jac had no idea how long she had stood outside her house that night, returning home from a party, her drug- and alcohol-addled brain looking at the scene like she was watching a movie. Precious minutes ticking by as everyone inside breathed in the toxic smoke from the flames that were devouring their home. Sometimes—a lot of the time—she felt she was just as guilty as her father. It was at the pub after their mother's funeral that Jac heard him, already drunk. 'She stood outside, watching us all burn— me, her sister and her mother. We could've all died, not just Izzy. It's all on her.'

Her dad refused to talk about the fire, but word got out that a lit cigarette left in an ashtray on the armchair in the lounge had started it. Izzy didn't smoke. Eddie and Jac did. And Jac hadn't been home that night. Rumours started up, twisting and multiplying, Eddie contributing, trying to save face in the small community, happy to throw his eldest daughter under the bus. It started off with Jac Morgan standing outside her house watching her family burn and then morphed into Jac being the one who started the fire. Coming home from a party drunk, abandoning a lit cigarette.

Jac looked over at Charlie. She'd kept quiet for the past seven years. She could keep quiet a bit longer. Charlie didn't need to know right now. Jac reached over to her, needing contact, and touched her forearm. She was worried about Charlie. Would she be okay? Jac needed to make sure she was. It would be her responsibility now. She brushed the pocket of her jeans, feeling the sharp edges of Iris's ring. Their way out. A new beginning.

They would stop somewhere, just as soon as they put a few more kilometres between them and the Gilmore Hotel. Charlie's clothes, which Jac had collected from the caravan, were in a bag on the floor. She shouldn't be in those weird clothes Lisa must have dressed her in for any longer than she had to be. Jac wanted to know the whole story, how Charlie had ended up at the hotel, what Lisa had done to her, but that, too, could wait.

'Where to from here?' Jac asked, attempting a smile.

Charlie pulled her hair from the tight ponytail. She took the headband off and threw it out the window, then did the same with the digital watch on her wrist. She wiped the lipstick from her lips and said, 'Anywhere but back there, and as long as I'm with you.'

'You got it,' Jac said. She had finally done what she'd always promised. She had come back for Charlie. It had taken too many years, but she had done it.

Jac glanced in her rear-vision mirror, Everly and the Gilmore Hotel long gone, and said a silent goodbye to all the ghosts. Jac and Charlie Morgan wouldn't be back.

FIFTY-TWO

Lisa

Sunday evening

IT WAS ALL OVER. She was gone and Lisa couldn't do anything about it. She felt the anger burning under her skin, pulsing in her head. The unfairness of it. After everything she had done.

Lisa smelled the smoke on her clothes, in her hair. She had been able to put the fire out easily. The table was ruined but, there was no lasting damage. Except that Paige had got away.

Straight after, Iris had been confused, and then her confusion gave way to her own anger. She wanted Paige, wanted to know where she had gone. She wouldn't settle, she wouldn't calm down. She blamed Lisa. Her words were vicious and cruel, and it took Lisa straight back to her childhood. She needed a break, a rest, a chance to breathe, free of Iris. And so, they had climbed the stairs, Lisa leading Iris to the soldiers' hallway. They were inside before Iris fully realised where she was.

Lisa stood over Iris who had kneeled on the floorboards and then stretched herself out until she was lying on her stomach, her forehead against the floor, muttering, caressing a notch in the wood. She shone the torch around room 12A. She hadn't had a chance to look around when she'd thrown Jac in here. Hadn't really wanted to. But now she could see it looked just the same. Why would it look any different? She thought, perhaps, her young mind had played it up, what it was like. She had often asked herself over the years, was it really that bad? The ghosts, the monsters, imagined and real. But it was that bad. The darkness. The heaviness. The hopelessness. Lisa sniffed the frigid air again—could she smell flowers? The perfumed aroma was tinged with rottenness.

'Why are we here?' Lisa could hear the anger in Iris's voice but there was an undertone of panic. 'Paige…' Iris said. 'She was just here. I saw her. I talked to her. Just for a little while it was like it used to be.'

'That's what I wanted,' Lisa said. 'But she's gone. I tried so hard…' Lisa's voice faltered, cracked as tears threatened, and she cleared her throat. 'I always tried so hard…'

'Why am I here?' Iris asked.

'Try taking a look at everything you have right now,' Lisa said. *Look at me.* 'Don't focus so much on what you've lost.'

'What I have right now?' Iris replied, her voice lowering to a snarl. She stood with some difficulty, leaning against the wall. In the torchlight, she looked every one of her seventy-nine years. The soldiers' hallway did that to you, Lisa remembered, it used to take something from you every time you were in it.

'I have *nothing.* Ever since Paige left, it's all been wrong. This place. It's not the same. It just isn't. And then you come back, you try and make it better and you fail, again and again. You're my perpetual punishment. Why are you here? *She* should be here. *Not you!*'

Lisa nodded, closing the door, taking the light; she felt like she had heard it all before. This was the best place for Iris, for now. Alone. Maybe it would do her some good. Maybe it wouldn't. She would wait and see. 'It's your turn, Mum. Remember, the darkness gives you time to think.'

* * * * *

ACKNOWLEDGEMENTS

THE WRITING OF *In Her Blood* was very much a collaborative effort and I have many people to thank who helped me turn it into the book I always envisioned it to be.

Thank you to my agent Vicki Marsdon for always being so enthusiastic and positive about my writing, and for always being available to talk things out when needed.

Thank you to my wonderful publisher, HarperCollins Australia, who made my writing dream come true once again. Huge thanks to Catherine Milne for your perceptive advice on an early draft of *In Her Blood* and directing me to the heart of the story. Special thanks also to Madeleine James, Jessica Friedmann, Kim Swivel, Rachel Cramp and Pam Dunne.

Thank you to Catherine Wallace, not only for my crash course in flute playing and music but more importantly for your support from the very beginning. It is very much appreciated.

Once again, thanks to Nathan Blackwell. Even though police procedure is thin on the ground in this book as Jac takes it upon herself to search for Charlie, you helped me work around the best and most believable way to keep the police out of the story so Jac could tackle it on her own.

The Gilmore Hotel is fictitious but is inspired by the Waitomo Hotel, which has closed down. Special thanks to Rangiiria Barclay-Kerr from Taharoa Holdings for letting me look inside the hotel and in doing so letting my imagination run wild.

To Craig Sisterson. Thank you for being such a wonderful champion of Kiwi crime writers. Your support for my books over the years (interviews, reviews, social media posts) is so appreciated. We're lucky to have you in our corner.

Where would we be without wonderful book shops? Many thanks to you all, especially Hamish and his team at Paper Plus Cambridge, and Rebecca and Sally and the rest of the team at Paper Plus Te Awamutu. Your support means a lot.

As well as to my wonderful sisters and brothers-in-law I've dedicated this book to, thanks, as always, goes to my mum and dad, Mike, Pip, Steven and Carol. And to my friends Libby and Carleen who are always there to listen over lunch or a wine.

Simon, Cate and Abbie, thank you for your constant enthusiasm and for putting up with my mutterings as I made my way through the structural edits and out the other side. Simon, thank you as always for your support, for knowing when to leave me alone and knowing when to lend an ear as I try to work through a slippery plot or characters who aren't behaving. I couldn't do what I do without you three.

To you, the reader. I know there's a lot of choice out there (salute to those teetering TBR piles), so thank you for choosing *In Her Blood*.

NIKKI CRUTCHLEY IS the author of *To the Sea* (HarperCollins, 2021). Prior to this, she self-published three police procedurals set in New Zealand, and was a finalist in the Ngaio Marsh Awards for her first two books. She has been published in *Flash Frontier*, *Mayhem Literary Journal*, *Flash Fiction Magazine* and in *Fresh Ink* anthology (published by Cloud Ink Press). She was longlisted and regional winner at National Flash Fiction Day in 2016, and at the 2017 National Flash Fiction Day she had two stories shortlisted and was regional winner.